# OUTCASTS OF VELRUNE

## by Isaac Crowe

*To Ella
Enjoy The Adventure!
Isaac Crowe*

Outcasts of Velrune

Copyright 2014 by Isaac Crowe

All Rights Reserved

First Print Edition: June 2014

Art by Nick Jordon Beja

Edited by Angela Bernardi

ISBN-13:978-149978282

ISBN-10:1499782829

## Acknowledgment

Thanks to my family and friends who read the early drafts of this book. My biggest thanks and my love goes to my wife who encouraged me to continue to write after seeing the first chapter. Spook also sends her thanks. If not for my wife, her role would have ended much earlier.

I can be found on the web at http://isaaccrowe.weebly.com

Enjoy the story.


## A note form the illustrator:

Hello my name is Nick Jordan Beja. I'm an artist (and average guy) from the Philippines. You can view my gallery at: http://nickbeja.deviantart.com or contact me at pur_doy@yahoo.com

Have a great day!

Outcasts of Velrune

# CHAPTER ONE

At six years of age, this was the first time Maxwell had left the city, or even its inner court. He had imagined the whole city to be like his finely hewed stone house that sat in a neat row with other homes. The endless, winding rows of poorly made apartments outside the inner court came as a disappointing surprise made even worse by the throng of people who flowed up and down the streets like rain in the gutters. Max breathed a sigh of relief when they reached the outer gates, despite the looks of concern from the guards.

The freeing feeling of leaving the city did not last long. They soon rode into a large rock canyon that had endless, twisting passageways branching off on either side. As his dad pushed them onward hour after hour, Max began to wish they had stayed in the city. His legs started to get sore from straddling the horse, and to make it worse, he couldn't ride with his dad. Instead, he rode with Mr. Penna, his dad's friend, who kept a firm grip on him.

Near dusk they reached a small, walled camp. A meager fire burned at its center. His dad placed them as far as he could from the fire's light. Maxwell started to wander off to explore the camp, but a firm grip on his shoulder stopped him.

"Max, stay close to us."

"But, I just wanted to see…"

"I know Max, but not tonight, okay?"

Max searched his father's face. His eyes burned with an intensity he had not seen before.

"Okay, dad."

Max sat down next to his dad, who relaxed a little, and handed a piece of bread to Mr. Penna.

"I'm sorry you are involved with this, Chiron."

Mr. Penna took the piece of bread. "You still have not told me exactly what has happened, Peter."

"And now is still not the time, I'm afraid. We must reach the other side of the dead lands before they realize we are gone."

"And who are *they*?"

"I have made enemies within the Protectors, Chiron."

"By helping the lacarna, I assume?"

Peter nodded, "Yes."

Chiron let out a soft chuckle. "I have broken a few rules myself, Peter."

Peter gave a small smile. "Your work in the auction houses has been invaluable, but I have taken actions in direct opposition to Lord Avram. Now I have endangered myself, my son, and my friend."

Mr. Penna grew serious. "I made my own choices; do not add me to your burden. As for you and Max, leaving the Protectors is wise. They have become corrupted."

Max saw a tinge of anger rise in his father. "Many of the Protectors are still good, Chiron, only misled. One day, I will set things straight. I must - for the lacarna and for Max. For now, we hide."

"You believe that if we stay out of the way they will leave you alone?"

"That is my hope. That is why we are going through the dead lands and then east to Hedgewood; few Protectors venture that way."

"And if you are wrong and they come after you?"

"Then we move again to some place even more remote. I must keep Max safe until he can stand on his own, until he can choose for himself whether to be involved or not."

Mr. Penna remained silent for a few moments. "Very well."

Peter nodded then turned to the camp entrance. "I'll keep first watch. If any messengers arrive we will leave immediately. Otherwise, we wait until first light." Peter turned to look over his shoulder. "My friend, if something should happen, teach Maxwell only what we both believe should be. The Immortals put the Protectors in place to provide justice and peace. Someone needs to hold onto that ideal even if it is false. When later he sees differently, I hope he will fix the things that I could not."

"I have my doubts things can be changed, Peter, but, as your friend, I will do as you say."

Peter nodded and turned back to the camp entrance. Max tried to follow his father, but Mr. Penna took his hand.

"Maxwell, come next to me. Your father does not need any distractions right now."

Max slid next to Mr. Penna and laid down to sleep for the night. He remained awake a while; however, as he watched his dad sit and stare up at the night sky.

In the morning they left the camp and rode out across the wasteland for several long days. Max wondered if they had enough food to reach wherever they were going. They had left in a hurry, packing little, and stopping for only a few minutes at a big stone church in a beautiful garden at the far edge of the city. There, his dad had left a small wooden box.

Max perked up when they finally reached a steep path leading up onto a grassy plain. The place seemed a lot more welcoming to him, but every now and then he caught his dad glancing nervously behind them.

Max grew more and more concerned as they rode through the night. His dad always remained calm and in charge. He recalled once when his dad stepped between two fighting men and scolded them like they were children causing a ruckus. His dad feared nothing, at least not until now. Max could feel it, and as the night wore on, he fell into a troubled sleep.

In his dream he stood in the streets of Mocnia, the city they had left. Before him stood a big dog that growled at him. Max took a step back. The dog inched forward. Max turned and ran as hard as he could. He stole a glance over his shoulder and saw that the dog followed close behind, barking. He could sense the dog's jaws snapping at his heels. Then he saw his dad running beside him. Max expected him to stop and chase the dog away, but his dad snatched him up instead without breaking stride. Max didn't understand why his dad didn't turn and fight the dog, but as he looked back, he saw several more join the first.

Max jerked awake to a shouting multitude. The horse shifted about underneath them. Mr. Penna's arms tightened around him. Max spotted swords that gleamed in the moonlight. His father sat on his horse surrounded by the shining swords. Peter drew his own sword and made two downward thrusts before several hands grabbed at his leg and pulled him to the ground. Max cried out, struggling against Mr. Penna's tight grasp. The men dove at his father. Fear swept over Max as the swords clanged together. Sparks flying from their impacts.

Suddenly, the attackers were shoved back, and in the center stood his father. The stories his father told him of the great Protectors appeared in Max's mind. Those heroic warriors who stood their ground and defeated everything that came their way. Max smiled. He knew his father would come out on top.

Max watched as several of the men rushed inward. With a sweep of his blade, his father easily struck them down. The others paused before turning and running off. The battle was over in minutes.

Mr. Penna relaxed the arm he had wrapped around Max. Max took a deep breath. They rode over to Peter, but before Mr. Penna could dismount, Peter waved for him to stop. Mr. Penna tried to smile, but Max heard the concern in his voice.

"It is hard to tell in the moonlight, Peter, but they seem to have given you a few wounds at least."

Peter, hunched over and breathing heavily, straightened and returned the half-hearted smile. "A few, but I'll manage. Those that got away may bring reinforcements. We need to keep moving. Are you okay, Max?"

Max nodded absently as he stared at all the dark spots on his dad's armor.

Peter looked down at his armor. The metal shimmered in the moonlight, except where the blood covered it. He shook his head.

"It's not mine, Max. It's from the bandits."

Max had his doubts.

Mr. Penna looked around. "Hedgewood is still a few days ride to the East; however, if I remember the map correctly, we are only an hour's ride from the road that leads to Pike. From there we go southwest for another hour to Pike itself where we can find a healer."

Peter nodded. "Alright, Pike it is."

With great effort Peter climbed back onto his horse. He seated himself and spurred the horse onward. They flew through the night. Max cringed at the loud hoof beats, afraid the bandits would be able to follow the sound. At the intersection of the southern road, the horses cornered hard, their hooves flinging dirt high into the air. Max held on tight and strained his eyes for any sign of a town.

Relief flooded Max when, at last, the light from the oil lamps of Pike shone in the distance. The light grew stronger, and houses began to take shape when, to Max's horror, his father's horse veered off the road. Max's mind raced back to the blood he had seen on his dad's armor, and his stomach twisted in fear. Mr. Penna jerked on his horse's reins and followed after Max's father.

"Peter! Peter, we are almost there. Try and steer Starlight back to the right."

"No," came a weak and labored response. "It's... too easy... to find. We... can't stop here."

Peter continued his course, skirting around the outside of the town. Mr. Penna pushed his horse harder and came up beside Starlight. He tried to grab her reins, but nearly lost his hold on Max in the process.

"Peter, we need to get you to a healer immediately."

Peter fought to speak every word. "Town...too close...farther."

"I don't know if there is another town, Peter!"

Peter nodded to the field in front of them. "Road."

Max saw a lone pair of lamps that marked the sides of another road leading out of the town. Max heard panic in Mr. Penna's voice for the first time.

"Peter, the map I had showed that road going back towards the dead lands."

Peter turned Starlight to follow the road. "This way."

Max recognized the determination in his father's voice. He knew Mr. Penna would not be able to stop his father. Mr. Penna knew too, as he spoke no more. Instead, he followed Peter along the road. Max tried to stay awake and keep an eye on his dad, but the panic of the battle and the fear of his dad's injuries sapped his strength. He began to drift off to sleep.

A strange voice jerked Max awake. "Bring him in here!"

Mr. Penna still held him, but they no longer sat on the horse. In front of him, several people helped his father down from Starlight. Max watched them carry him into a nearby house. From behind him, a loud thump made both he and Mr. Penna jump and turn. On the ground lay the horse they had been riding, struggling to breathe.

A calm, authoritative voice rang out over the crowd. "Bring the others."

Several hands grabbed hold of them. The villagers ushered Mr. Penna and Max through a second doorway in the same house where they had taken his father. Inside, the villagers led them to a few chairs against one of the walls. Mr. Penna seated himself and held Max in his lap.

The villagers wasted no time in bombarding them with questions. "Who are you?" "Where did you ride in from?" "Were you attacked by bandits?"

The commotion overwhelmed Max. Mr. Penna struggled to answer. After a few minutes, a man stepped in from the adjoining room, hushing the crowd of people. He then turned to speak to Mr. Penna.

"Your friend has been badly hurt. Luckily, our Healer is one of the best and most determined around. She will fix him up, but, for now, all we can do is wait."

Mr. Penna nodded his head wearily. "Thank you."

"Now, I do have a few questions for you, as we are not used to having strangers show up in the middle of the night; at least not the friendly kind. But first…" The man turned his attention to the crowded room and motioned the people toward the door. "All right, everyone out."

The disappointed villagers followed the order and left the house one by one. The man watched them leave. When the last was out he gave a bemused smile.

"That means you too, Evangeline."

Max heard a small voice from behind a large cabinet in a far corner of the room.

"Aaahh."

A little girl, perhaps six, stepped out. She had cat-like ears that sat atop her head. A long tail came into view as she edged closer. Max remembered seeing others like her back in the city, but only at a distance since few were allowed into the inner court.

The little girl clasped her hands together and tried to plead her case. "I want to stay. I'll be quiet."

"No, Evangeline."

The girl hung her head in disappointment. The man smiled. "I have an important job for you to do instead."

The little girl bounced up and down. "Really?"

"Yes, I need you to go over to your home and have Mrs. Tassi round up some food and tea for our guests. I know they will really appreciate it later when we are finished. Can you do that for me?"

"Yep! You bet!"

Evangeline looked squarely at Max, who now saw one eye was green and the other blue, and waved. "Bye." She ran out the door, her tail trailing straight out behind her.

With the room now clear the man focused his attention back to Mr. Penna. "Well now, with things a little calmer, perhaps we can get down to business. I am Aric, the mayor of Swiftwater."

He reached out his hand. Mr. Penna grasped it.

"I'm Chiron Penna. The man you care for is Peter Laskaris, a lieutenant of the Protectors. This is his son; my godson, Maxwell."

The mayor gave Maxwell a polite nod.

"You've had quite a night little one. Don't worry. Your dad's going to be fine."

Max only returned an empty stare. With the villagers gone and the reassurance that the Healer would take care of his dad, sleep began to overtake him.

The mayor smiled and began to ask Mr. Penna all sorts of questions. The first few the villagers themselves had asked, but the mayor soon probed deeper. The conversation faded as Max drifted off to dreams of playing hide and seek with the strange little cat girl.

It had been two years since the night Max and his father arrived in Swiftwater. The Healer, with her home-brew of salves made from local plant life, had worked wonders for his father. Within weeks he was up and moving about. However, a few of his deeper wounds never did heal completely. They left him with aches in his bones that, at times, made it difficult for him to move.

While Max's father recovered, the villagers put them up in an old house abandoned by another villager who never returned from a trip across the dead lands. The villagers also supplied them with anything they needed, often brought over by the little cat girl, Evangeline. Max liked it when Eve came over because she always wanted to play games with him.

Once Max's dad regained his strength, he began helping the villagers in return for their kindness. Soon the villagers accepted Max, his father and Mr. Penna as one of their own. Max, unsure of when they would leave, took full advantage of life outside of the big city they had come from. He spent day after day exploring the village and playing by the Swiftwater River, often with Eve. Other times he helped his dad around the village, something he never got to do back home. He could tell his dad enjoyed the village also. Here he laughed freely and even skipped work at times to play with Max. All this made Max's decision easy when his father asked Max if he would like to stay in the village for good.

Mr. Penna also decided to stay and took to teaching the children in the village. Max found his own place in the village. He would help Eve at her mother's cafe. It wasn't a fancy place, but Mrs. Tassi provided good food and cool drinks. She made everyone feel welcome too, making the cafe the place that everyone gathered to relax and talk.

Chores finished, Eve, an endless ball of energy, she would proceed to drag Max along on whatever whim came to her that day. He rarely had much choice in the matter. It didn't bother him though. Most of the time he would have gone anyway. She was odd, and he liked that.

Max's friendship with Eve did have one downside; her constant attempts to surprise him. She was agile, and the thin coat of fur on the bottom of her feet made it almost impossible to hear her coming. Despite her fiery red hair and her long tail of the same color, he always noticed her a moment too late. Before he knew it, he often found himself lying on the ground with her perched on top of his chest.

After living the village for a year, the villagers made Max's father sheriff. Not that the town needed much of one, but from time to time trouble did arise. Tonight was one of those times. His dad had carried Max to bed and tucked him in when a loud knock came at the door. A man shouted.

"Mr. Laskaris, I've spotted a bandit in the village not far from your house."

Max did not recognize the man's voice. The image of the

battle on the road flashed through his mind. Max gripped the blanket. His father rubbed Max's head and smiled.

"I'm sure it's nothing. You stay here. I'll be back in a few minutes."

"But..."

"It's only one. I think I can handle that. Don't you?"

Max gave a weak smile. "Yeah."

Peter left Max's room. Max heard the front door open and a conversation start. He listened intently, but the voices faded as his dad and the stranger moved away. Without warning a loud whisper came from the open window next to his bed.

"Max!"

Max practically jumped out of his skin, despite having recognized the voice. He took a deep breath to calm himself while Eve climbed in through the window.

"Eve, I told you, don't sneak up on me like that."

"I'm sorry, Max, but we've got to get out of here."

Max's eyebrows furrowed. "What? Why?"

Eve took hold of her tail. "It's not safe. Please come with me."

Max smiled. She always grabbed her tail when she felt nervous. "Eve, you're silly. Dad will return any minute."

"No, Max, something is wrong. Please come with me."

Max's smile faded away. He swung his feet over the edge of the bed. "I need to check on dad."

Eve grabbed Max's arm. "No, Max, you must come with me."

Max had never seen Eve so scared. His heart raced. He stood and tried to run after his dad, but Eve pulled him back and shoved him towards the window. Max hit the sill and tumbled out. Behind him, Eve nimbly climbed out. He regained his footing only to have Eve grab his hand and pull him along. She took him behind several houses then cut between a pair of them. Max had seen no one else until they crossed the main street in town. Here, he glanced to his right and saw a large number of men standing outside of his house, none of them from the village. He tried to stop in order to find his father, but Eve jerked him along into the cafe. She took him in through the kitchen, back to a row of cabinets that lined the floor. She opened the door to one of them.

"Get in, Max"

Max didn't move. "Those men out there…?"

Eve shoved Max into the cabinet. He managed to turn round to face Eve. The fear he had seen earlier had disappeared, replaced by a fierce determination. As he watched, claws shot out from the top of Eve's hands, extending several inches beyond her fingertips. A chill ran down Max's spine.

*She has claws? Why didn't she tell me she had claws?*

Eve spoke in a soft tone, contradicting the sharp weapons she had just revealed. "I'll be right here, Maxy."

Eve closed the cabinet door. He heard the lock slide through the handles. Max tried to shake his head clear.

*What is happening? One moment I'm in bed and the next I'm crammed into a kitchen cabinet. Now Eve's turned into a wild beast.*

Shouting came from outside the cafe, dulled by the walls and cabinet door. Max knew those sounds. He had heard them the last time bandits had attacked his father. Now, though, he could not even watch. The shouting stopped. He had never experienced such silence. He tried to open the door, but it wouldn't budge. After what felt like an eternity of dark silence, he heard the individual shouts of villagers calling for someone. He didn't hear his father's voice among them. Finally, Mrs. Tassi's relieved voice came from outside of his hiding place.

"Eve, there you are. Do you have Max with you?"

Eve didn't respond. Max wondered if she was still there. He tried to speak himself but found his voice gone. Mrs. Tassi spoke again in her caring tone she reserved only for Eve. "It's okay sweetie. They're gone. No one is going to hurt Max."

"He's in here, mother."

The small, weak voice sounded nothing like Eve. Max reeled. In one night she had been scared, then fierce, then as fragile as he had ever seen her. His heart rose into his throat.

*What happened tonight? What happened to dad?*

Footsteps approached the cabinet. The door opened. At first

the light from the kitchen blinded him, but slowly his eyes adjusted. Mrs. Tassi crouched in front of the cabinet.

"You can come on out now, Max."

Max crawled out of the cabinet as best he could. When he emerged Mrs. Tassi picked him up and held him. Eve stood over to the side. Her claws remained out, but the tears that now flowed had put out the fire in her eyes.

Mrs. Tassi laid a soothing hand on Eve's. "It's okay, Eve. It's over. You protected him. Now why don't you put those things away?"

Mrs. Tassi forced a tiny smile on her worn face. Eve sheathed her claws and wrapped her arms around Mrs. Tassi.

"That's my girl. Now, go outside and find Mr. Penna and bring him back here."

Eve hesitated for a moment. She turned to Max, looking lost for a second, then ran out of the kitchen.

Max swallowed hard and found his voice again. "Where's my Dad? Why did you send Eve for Mr. Penna instead of Dad?"

Mrs. Tassi took a deep breath and let it out. She stroked the side of Max's face as tears ran down her own.

"I'm afraid your father can't come, Max."

As Mrs. Tassi carried Max out to one of the tables, his mind raced. *What did she mean, dad couldn't come? Was he hurt again? If the Healer was taking care of him, why can't I go there?*

Max started to get angry. He wanted to see his father. Mrs. Tassi sat down in a chair and began to rock slowly back and forth. Max's anger faded, replaced, once again, by fear. Footsteps sounded at the door to the cafe. He twisted in Mrs. Tassi's arms to see Mr. Penna standing before him with Eve peeking round from behind. Mr. Penna crouched in front of him.

"Maxwell, my son."

Mr. Penna held out his arms. Mrs. Tassi let go of Max and he reached for Mr. Penna.

"Where's dad?"

Mr. Penna took Max tightly in his arms. "Though both of us thought him to be more, your father was indeed a mortal man.

Tonight others have taken him from us. I can only give you myself in his place. I am sorry, Maxwell."

Deep in himself Max had known what had happened. He clenched Mr. Penna and sobbed. He felt Mr. Penna cry with him as Mrs. Tassi and Eve embraced them both.

## CHAPTER TWO

Max stared out the window at the cafe down the street, wishing Mr. Penna would hurry and finish the lesson. It was a sunny day outside, and he wanted to enjoy it, but he doubted Mr. Penna would let him out early. Since becoming his sole guardian after Max's father, Peter, died eight years before, Mr. Penna insisted on his studies.

"Maxwell. Maxwell! Are you paying attention?"

Max turned quickly away from the window and faced the front of the room where Mr. Penna stood, arms crossed, shaking his head.

"As I was saying, Maxwell Laskaris," Mr. Penna sighed, "the Lifestone can create life itself, and its use is responsible for this world we now live in."

"Isn't the Lifestone just a fairy tale, Mr. Penna? I mean, no one has reported seeing it in centuries. Besides, why would we even need it? Things are fine here with the Protectors watching over us."

Mr. Penna massaged his forehead as he turned away from Max. "You and your ideas about the Protectors again. You know, your father exemplified their good qualities. There are few others like him." Mr. Penna faced the window, "I never had a better friend than your father and I promised him I would teach you as he wished. I hope he was right." Mr. Penna let out a long sigh and turned back around. "I suppose it is getting close to practice time and that crazy lacarnian girl will be waiting for you. That is enough for today. You are excused."

Maxwell didn't give Mr. Penna a chance to change his mind. He leapt up from his seat, ran out of the house, and headed for the cafe down the street.

*Eve, or, as Mr. Penna calls her, 'the crazy lacarnian girl', should have finished her chores by now. I'll grab Eve and head to Tyco's for sword training. After a full day of lessons from Mr. Penna, I need a little action.*

The villagers knew Max's routine as well as he did. Mr. Penna might be his caretaker legally, but the whole village acted in his father's place. He liked having so many people care for him, though they often tried to protect him too much. He didn't complain about it, not after Mr. Penna told him they did so because they felt responsible for his father's death. In fact, it helped drive him to be even more like his father, to show them he could stand on his own. His body was already on its way to being a carbon copy; the same dark, unruly hair, brown eyes and even the same slender, muscular body. He still had a couple of inches to go to reach his father's height of 6 foot, but that was only a matter of time.

Now he just had to work on acting like his father. He already helped the villagers by running errands and repairing equipment. He even acted as "sheriff" for the other kids, breaking up fights and settling arguments. While it cost him some friends, the villagers had begun to look at him with the same respect he had seen them give his father. Unfortunately, as soon as he brought up his sword training, they went back to treating him like a little kid. Thankfully Mr. Penna had the final say on his dream of becoming a Protector, although, at times, even he acted reluctant to allow him to train.

Max put his thoughts aside as he reached the café and went inside. "Eve! Come on! Let's go!"

Mrs. Tassi grabbed Max's shirt and pulled him to a halt. "Land sakes, Maxwell! Watch where you're going!"

"Oh, sorry, Mrs. Tassi. Hey, where's Eve?"

"She's in the storeroom trying to get rid of a mouse for me."

"Is she done with her work for today?"

"She is if she can get rid of that filthy rodent."

"Thanks, Mrs. Tassi."

Max worked his way past the tables and customers, back towards the storeroom, opened the door, and stepped in.

"Hey, Eve, I hear you...have a ...rodent...problem?"

The room was almost completely dark, only a few small slivers of light seeping in around the edges of the covered windows. Max turned and started to step back outside of the room, but stopped when he heard a low, quiet growl from behind him. Max sighed and his shoulders slumped.

"Le...Let's think this through, Eve." Max started to turn back. "You really don't wa-"

Max finished his turn in time to see a dark shape spring out from behind one of the crates in the storeroom. The thing lunged straight for him. The impact knocked him out of the room and onto the floor in the hallway. It took a few seconds for Max to regain his breath. As he did he heard the faint breathing of the thing on top of him. Max rubbed the stars out of his eyes and focused on the face that hovered inches from his own.

"Hi, Eve."

Eve laughed. "Hi, Maxy."

"You know, normal people shake hands rather than pouncing when they greet each other."

"Well, thank goodness I'm not normal then. I mean, what fun would that be? Besides, it's not my fault that you don't pay more attention to your surroundings."

"You know I can't see in the dark like you can."

"See you? I heard you when you came into the cafe, smelled you from there too." Eve waved her hand in front of her nose and laughed again. "When's the last time you took a bath? Besides, think of the pouncings as extra training." Eve put on a more serious tone much like Tyco's. "Learn to observe your surroundings."

"Alright, alright, you win. You also do a good impression of

Tyco." Max let out a groan. "Now could you get off of me? You may be light on your feet, but you still weigh plenty when you're crouched on my chest like this."

Eve stood up and offered a hand to Maxwell. He took it, and she helped him up. Max dusted off his backside.

"Weren't you supposed to be after a mouse, anyways?"

"Yep! Caught him shortly before you showed up. It made a nice little snack."

Eve licked her lips as if she'd just eaten a delicious piece of pie. Max scrunched his face up in disgust.

"You're kidding, right?"

Eve just smiled. "Well, I am part cat after all." She didn't need to tell him that. He was well aware of it. He had become accustomed to the ears and tail during their friendship, but her cat-like behavior still amused him. On sunny days he would often find her lying on top of a house fast asleep. At night she ran around in the fields chasing moths and bats.

Eve had an insatiable curiosity as well. She would crawl in holes, trudge through ditches, and climb anything in sight so that no place went unexplored. Her clothes, a loose shirt with two pockets and a line of buttons up the front plus a pair of baggy pants, all well-worn and ragged, testified to these adventures. Max, on the other hand, often came back with an assortment of scratches, cuts and various bruises. At least someone in this town let him get into trouble. Of course, she always had to get him back out of it. He smiled. Except for one misadventure where she fell in the pond. He'd told her that branch wouldn't hold, but she really wanted to catch the butterfly.

As Max's thoughts circled back to considering what a live mouse tasted like, Mrs. Tassi came down the hallway. "Well, did you catch that filthy rodent?"

"Yep, sure did, Mrs. Tassi." At this, Eve brought her tail around, the end of which wrapped around a small mouse. "She's just a little one."

Mrs. Tassi took a half step back and raised her voice a little. "I don't care what size it is. Just get rid of it! Then you can go play with Maxwell till closing this evening."

"Okay, Mrs. Tassi." Eve turned and flashed a devilish grin to a stunned Max. "You didn't think I'd actually eaten it, did you, Max?"

Eve, humming to herself, walked out the back door of the cafe. Max shut his mouth and followed her. Outside, they headed to the edge of the village where Tyco lived.

Bemused, Max studied the white and brown mouse still entrapped by Eve's tail. "So, what are you going to do with your furry little friend?"

Eve lifted her tail over her shoulder and dropped the mouse into her hands. "Mmm, don't know. Maybe I'll keep her as a pet."

"A cat keeping a mouse as a pet?" Max shook his head in disbelief. "You know, everyone already thinks you're crazy. Do you really want to add this as well?"

Eve turned her nose up and smirked. "They only think that because I hang around with you."

"Hey, now…"

Eve had a talent for interrupting Max at times like this. She pointed ahead of them. "Looks like Tyco is out and waiting for us."

"Hey, don't go changing the subject."

Eve ignored him. "Looks like someone else is there with him. Wonder who it is?"

Max followed Eve's gaze and saw Tyco standing in front of his house speaking with a stranger. "Don't know. Guess we'll find out. Let's go."

Max picked up his pace while Eve lingered behind, a wry smile on her face. "Okay, okay." She gently put the mouse into her shirt pocket. Eve turned her ears forward and followed after Max. With the wind blowing towards her she could faintly hear the conversation between Tyco and the stranger.

The stranger, who wore a dull gray cloak with the hood pulled up over his head, nodded in their direction and leaned over to Tyco. "That him?"

Tyco glanced up at her and Max. "That's him."

Eve saw the stranger spit out a piece of a foul substance that he was chewing. "Who's the stray?"

"The cafe owner bought her years ago. From what I've gathered, she's the one that hid Maxwell the night the bandits killed his father. They're close friends."

Eve could see the disgust form on the stranger's face. She started to tense up, but stopped herself when the stranger focused in her direction.

"Will she be a problem?"

"She might want to go along."

The stranger's mouth formed a brief, crooked smile. "Humph. I suppose we could accommodate her." The smile disappeared. "You know what to do, then?"

Tyco nodded to the stranger. "Yes, I've got it."

"Then I'll get things ready. I'll see you in a week."

"I'll have him there."

The stranger walked to the side of the house and mounted a large black stallion tied there. Eve and Max climbed over the fence that separated the field from Tyco's house as the stranger rode off. Maxwell walked up to Tyco.

"Who was that?"

"A messenger."

Eve watched the stranger ride out of sight. "The horse was beautiful, but he gave me the creeps."

Tyco nodded. "Riding across the south end of the dead lands can do that to a person."

Eve shook her head. "I don't know, he seemed like he belongs in the dead lands to me."

Tyco glared at Eve, but she still faced in the direction of the departed stranger.

"It is none of your concern, lacarnian."

Eve turned towards Tyco, an inaudible growl emitted from her chest. Max, able to sense the low growls after years of friendship, changed the subject.

"So, what are we practicing today?"

Tyco broke his gaze from Eve and smiled. "Nothing new today Max, instead I want to assess what you've already learned. Go get the practice swords and meet me in the circle for a match."

Tyco moved toward a large circle drawn in chalk not far from his house. Max faced Eve. "I know Tyco doesn't like you much, but you usually put up with him a little better than that."

Eve looked over at Tyco. He was standing close enough that he might overhear her, so she kept to a whisper. "We don't know much about Tyco, and I think that stranger is trouble."

"Tyco is a Protector. He's not going to harm us."

"Max, there are things you don't…"

Tyco shouted at Max from inside the circle. "Maxwell, we're wasting daylight."

"Coming, Tyco." Max leaned over to Eve. "I'm sure it's fine. If I'm wrong, you can tear the messenger to shreds later. Deal?"

Eve huffed. "Fine."

Max laughed and ran into the house where he grabbed the wooden swords that Tyco and he used for training. He rushed back out and over to the large circle. Eve walked over to the fence next to the field and seated herself on the top bar. She tried to put aside the conversation between Tyco and the stranger. She enjoyed watching Max fight and did not want to be distracted; however, her thoughts still wandered.

The villagers knew little about Tyco. They guessed that he was in his late thirty's. He stood six feet tall with broad shoulders and well-built muscles. His skin was weathered a bit, and his hands had the beginnings of permanent calluses.

He had arrived alone in the village a few years back. He had retired from the Protectors after a back injury prevented him from performing the rigorous usual duties of service. The villagers, having expected him to be like Max's father, invited him to stay in the village. However, his gruff demeanor and lack of interest in Swiftwater's affairs soon disappointed the villagers, but he did prove to be helpful in repairing houses, carts and the like. He also ventured to the woods a couple of days ride to the east to gather supplies.

Tyco's arrival had thrilled Max. Until that time, he had no one to teach him proper fighting techniques. When Max had first asked, Mr. Penna forbade the training; however, after several months of Max's begging, he finally allowed it. Tyco had jumped at the chance to mentor him.

Tyco started by first assessing Max's natural abilities to best determine his fighting style. After a good bit of trial and error, Tyco discovered that Max fought best with only light leather armor while carrying two short blades. Max had speed, but not much strength. Tyco, on the other hand, had strength to spare. His weapon of choice was a two-handed long sword. Though slower to maneuver, the weapon's length provided a good block to Max's two swords and also allowed Tyco to deliver powerful blows.

Over the past two years, Max's skill had improved greatly. He now at least presented a challenge to Tyco. Tyco; however, never ran out of new tricks. The increased volume and frequency of the clashing swords broke Eve free of her thoughts and she focused on the fight. It appeared Max had held his ground so far. Eve knew that would change at any moment. She had studied Tyco enough during these sessions that she could predict his movements better than Max. She wished she could have a go at Tyco, but, for now she watched Max try his best.

Max swung at Tyco with his right sword; with his left held in defense. Tyco angled his blade to block Max's. The two wooden blades made contact with a loud thunk. Tyco pushed forward with his sword which shoved Max's back and also blocked his left sword. Max hesitated for a moment, his lack of experience leaving him unsure of how to get out of this situation. Tyco took the advantage and placed his right foot behind Max's leg. With another further shove he tripped Max and sent him to the ground. Max blinked a couple of times from the jolt and found the tip of Tyco's wooden sword at his throat.

"Well done, Max. You did better than I had hoped."

Tyco tossed the wooden sword to the side and extended his hand to Max. Max grabbed Tyco's hand and let Tyco pull him up.

"There's still a little daylight left, teach me that move you just used."

"Sorry, Max, I have to get ready to leave in the morning."

"Oh, are you going to the forest for supplies?"

"No, to Protector Headquarters in Moenia."

Eve joined the two. "The messenger, right?"

Tyco nodded. "He said training has grown lax and Lord Avram has requested my input to correct the problem."

Eve's ears twitched, the earlier conversation coming back to her. "Why, after three years, have they requested your help?"

"I've been sending them information on my training with Max. I guess they liked what I've accomplished. It's a shame you can't come along, Max, so I can show them how well it's worked."

Eve saw Max's eyes light up at the thought of a chance to go to Protector Headquarters. She cut off his next question. "It's too dangerous, Max. The dead lands take a week to cross and it's filled with Bandits."

Eve saw Tyco smile and knew he had set her up. She grabbed the end of her tail in nervousness as he closed the trap. "The dead lands are dangerous, unless you follow the northern route along the river. Up there the Protectors have several small, armed camps along the way making passage much safer."

Eve could feel the excitement building in Max. She tried one other thing even though she had a feeling Tyco was ready for it. "Mr. Penna won't let you go, Max."

Max groaned. "You're probably right, Eve."

Tyco acted like he was thinking hard for a moment, but Eve could tell he had been ready for that objection too. "Mr. Penna could be a bit of a challenge, Max. I know his weakness though. If you really want to come with me, I think I can persuade him."

"You'd do that, Tyco?"

Tyco clasped Max on his shoulder. "You would be helping

me by going. Let's go see what we can do."

As the two headed back towards Mr. Penna's house, Tyco shot Eve a crooked smile, the sight of which made her feel sick to her stomach. She followed after them, hoping to come up with another idea to stop Max from going. When they reached the house, they found Mr. Penna in his study.

"Nose buried in a book as usual, I see."

Mr. Penna eyed Tyco over the top of his book. "Good evening, Tyco." Mr. Penna smiled at Eve. "A very good evening to you, Miss Evangeline."

Eve shifted her weight from one foot to the other, still trying to think of what she could do. "Good evening, Mr. Penna."

Mr. Penna noted Eve's discomfort, marked his place in the book, and set it down. "So what brings you three here?"

"I need to go to Protector Headquarters to oversee their training. Max would like to go with me. I would like that as well. It would allow me to show the results of certain training techniques first hand."

Mr. Penna scratched at his short beard. "I'm not sure that's a good idea. It would take a few weeks, at least. I do not think Maxwell is ready, not to mention delaying his studies for that long of a time."

"I can assure you, Mr. Penna, that the road along the river is quite safe. Besides, Max has come a long way in his training, which is the very reason I would like to take him. He's not to be easily trifled with. As for his studies," a wry smile formed on Tyco's face, "as you well know, he's not going to find a better library than the one in the capital. Maybe there's something we could pick up for you?"

"Training and a real fight are two different animals." Eve started to relax. "On the other hand, the library at Moenia has a lot of literature I would like to have here in the village, and I suppose the boy does need to at least see the city."

Eve's heart raced. She hadn't thought he would even consider letting Max go. *If I tell Mr. Penna of the messenger's conversation with Tyco, surely Mr. Penna will stop Max.* Eve twisted her tail in her hands, ignoring the pain. *But I can't let Tyco know I heard the conversation. Maybe...*

"Tyco, did the stranger who delivered the message say how long you would be gone? He rode off into the dead lands before we could reach you."

Eve saw Tyco's eye twitch and knew she had thrown him off.

"No, Evangeline, he did not, but I don't think we would be long."

Mr. Penna studied Eve carefully. With his attention on her, she stared right at Mr. Penna and took a risk. "You said you told the Protectors about Max's training already didn't you? Wouldn't the messenger have asked for Max specifically if they wanted to see him?"

Mr. Penna stroked his beard. "Hmm, so you told them about Max. Well, I suppose they will be eager to see him. Perhaps he should indeed go."

Eve barely kept herself from falling over. *How did he miss my hint*?

Mr. Penna smiled. "He may go, and so will I."

Eve sighed knowing he had caught her hint after all.

She smirked at the lost expression forming on Tyco's face due to this unforeseen complication. He tried his best to recover.

"Mr. Penna, that's not really necessary."

"Nonsense, Tyco, someone needs to keep the boy focused."

"But, Mr. Penna, we will be riding pretty hard for most of the trip."

"Oh, I'll keep up fine."

Eve tried not to laugh when Tyco, sighing, resigned to Mr. Penna's decision. "Okay then, I'll see you at the stables at first light. Good evening to you, Mr. Penna, Max."

Eve watched in satisfaction as Tyco left. She would have liked it better for Max not to go at all, but with Mr. Penna along, not much could happen. She looked back at Mr. Penna and found him studying her once again.

"Evangeline, my dear, I assume you will be joining us."

Eve froze. Max turned to her. "Of course you are, right?"

Eve looked back and forth between the two, her ears quivering. *I can't go back to Moenia, not with Max. Besides, he'll be safe with Mr. Penna. Won't he?* "I…I don't want to go."

"Ahh, come on, Eve. You are the one always wanting a new adventure, after all. Besides, it'd be a lot more fun with you."

Eve shook her head and backed towards the study door. "No, no, I don't think I want to. Mrs. Tassi wouldn't let me anyway."

"Are you sure, Eve?"

"Yes, I'm sure. Well…good night." Eve turned and ran out of the house.

Max stared after Eve. "What got in to her?"

Mr. Penna stood and placed a hand on Max's shoulder. "Moenia is a very different place from our little village, Maxwell. You will find that out for yourself soon enough. Well, we both better start packing. The sun's already set and we have an early start tomorrow."

Max ran to his room to begin packing. *I finally get to see Protector Headquarters, but I wish Eve was coming with us. We've done everything together. Maybe she didn't want to be around Tyco that long. He was rather mean to her today, more so than usual, but she usually ignores him. I guess I'll have to tell her about it when I get back. I can't pass this up, it's another step closer to dad.*

After finishing packing, Max lay late into the night with dreams of standing with other Protectors, ready to respond to anyone in need of help.

# CHAPTER THREE

Mrs. Tassi bustled about the cafe setting up tables. "Sun will be comin' up soon."

"Yeah," murmured Eve. She sat in a chair, arms wrapped around her legs, her knees pulled up to her chest.

Mrs. Tassi stopped for a moment. "I'm sure I can find someone to help out here for a few weeks."

Eve's mind wandered to some far off place. "I can't help him out there."

Mrs. Tassi turned to face Eve. "I seem to recall a little girl who didn't want something to be found; her teeth bared, claws extended, ready to take on a whole horde of bandits." A little smirk, the one Eve had unknowingly copied over the years, formed on Mrs. Tassi's lips. "I don't think the fact she might not be able to actually take them on ever entered her mind."

Eve looked up at Mrs. Tassi. "I didn't know what I was doing."

"You knew you aimed to protect Max, no matter the cost." Mrs. Tassi sat down in front of Eve. "And from what you said about that messenger, you may need to do it again." Mrs. Tassi gently took one of Eve's hands. "What's stopping you?"

Eve started to whimper. She looked down at the floor. "Nobody cares about the laws against the lacarna out here, but in the city I'll be watched wherever I go. To make it worse, Max is going to the Protector's Headquarters. I can't go there. I won't be able to help him, and when Max finds out that I'm the enemy; that Protectors don't associate with lacarna…" Eve shook her head. "If I go, I'll only be sent away. It's easier to stay here. Then I won't have to see him when he finds out about the lacarna…about me."

Eve brought her tail around, tightly grabbed hold of it with her free hand, and softly cried. Mrs. Tassi, still holding onto Eve's right hand, leaned over and put her arm around Eve's shoulders.

"Do you honestly think that boy would send you, his best friend, away?"

"He has to if he wants to become a Protector."

"Eve, I thought you had figured out by now that people always do what they want to. If anyone says someone made them, it's only because they were too weak to do anything else. Think about Max's father. Did you ever see him back down, even in the end? Then there is Chiron, who has cared for Max all these years. He certainly broke rules when he helped us adopt you, a lacarna.

Eve's ears perked up, she stifled a sob. "What does Mr. Penna have to do with me?"

"I don't know much, but he worked for the Protectors when he helped us get you out of that awful market. The rest you need to ask him about."

Eve slouched. "But, just because you guys broke the rules doesn't mean Max will. It's his dream to be like his father, to be a Protector."

"Don't you remember how well Max's father treated you? Max got to see that, and Mr. Penna has done everything to teach that boy how to make up his own mind about things. Max has also had you, Eve. He's seen someone first hand fight for what they believe in. He's even had a lacarnian risk her own safety for him. A thing like that is not easily dismissed. Can I promise you what Max will ultimately do? No, but he deserves a chance; the same chance you want for yourself. Until then, if you care about him that much, fight for him like you did all those years ago, no matter the cost."

Eve's voice steadied. "But, how am I even supposed to get into Moenia? A lacarnian can only enter with their owner."

"I'll transfer ownership to Mr. Penna or Max."

"No!" Eve bit her lip and looked down. "I mean, I've never belonged to anyone else." Eve stamped her foot and stared back at Mrs. Tassi. "And I don't want to either! You're my mother."

Mrs. Tassi let go of Eve's hand and stood up, smiling. "There's my girl. Eve, that piece of paper never legally made me your mother, only your owner, and you know it. Your father and I decided you'd be our daughter and not some slave. I tell you right now, as long as you'll have me, I'll be your mother whether I own you or not. Now, I'll take care of the details with Mr. Penna. You hurry up and go pack. There isn't much time."

Eve got up from the chair to walk towards her room. The sound of her mother's agitated voice stopped her. "Oh, and Eve, for goodness sakes, get rid of that mouse or take it with you. But whichever it is, don't you dare leave it here."

A smile formed once again on Eve's face. The anger in her mother's voice sounded a little too forced.

## CHAPTER FOUR

The first light of dawn had appeared in the eastern sky when Max and Mr. Penna arrived at the stable. Tyco was waiting for them next to his horse, his things already packed.

"The stable master has Starlight saddled up for you, Max. I'll help you get your gear fastened. As for you, Mr. Penna, he has a couple of horses for you to choose from. He's in the back of the stable."

Max walked up to Starlight. "I sure hope Starlight will be okay. I've never taken her on such a long ride before."

Mr. Penna laughed. "She will be fine, Max. She has seen far more country than you can even imagine. After all, she was the one that brought your father here so many years ago." Mr. Penna turned and started for the stable. "Now, I shall go and see what our fine stable master, Hektor, has for me."

While Mr. Penna sought out Hektor, Max inspected Starlight. He never grew tired of looking at her. Her coat was pitch black. Here and there she had small white circular patches. From those circles, thin, short strips of white hair stretched out in various directions. These patches closely resembled the stars shining in the night; thus her name, Starlight. Her coat, well groomed over the years, still held a beautiful shine. Max had a feeling Hektor loved her as much as he did.

Tyco helped Max fasten his bedroll and traveling pack onto Starlight's back. He brought the most basic of necessities. Max was tightening the last strap when Mr. Penna came out of the stables riding a rather plain looking brown mare.

Tyco furrowed his eyebrows. "I've never seen that horse before."

Mr. Penna chuckled. "She belongs to a merchant in Moenia. The mare injured her leg when he was here a few months back. He left her with Hektor to mend. Hektor took good care of her and now she's ready to be returned to the merchant. Seeing how we are going to Moenia, I volunteered to deliver her."

Tyco grimaced. "In other words, you got a free ride."

Mr. Penna winked at Max. "Precisely."

Tyco mounted his own horse, Teak, a large brown stallion with a white blaze of hair on his head. Max could only imagine the foals he and Starlight might have because the two would not have anything to do with one another.

Tyco gripped Teak's reins. "Well, are we ready then?"

Max's gaze wandered up the street. "Yeah, I guess so."

Tyco, impatient, chided him. "Then you might want to try getting on the horse. We'll move quicker that way."

"Yeah, okay."

Max mounted Starlight and moved her beside the other two. They faced out towards the open countryside. The morning dew sparkled in the sunlight, but Max sat unaware of its beauty.

"I thought she would at least come and say goodbye."

Tyco nodded his head. "Good. It's just as well that she didn't."

Max looked oddly at Tyco. "What do you mean by that?"

"You'll see soon enough. Besides, it's time we got moving."

Tyco nudged Teak with his heels.

"But..."

Mr. Penna smiled. "Do not worry about it, Maxwell. Tyco likes things neat and orderly. We both know that is not exactly Evangeline's style."

Mr. Penna followed Tyco. Max didn't feel that's what Tyco meant, but he wasn't going to contradict Mr. Penna. Instead he leaned forward in the saddle, preparing to follow the others, when he heard someone call his name from behind. Turning, he saw Eve running up the street towards them.

"Hey, Maxy! Wait up!"

Max turned Starlight around, a smile forming on his lips as he also saw Mrs. Tassi running a good distance behind Eve. Max laughed at the sight. He had yet to meet anyone who could keep up with Eve when she was in a hurry. Eve reached Max in no time, not even winded by the run.

"What's the big idea, trying to leave before I could get here?"

Max felt a little ashamed that he had thought she wouldn't come and say goodbye. "I thought you might have had more important things to do than to see me off."

Eve grinned slyly. "You bet I did, but then I figured as helpless as you are there was no telling whether you'd ever make it back alive or not. So, I figured I had better get my last goodbye in while I had a chance."

Tyco and Mr. Penna had heard the commotion and came up behind Max. Mr. Penna nodded at the bedroll and backpack Eve had slung behind her.

"Good morning, Miss Evangeline. I see you have decided to come along with us after all."

"Yep!"

Max had not expected that. He had missed the backpack when she arrived. He only knew that last night she certainly did not want to go. Now he was confused, which happened a lot around Eve.

"I thought you only came to see us off."

Eve swung the backpack down to the ground. "You really aren't very observant, are you? Worse yet, it's not even dark this time."

Max's face flushed red. "Now wait..." but before he could finish Mrs. Tassi arrived, somewhat out of breath. Tyco used the opening to speak.

"I'm glad you could make it in time to say goodbye, Evangeline. Unfortunately, I'm sorry to say, you won't be able to go with us since the only horses Hektor has left need to stay here for the villagers."

Eve shrugged, unconcerned. "That's okay, Tyco. I can walk."

Tyco snorted. "Walk! It's over a week's time, even by horseback, to the capital."

Eve got annoyed. "Unless you plan on riding full out the whole way, I'll have no trouble keeping up."

Mr. Penna broke in before things could go further. "I'm sure you can, Evangeline. Besides, you can ride with Maxwell for at least part of the trip. Starlight will hardly notice the difference."

Eve perked back up. "That sounds great, Mr. Penna." Eve narrowed her eyes at Max. "At least *someone* doesn't think I weigh too much."

Max threw his arms up. "You were crouched on my chest!"

Having finally caught her breath, Mrs. Tassi said. "Well, now that that's settled, you'd best be on your way."

Behind them Tyco turned Teak back around and start off again, but not before Max saw the agitation in his face. He wondered why it bothered Tyco so much that Eve decided to join them.

*Oh well, maybe he's just grumpy in the mornings. I know I prefer to sleep in.*

Max reached down and helped Eve up behind him. She squeezed tight against his back, surprising him. Usually she left a little space between them, but that was without the packs strapped on Starlight. Max felt a little awkward and caught a funny grin on Mrs. Tassi's face. He looked away and she cleared her throat.

"Well, now that you two are comfy, I brought a little of my cooking for you."

She reached into the basket she had been carrying and brought out a cloth bundle. Max took the bundle and passed it under his nose.

"They're biscuits I made this morning. Since they're fresh, they'll be good until you reach Moenia. Be sure to save them until you get close. Trust me, after a few days of those travel rations you'll be ready for some of my biscuits."

"Okay, Mrs. Tassi, we'll wait. Thank you."

Max put the bundle in one of the side packs fastened to Starlight.

"You'd better. Now," Mrs. Tassi held out her hand, "that will be one silver piece."

Max jerked straight which caused him to bump Eve who shoved him back. "A silver piece?"

Mrs. Tassi stifled a laugh and did her best to act serious. "You didn't think those were free, did you? I do run a cafe, after all. Can't just be giving food away."

Max's shoulders sagged. "But a whole silver piece. Don't you think that's a bit much?"

"Just think of it as back pay for all the food you've helped yourself to over the years. With you taking off across the dead lands, who knows when I'd ever get my due."

"But…"

By this time, Mr. Penna had begun to laugh so heartily he needed to grab his saddle horn to keep from falling off the horse. "Just pay her, Maxwell. You are not going to win against Mrs. Tassi."

Max knew Mr. Penna was right. He gave in and dug one of the few silver coins he had out of his pocket.

"Okay, here you go."

"Thank you, Max." Mrs. Tassi took the coin and put it in her apron pocket. "Oh, I almost forgot." She reached back in the basket and pulled out a smaller bundle. "This is for you, Eve."

Eve reached down and took the bundle from Mrs. Tassi. She peeped under the wrappings and giggled a moment before a more contemplative look appeared. "Thank you, Mother."

Mrs. Tassi smiled brightly at Eve. "You're welcome."

Max tried to turn around to face Eve but with her so close behind him he couldn't. "What is it? When did you start calling Mrs. Tassi Mother?"

Eve put the bundle in her pocket. "It's none of your business. Let's get going."

Eve kicked her heels into Starlight, who jolted forward at a fast trot. Max quickly faced forward to steady himself, but shouted back at Eve.

"I'm starting to think it was a mistake asking you along."

Eve laughed merrily. "And just think, it's only the first day."

Max shook his head as he got Starlight to slow down. His thoughts swirled around the adventure ahead while Eve strained to hear the conversation between Mr. Penna and Mrs. Tassi back at the stable.

"Do not worry, Mrs. Tassi. I will wait as long as possible to tell him about Evangeline's papers. He won't like it at first, but I think he will understand soon enough. He is much like his father."

"Thank you, Mr. Penna."

Mr. Penna chuckled. "I will say, you are a sly one, Mrs. Tassi. It is no wonder why that girl gives Maxwell so much trouble. She is your daughter through and through, adopted or not."

"I've done all I can for her. She's on her own now."

"Not if Maxwell becomes…"

Starlight carried Eve out of hearing distance, but that was fine. She had heard enough. Both Mr. Penna and her mother had faith in Max. She had to trust them that things would turn out okay. Eve, though she had no fear of falling, wrapped her arms around Max.

## CHAPTER FIVE

Tyco kept them at an easy pace as they left Swiftwater. To the west of them loomed the dead lands, beyond which lay Moenia, the capital and their eventual destination. To the north and east stretched open plains in which Max and Eve had spent most of their childhood riding and playing. The safest way to cross the dead lands lay towards the north at the Clanrye River.

Max grew excited at the thought of seeing the river and everything that lay beyond. Starlight picked up on Max's excitement and began to trot. They had not gone far before hearing a shout from Tyco.

"Slow it down a little there, Max."

Max pulled back on Starlight's reins. "Whoa!" Max turned to look back at Tyco. "Sorry, guess Starlight is a little excited."

Eve giggled. "Yeah, it's all Starlight's fault. I'm sure she's very excited to go and see the capital."

Max turned to look over his shoulder. "You know, you could be walking right now."

Eve smiled. "Yep, and I'd probably get there quicker."

Tyco and Mr. Penna caught back up to Max. They now rode three abreast. Tyco eyed Starlight.

"Starlight's a fine horse, but she'll need that energy for crossing the dead lands. It is not a path you mosey along on, enjoying the scenery as you go."

"But don't the Protectors have camps along the path?"

"They do, but they are spaced far enough apart that you need to keep moving from first light till dusk in order to make it from one to the next. Otherwise, you'll be caught out in the dark between camps. Nighttime in the dead lands is a very unpleasant experience."

"What about those who don't have horses?"

"If you absolutely have to travel by foot, then you do so in large, well-armed groups. However, Protectors provide horses for rent on both sides of the dead lands."

Eve let out a snicker. "Well isn't that nice of them. Let me guess, you have to pay a fee at each of the camps along the way as well."

"It helps pay for the cost of having members of the Protectors stationed at the camps." Tyco nudged Teak a little ahead of the others.

Eve snorted in disgust. Max elbowed her and spoke up so Tyco could still hear him. "Makes sense to me. It's like paying to stay at an inn."

Max could feel the cold stare from Eve. "I suppose, as long as it's a fair price."

To ease the tension, Max had Starlight slow a bit until they were several lengths behind Tyco and Mr. Penna where he began telling Eve what he thought they might see on their trip. She held silent at first, but soon joined with her own ideas.

In the early evening when they stopped to make camp. Not long after everyone had dismounted, Mr. Penna called out to Eve.

"Evangeline, can you come over here and give me a hand please?"

"Yep!"

Eve walked over to Mr. Penna, who had stopped a little short of the others. He leaned over and whispered something to her before she began to help him unpack. That surprised Max. Usually he had to do the grunt work. He shrugged his shoulders and went to work unpacking his own things.

*What are they up to?*

Max finished unpacking about the time Eve and Mr. Penna, with the mare in tow, rejoined the rest of them. Mr. Penna tethered his mare to Teak and left them and Starlight to graze. Tyco and Max had no fear of them running away; both had long since proven dedicated to their masters.

Everyone sat down together in a circle to enjoy a meal of dried meat and fruit before the sun set. By the time they finished, the stars and moon had appeared in the clear night sky giving them light to see by. As they enjoyed the cool night, Max watched Eve take out the small bundle Mrs. Tassi had given her. She carefully unwrapped it, revealing a wedge of cheese. Max's eyebrows furrowed.

"I didn't think you liked cheese, Eve?"

"I don't," Eve gave her usual mischievous grin, "but it's not for me."

"Then who?"

Eve reached into her shirt pocket and pulled out a brown and white mouse. With an expression that dared Max to say something, she placed the furry little thing on the ground in front of her.

Max sat in complete disbelief. He watched Eve as she broke off a piece of the cheese and held it out in front of the mouse. It took the cheese immediately and started to nibbling. Eve lay down on her stomach, propped her head up in her hands and watched her new friend eat. Max shook his head. At times he really did think she was crazy.

"I'm not sure which I'm having a harder time believing: that you brought that thing with you or that Mrs. Tassi actually gave you cheese to feed it."

Mr. Penna, who sat next to Max, watched Eve and her mouse as well. He let out a soft chuckle.

"Despite her fussing, Mrs. Tassi has quite a soft spot for all creatures of Velrune, though I doubt it was for the mouse in this case." Mr. Penna broke out into a hardy laugh. "People, on the other hand, should be wary of her."

Max sighed. "Well, I guess if the little guy is coming with us we might as well give him his share."

Max reached into his saddle pack and brought out a piece of bread. He broke off a corner and tossed it over to the mouse. The crumb barely touched the ground before the mouse snatched it, ran over to Eve and hopped back into her shirt pocket.

Eve giggled and looked over at Max with a twinkle in her eye. She gave him an odd smile that he had not seen before.

"Thanks Maxy."

Max tried to figure out the her expression and only half paid attention as she continued.

"Oh, and, by the way, her name is Spook."

Still confused, Max jumped when Tyco interrupted them. "I think it's about time we got to sleep. After tomorrow, we have a lot of hard riding ahead of us. We'll need all the rest we can get."

Tyco stood and walked over to his bedroll. He lay down and quickly went to sleep. Eve rolled over onto her back, so as not to squish Spook, and soon fell asleep herself. Max shook his head and heard a soft chuckle from Mr. Penna.

"I don't understand her, Mr. Penna."

"Nor will you ever, Maxwell, not completely. Do not worry though. It is more important that you try, not so much that you actually do. Over the next couple of weeks you must remember that."

Max shook his head again. "I don't understand you either. Do you ever just say what you mean?"

Mr. Penna rocked back, slapping his knee and laughing. "There are times you are so much like your father, Maxwell."

Mr. Penna faced out into the open plains and grew somber. "I believe Mrs. Tassi has put her trust in the right person."

Max wondered what Mrs. Tassi had to do with the conversation. "What?"

Mr. Penna cleared his throat as he shook off the thought. "Tyco is right, Maxwell. We will need our rest. Get to sleep."

Max sighed. He knew he wouldn't get any more information.

He flopped down on the ground and fell asleep. Dreams of cats and mice playing together all across Velrune filled his night.

The next morning, the four repacked their gear with Spook supervising from atop Eve's shoulder. Max mounted Starlight and bent to help Eve up behind him. He noticed at once that she now wore a pink band around her neck. It was about a half inch in width and had a small pink stone set in the front.

"I've never seen you wear that before."

Eve crossed her arms. "Mrs. Tassi gave it to me before we left. It's popular to wear them in Moenia."

Max looked at it with some amusement. "If you say so."

To Max, the band resembled a collar you would find on someone's pet. The stone looked smooth and seemed to give off a very faint glow unlike anything Max had previously seen. Eve's crossed arms, however, warned him to drop the subject. He helped her on the horse.

The landscape changed little as they rode north, so Max grew excited when in the afternoon he spotted a line of trees that spanned the horizon.

"Finally, we're getting somewhere."

In response, Max heard the familiar, dry, voice Mr. Pennas used in his classes.

"That would be the river Clanrye. The Clanrye starts as a spring in the mountains to the far northeast. Several springs empty into it as it winds down the mountains and across the plains. It then flows over the cliffs and into the dead lands, sustaining the camps below. We will be crossing it shortly before the dropoff as the trail down lies on the other side."

Max rolled his eyes. "You really do plan on stuffing me with as much information as possible on this trip, don't you?"

Mr. Penna laughed. "There is always something to be learned, Maxwell."

The four soon reached the edge of the river. Tyco scanned the bank.

"There should be a ferry somewhere near here that we can

use to cross."

Eve stared nervously at the rushing water and moaned. "A ferry? I was sure I remembered crossing over on a bridge."

Tyco looked back at Eve. "You most likely crossed at Hedgewood. Unfortunately, that is almost a four day ride to the east." A grin formed on his face. "We'll understand if you're too frightened to cross and continue with us."

Eve's eyes stayed fixed on the river as it cascaded down the steep slopes not far to their left. She gave a slight quiver. She really didn't like Tyco.

"No, I'm going."

Max twisted around on the horse.

"When did you cross the river, Eve?"

Eve's voice was distant. "Back when Mr. and Mrs. Tassi brought me to Swiftwater."

The grin left Tyco's face and he started riding towards the east. "Let's head up the river a bit. The crossing shouldn't be far."

Max tried to question Eve further, but he could not draw her attention. Before long, they came to a dock with a large winch. On the far side of the river, Max spotted the ferry. Tyco nodded towards it.

"There it is on the other side. We'll have to pull it back using the winch."

Tyco dismounted Teak, walked over to the winch and began to turn the attached wheel. Everyone else, except Eve, got off of the horses. She turned to Mr. Penna.

"Um, just how wide is the river?"

Mr. Penna answered without hesitation. "Three hundred and twenty feet; give or take a few feet."

"A-and how deep?"

"Twenty-five feet in the center."

Tyco looked up from the winch, that unpleasant grin back.

"Sure you want to go with us Eve? If you're not careful you might end up going for a swim. Well, I guess lacarnians don't swim, do they?"

Mr. Penna turned to Eve.

"Don't worry, Evangeline, a properly weighted ferry is very safe. You will be fine."

Max reached out and helped Eve off of Starlight. "Yeah Eve, don't worry. I personally have no intention of going for a swim, so I won't let you either."

Eve slid off the horse. She wondered if Tyco came this way on purpose just to try and make her turn back. She shivered again as the small ferry reached the dock.

"That looks awfully small for all of us and the horses to fit on."

Tyco inspected the ferry. "Well, it was built to only carry two riders and their horses. We'll need to make two trips. Mr. Penna and I will take Teak and the mare. The ferry is made so you can pull it along the ropes strung over the river. Once we are across, Max, you will have to use the winch to bring it back. When you and Starlight are on, Mr. Penna and I will use the winch on the other side to pull you over."

Eve crossed her arms "And me."

"We'll see." Tyco grabbed Teak's reins and led him onto the ferry.

Mr. Penna sighed. "You will be fine, Evangeline." He led the mare on to the ferry and together he and Tyco began to pull it across the river.

Max watched them cross. "It sure is a lot bigger than the Swiftwater River at home, and a good bit deeper too."

Eve's voice cracked. "Yep."

Max grimaced. *That was a stupid thing to say.*

Eve stood trembling, her tail tight in her hands. Max gently took hold of her arm. "You've worked hard on your swimming. You've gotten pretty good at it."

"Yeah, but the water in the Swiftwater is only chest deep, and I wasn't even in the river, it was a small pool off to the side."

Max let go of Eve's arm and laughed. "And yet you still almost managed to drown me."

Eve stared down at her feet and mumbled. "I'm sorry."

Max wondered what else might be bothering Eve. It was unlike her to be so nervous. He remembered the first time she waded into the little pool by the Swiftwater River. She had shaken with fright, but had still made jokes. Now she stood silently with her head hung low.

Max didn't know what else he could say, so he remained quiet for the next several minutes. A shout from across the river brought him back to the present. He faced the far bank and saw that Tyco and Mr. Penna had reached it. They signaled him to bring the ferry back across.

Max stepped up to the wheel for the winch. "Come on, Eve, our turn."

Together they worked the winch to pull the ferry back over to their side. Max led Starlight on to it then turned to check on Eve. Her trembling had resumed. She stood firmly on the edge of the bank.

Max tried to reassure her. "You'll be fine, Eve."

"May...Maybe...I...I should just go home."

Max scratched his head then tried a different tactic.

"I suppose it would be less of a hassle if you did. I'd get into a lot less trouble, and it would certainly be nice not to have to worry about getting pounced on every time I walked by a dark corner."

Eve's shaking subsided a little. "You would get into plenty of trouble by yourself. I'm the one always getting you out of it."

A wry smile crept onto Max's face. "If that's the case, you sure have a funny way of doing it. I think you're confused on what helping means."

That did it. The fire in Eve's eyes flared up.

"Maybe I should stay here, and you can get out of your own trouble then."

"Maybe so, but I've got a better idea. Why don't you let me help you get across this river and show you how you're supposed to get someone out of trouble? Then, just maybe, I'll let you come along and see if you can do any better."

Eve turned her nose up. "I...I suppose we could try that

instead."

"Alright then."

Max stepped off the ferry and walked over to Eve. She didn't look as scared, but he could still feel her trembling when he took her hand. Eve, tail in hand, tightly wrapped her other arm around Max's waist. Together they walked to the ferry where they boarded, moving opposite of Starlight. Max sat down with Eve, her grip around him even tighter.

"Now then, all we have to do is let Tyco and Mr. Penna do all the work while we take a nice ride across."

"Kay."

Eve sat stone still the breadth of the river, not making the slightest peep. The ferry soon reached the dock on the other side where Max guided Eve off the ferry. Once on the shore she stopped shaking. Her tail, badly ruffled where she had held it, waved back and forth behind her once more.

Tyco and Mr. Penna had already mounted their horses. Max let go of Eve and went back for Starlight. He led her off the ferry and climbed into the saddle. Mr. Penna gave Eve the pleasant smile he reserved only for her.

"For a minute there, Evangeline, I did not think you were going to be joining us."

Eve smiled back. "For a moment, I wasn't sure either."

Eve turned and looked at the path that led down into the dead lands. One last shiver ran down her as she thought about what lie ahead.

*Well, I've come this far, and I'm not going back across that river again. Might as well see what happens next.* She took a deep breath, held it for a second, then let it out.

"Well, let's get going."

Without any further hesitation, Eve walked west towards the narrow path that led over the cliff wall. The quick change caught Max off guard. She reached the edge of the path without him realizing it.

"Don't you want to ride, Eve?"

Eve paused and looked back over her shoulder. "Sorry, I can't now."

*Why do I even try to understand her?* "What do you mean you can't?"

Mr. Penna cleared his throat. "The path up ahead is narrow and somewhat steep. It would be too dangerous for both of you to be on the horse."

Eve smiled at Mr. Penna. "Thanks Mr. Penna, but it's okay." She faced Max and crossed her arms. "I'm not allowed to ride horses." She did an about face and continued down the path.

"Huh? Not allowed? But you rode this far."

Tyco grunted. "Iacarna are not allowed to ride horses. Unfortunately, there are not enough Protectors to enforce the laws on this side of the dead lands." The smirk reformed on Tyco's face. "There will be in the camps though. She'll have to abide by the law from here on in." Tyco nudged Teak and started down the path.

Max turned to Mr. Penna. "There's actually a law that she can't ride a horse? Why?"

Mr. Penna sounded rather disgusted. "You will soon find out there are several laws concerning the Iacarna. Few for which I can find a good reason. Perhaps it is something you can inquire of the Protectors once you meet them in Moenia. They are the ones responsible for most of them, after all."

With that Mr. Penna urged his horse after the others, leaving Max with all kinds of questions. *Can't anyone give a straight answer?*

Max nudged Starlight to follow Mr. Penna. *I guess I'll find out for myself soon enough.*

## CHAPTER SIX

The narrow path into the dead lands forced the group to travel in single file. Eve led the procession, finding the steep, crumbling trail of little concern. The rest kept to themselves, their focus on every step their horses took down the zig-zagging path. They reached the bottom just as the last few rays of sunlight faded from the sky.

Before them lay the first encampment. A low stone wall curved out from the cliff face to surround the camp, providing a boundary from the dead lands beyond. At its center, a large bonfire blazed high, illuminating three poorly made stone buildings positioned equal distance from the flames. At the far edge of the fire's light stood several rickety wooden shacks.

Mr. Penna leaned over to Max. "The building next to the cliff wall is the inn. The one closest to us, the stable. The third is the guardhouse."

"It's a lot bigger than I expected."

"It has the towns of Hedgwood and Pike to support it."

"What are the wooden shacks?"

"Peddlers built them. They sell last minute supplies to those who are about to cross the dead lands. Their goods are rather expensive in order to take advantage of forgetful travelers. That is why I made sure we had everything we needed before leaving Swiftwater."

Tyco pointed at the guardhouse. "All travelers passing

through the dead lands report to the guards first. It makes it easier to notify families when someone turns up missing."

They moved towards the guardhouse, passing the bonfire along the way. Tyco nodded in its direction. "Most travelers set up camp next to the fire. We'll be staying in the inn, however."

When they reached the stone building, Tyco dismounted and went inside. Max and Mr. Penna dismounted as well and waited for Tyco to return. Eve wandered over to the building and leaned against it. She was trying to hear the conversation inside without Max and Mr. Penna catching her doing so. An unknown man spoke.

"Lieutenant Biros, we've been expecting you."

"Well, here I am, along with three others, one of which is a lacarnian."

"That is more than we were expecting, Sir."

Tyco growled. "Plans have changed."

"Yes sir. Is the fleabag at least registered?"

"Of course she is, now what about our rooms."

"There are still two rooms left, Sir. Each has two beds."

"Fine, we'll use both."

The door to the outpost began to open. Eve hopped away and ran over to Max and Mr. Penna before Tyco stepped out.

"I have registered us and it seems there is still one room open in the inn."

Tyco faced Max. "It has two beds, so as long as you don't mind sharing with Mr. Penna we're good."

He then turned to Eve. "It looks like you will have to be outside again."

Eve stared at Tyco. "Only one left? Didn't seem like there were that many people here."

Max shook his head. "Wait a minute, Tyco. Can't you and Mr. Penna share a bed? Eve can have the other one and I'll stay on the floor."

Tyco smiled. "Sorry Max, I'm a loner."

Eve tilted her nose up. "It's okay Max. I'd rather stay outside anyway."

Before Max could get in another word she grabbed her bedroll from Starlight and took off toward the campfire.

Tyco clapped his hands together. "Well, that settles that, shall we go?"

Max watched Eve as she walked past some other travelers and stopped in a vacant area on the far side of the campfire. "Actually, I think I'll stay out here as well."

Tyco's voice grew stern. "Don't be ridiculous, Max. You'll need a good night's sleep."

"I'll be fine out here, and I'm sure Mr. Penna would rather have the bed to himself." Max took Starlight's reins and followed after Eve.

"Max, get back here!"

Max ignored Tyco, reaching Eve just after she had finished unrolling her bedroll.

"It looks like you've found a nice spot."

Eve looked up in surprise. "What are you doing here?"

Max laughed and began to unpack his things from Starlight. "Thanks for the welcome."

"Sorry, Max, it's just that I haven't known you to turn down a bed."

"Normally no, but haven't you noticed how much Mr. Penna snores? The last thing I want is to be trapped in the same bed as him."

Eve giggled, beyond Max she saw Mr. Penna walking towards them. "Actually, I hadn't really noticed. Just how bad is Mr. Penna's snoring?"

"Oh it's awful, I'm lucky I haven't gone deaf."

"Is that so?" Max nearly jumped out of his skin at the sound of Mr. Penna's voice.. He spun around and saw Mr. Penna a few feet away.

"Mr. Penna, I thought you went over to the inn with Tyco."

Mr. Penna crossed his arms. "So I gathered."

Eve burst out laughing..

"You saw him coming didn't you?"

"Yep!" managed Eve between laughs.

Mr. Penna gave a deep, hearty laugh.

"Why did you follow us, Mr. Penna? Aren't you going to stay in the Inn?"

"It is a beautiful night, Maxwell. I thought I might enjoy the outdoors. That is, if you will have me, snoring and all?"

Max shook his head and went back to unpacking his horse. Mr. Penna gave a chuckle and did the same. When Max finished he started to take Starlight to the stables. Mr. Penna stopped him.

"Leave Starlight here, Maxwell. The prices for the stables are outrageous. I am afraid Evangeline was on the right track yesterday. The Protectors have a nice little market going for themselves."

Max dropped the reins and helped Mr. Penna unpack instead. Once finished, the three sat down to eat. Eve let Spook out, giving her some of the cheese Mrs. Tassi had sent. The little mouse devoured it then ran around picking up everyone's crumbs. Max watched for a while before voicing what had been eating at him since crossing the river.

"You know, Eve, we've know each other so long that I'd stopped thinking about the fact you're a different race. I mean, sure you've got ears and a tail, but, to me, that's like someone else having freckles or a big nose. I guess I really don't know what the lacarnians are." Max studied Eve's red tail and ears. "Guess that means I don't know what you are. It never really mattered to me."

Eve smiled and shrugged her shoulders. "I don't really know a whole lot myself. I don't remember much before coming to Swiftwater. I know I was in a forest first. Then I remember being squeezed in a room with others like me in the city. Then I was handed over to Mr. and Mrs. Tassi and taken on a long ride to Swiftwater. Anything I know about what I actually am as a lacarna came from Mr. Penna."

Max turned to Mr. Penna. "Why have you never told me about Eve's people? You've been relentless about everything else with my education."

Mr. Penna sighed, "Because I made a promise to your father, Maxwell, to let you learn for yourself about the lacarna. It may have been a mistake, but he was adamant that you form your own opinion of them."

Max swallowed hard, "My father? But why? Are they really that different from us?"

"Not so much now, but at one time, yes."

"When was that? What did they used to be like? Why did they change?"

Mr. Penna laughed. "Are you actually asking for a lecture? I never believed I would see the day."

Max didn't laugh, which caused Mr. Penna to grow serious once again.

"All right, so be it. There are not a lot of detailed facts about our planet so I will give you what is common lore of Velrune. I will do my best to keep my own thoughts out of the picture. What you do with this information in days to come is up to you."

Mr. Penna cleared his throat and began.

"It is said the Creators came from the outer reaches of the cosmos. When they came across Velrune they found it very appealing and decided to make it there home. They first populated the planet with a variety of wild beasts and plants. Little thought was given to the overall design, resulting in chaos. To bring order, they decided to create a more intelligent creature, one they could communicate with. They would need to make this new creature strong, agile and quick in order for it to survive. Thus they created the lacarna." Mr. Penna winked at Eve. "The first lacarna were different from what you see now, Maxwell. They were designed as an animal, like a large panther, but the Creators gave them the ability to change form. In this other form, they stood on two legs and could speak the language of the Creators.

"The lacarna's strength and intelligence soon brought order to the previous chaos. Velrune became a welcoming place, enough so, that many of the Creators decided it was time to live on it.

"It is unclear how much time passed before the Creators decided to make us, humans. Why they made us is unclear as well. It is believed the lacarna leaned to far towards their beast-like natures whereas that the Creators wanted a being more like themselves. Whatever the reason, humankind came to be and time continued to pass.

"The humans multiplied and spread across Velrune. Their relationship with the Creators began to change as they began to worship them as gods. It was during this time that the Creators living on Velrune became known as Immortals. The humans named them this to separate them from those that were said to exist in the cosmos.

"When the humans began to worship the Immortals, they denied the lacarna the right to see them, thinking of them as nothing more than beasts. The lacarna grew angry and demanded to see the Creators. When the humans continued to deny them access, war erupted.

"It was a short war. The lacarna nearly wiped out the humans before the Immortals put a stop to it. They realized it was their error in letting the humans take things so far. It had not been their intention to be worshiped. To return peace they decided three things. First, the Immortals spread out to live with both the humans and the lacarna. Second, they instituted a ruling body made up of members of both races. This ruling body they called the Protectors. Finally, they encouraged the two beings to live and work among each other.

"Over time, the two races did mix and things remained in order. However, after approximately six hundred years, the Immortals suddenly disappeared. Rumors as to the reasons behind their disappearance spread, each race blaming the other.

"As the accusations increased, war broke out again. This time the sides were more evenly matched. The lacarna had lost many of their beast-like qualities from mating with the humans and the humans had much greater numbers.

"The war raged on for several years, each side losing most of their population. Finally, both sides near extinction, the Protectors were able to bring about peace with the following proposal. The lacarna would stay in the distant wilds or dense forest areas. Any lacarna entering a settlement could do so only if accompanied by a human. Likewise, humans would stay in the open regions and in the settlements that had already been built. They were not to enter the forest unless escorted by a lacarna. The two races were free to marry one another but such unions were needed to be registered with the Protectors."

Mr. Penna dropped out of his lecture tone and focused on Eve and Max. "Those are the terms that each race lives by today."

Max tried to process Mr. Penna's story. "I guess I can understand the Protectors' terms at that time. But, why still today?"

"Many humans still fear the lacarna, Maxwell."

"Yeah, but I'm not afraid of Eve. Besides, what does that have to do with what Tyco said about a law against a lacarnian riding a horse?"

"I am afraid any more comments I have would only break my promise to your father Maxwell. I will end this conversation with one last fact. There have not been any lacarnians in the Protectors for a long time."

Max shook his head. "I don't understand, Mr. Penna. I don't understand why my father would have you make such a promise, or why the Protectors would place so many restrictions. I mean, Eve is one of the nicest people I know. The only time I've ever even seen her bare her claws is when she was protecting me."

"I am glad you have Evangeline, Maxwell. She is pretty typical of her race." Mr. Penna let out a soft chuckle. "Not that I would ever accuse Evangeline of being typical."

Eve's cheeks pinked a little. Mr. Penna continued.

"I have met many lacarnians, Maxwell; all friendly. Once, your father and I were even honored guests in one of their forest villages. However, many people only know what the Protectors tell them."

Mr. Penna paused in thought, becoming very serious. "About Evangeline's claws, Maxwell, never tell anyone that she has them. It is strictly forbidden for any registered lacarna to have them. In fact, their claws are removed before they are allowed to enter a city."

Max stared in disbelief. "That's awful...but, why then does Eve still have hers?"

A smile crossed Mr. Penna's face. "My guess? Someone forgot to check when they first registered her."

Max brought his attention back to Eve, who sat with her head bowed, scribbling absent-mindedly in the dirt.

"I can see now why you didn't want to come with us, if people really are that afraid of the lacarna, but why didn't you tell me?"

Eve raised her head. Tears filled her eyes. She could barely be heard. "I didn't know how, and I didn't think you would be my friend anymore."

Eve quickly looked down at the ground again. Max stumbled for something to say He hadn't seen Eve cry since the night his father died.

"Shoot, Eve, there have been times when I could have sworn you were the devil himself. The fire in your eyes when you get an idea for an adventure; that red hair of yours blowing about, yet I never stopped being your friend. I knew you would never hurt me. Finding out your long lost ancestors were wild beasts or that there are a few stupid laws your race has to follow isn't going to change that."

Eve looked up at Max and stared at him for what seemed like ages. He began to wonder if he would survive until morning. He was pretty sure she would never hurt him. At long last, she made a sound that fell between a sob and a laugh.

"I think that had to be the worst attempt at trying to cheer a person up that I've ever heard."

Max, relieved, let out his breath. "That's what you get for making me try to, with your crying and all. Hopefully you'll remember this and never do that to me again."

Eve laughed and wiped the tears from her eyes. "I'll try my best not to. I don't think I could take that again."

Mr. Penna, who had watched the two in silence, gave a slight nod. "Well, things seemed to have worked out nicely. Not that I had expected any different, being Peter's son and all. Alright then, time for bed."

Mr. Penna laid down and started snoring. Max had a feeling he was faking to avoid further questions. He shared a look of confusion with Eve before laying down himself.

## CHAPTER SEVEN

Max gazed up at the night sky as he lay on the bank of the river. His mind drifted among the stars. He felt a light breeze blow across him, carrying with it a distant voice. Max propped himself up to listen.

"Maaaxxxxyyy!"

Max smiled. Now he remembered. Eve wanted to work on her swimming tonight. This would make the third night in a row. She had come a long way since she first asked for his help several weeks ago.

Water was the only thing Eve feared, not even wanting to dip so much as a toe in it. If Max went fishing or swimming, she would stay on the bank and watch. Now she had changed her mind, wanting to face her fear, but only when no one else would be watching. So, here he was, on the bank of the river, waiting for her arrival.

"Hey, Maaxyyy!"

Max sat all the way up and saw Eve running across the fields towards him, strangely illuminated by the moonlight. The smile on his face grew bigger. Eve definitely made life more interesting. Joyful and energetic, she always brought with her a new adventure. Whether it was climbing trees, investigating the quarry or chasing animals, she went at it with full force. He often had a hard time keeping up with her.

Here, at night, next to the water, that changed. The water

made her cautious, almost timid. Here, he took the lead, guiding Eve carefully into the river. It was during this time that he had noticed things about Eve he never had a chance to before. To his surprise, behind her usual fierceness lay a delicate, quiet side. He thought she wore perfume, although he really couldn't imagine her doing so. Either way, he couldn't deny the faint scent of earth and flowers around her that reminded him of spring.

Eve's voice grew louder, shaking Max loose of his thoughts. "Come on Max."

Max's smile faded. *Why is she yelling like that? She'll wake everyone up.*

Eve's voice grew louder still. "Come on Maxy. Wake up!"

Max furrowed his eyebrows. *Wake up, what does she mean? Why isn't she slowing down?*

Max realized Eve's intention too late. He cringed at the impending impact.

"No, Eve! Wait!"

Eve leapt into the air, "Maxy, Wake! Up!" and landed with her hands and feet hitting him square in the chest. Max fell back onto the ground with a jolt.

Max woke with a start from a deep sleep. He rubbed his eyes then opened them to find Eve's face inches from his own.

*Well, now I know what the yelling was about,* Max rubbed his chest, *and why it hurt when she hit me.*

"You know, Eve, most people use cold water to wake someone up."

Eve giggled. "Well, your face could use a good washing, but pouncing is so much more fun."

"For you, maybe, but you've got me dreading it, even in my dreams."

"Oh, really? I was in your dream?" A devious grin formed on Eve's lips. "What was your dream about?"

Max blushed and turned to face the starry sky overhead. "Why did you wake me? It's still dark out."

"We have to be packed and ready to go at first light, remember?"

Eve shifted back into Max's line of sight, staring at Max intently. Above her, her tail waved back and forth in a slow motion.

"Now, what about your dream?"

Max had seen her behave this way when some creature had piqued her curiosity. She could watch them for hours. To his relief, Mr. Penna spoke from behind them.

"I see you have finally gotten Maxwell to wake up, Evangeline. Good, you can help me finish packing while he gets Starlight ready."

"Well, you heard him, Eve. I'd best be getting ready. Would you mind getting off of my chest so I can get to work?"

Eve searched him with her eyes for a weak spot she could attack. Max focused on her face, trying not to think about his dream. After a moment, she gave up and stuck her tongue out at him. With reluctance, she got off of Max to go help Mr. Penna. Max got to his knees and breathed a sigh of relief. He secretly thanked Mr. Penna for the interruption as he worked on rolling up his bed. He had just fished tying it to Starlight when Tyco, frowning, arrived riding Teak.

"Hurry it up. We need to leave camp before the sun is above the horizon, which means you have about fifteen minutes."

Tyco rode to the west side of the camp where Max could see that a few other people had gathered. The three quickly finished packing. Mr. Penna and Max mounted their horses and rode over to join Tyco, Evangeline following on foot. Tyco, who had been speaking with the other travelers, turned as they arrived.

"I hope you're ready. It is going to be a long five days. We will ride from sun up to near sundown, stopping only for lunch and a short rest or two."

Eve, her usual chipper self, chimed in. "Nooo problem."

She began to perform various stretches in preparation for the long walk, fascinating Max. She reminded him of a cat waking up from a long nap in the sunlight. Her flexibility never ceased to amaze him.

Max heard Tyco's voice. "Are you ready, Max?"

Distracted by Eve, Max had forgotten his surroundings. He shook his head to clear it.

"Huh?"

He saw Tyco giving him a cold stare. "You need to be more careful of such…distraction. I asked, 'are you ready?'"

Max swallowed, "Yes, sir."

"Good." Tyco nodded towards the other travelers. "I spoke with these three briefly this morning at the stable where they were renting horses. The two men, Zeth and Bastiaan, are diggers. The girl is an acolyte in the Children of the Immortals. We've agreed to ride together. In the dead lands, the bigger the group, the better your chances of not getting picked off by animals or bandits."

Tyco spurred Teak to face towards the dead lands. "The path will be narrow for most of the way. We'll ride in pairs. Max, you're with me. The diggers and the acolyte will follow with Evangeline and Mr. Penna bringing up the rear."

Max cleared his throat, nervously. "I'd rather stay in the back with Eve."

"No, Maxwell…"

Mr. Penna interrupted. "Perfect, I'm afraid the dust in the back might be too much for me. I will be better off up front."

Mr. Penna nudged his mare in the side, moving her forward at a trot before Tyco could raise another objection. Everyone else fell in to place for the long trip. Before them, the sunlight from the new day began to spread across the dead lands.

The party maintained a constant pace for the next several hours. No one seemed inclined to speak, giving Max plenty of time to observe the surrounding landscape. They followed a trail worn smooth by years of use. To their left, at most fifteen feet wide, often times less, flowed the Clanrye River. Long, scraggly grass, the only vegetation Max could see, grew sparsely along its banks. To the right, large rock formations littered the dry and sun-baked valley. Some of the rocks formed tall spires while others formed large archways. Together they formed canyons that snaked their way through the land.

Max turned his curiosity to the other travelers. He had heard of diggers before, several having come to Swiftwater to poke around the quarry in hopes of finding some relic from the past. The two that rode with them now were typical of their profession. They appeared to be in their fifties, had long graying beards and wore dusty, weather worn clothing. Packed on their horses were the pickaxes, shovels and other tools that represented their trade.

The woman, the acolyte, presented a bigger mystery to him. He had never heard of the Children of the Immortals.

*Are they some secret organization working with the Protectors?*

The cape and hood hid the woman's features as if she did not want anyone to take notice of her nor did she take any notice of him. She rode her horse with confidence with the diggers following behind her.

At noon, Tyco brought them to a stop. "Dismount and let the horses drink from the river. Meanwhile, grab some lunch. Be packed and ready to leave again in half an hour."

Maxwell hopped off Starlight and led her over to the water. He gently patted her on the shoulder, speaking softly.

"How are you holding up, old girl?"

Starlight lifted her head, snorted at him, then went back to drinking water. Just as he had suspected, she would have little trouble with the trip. He turned his attention toward something that did have him concerned.

"And how are you holding up, old girl?"

Eve had sat down next to the water's edge at their arrival. She had one shoe off with the other soon to follow.

"Okay enough to knock you into the river if I wanted to. You know I can keep up with Starlight. We've raced plenty enough times."

"Yeah, but those were short sprints, and this is for five days straight."

Eve stood up and took a couple of steps into the Clanrye. She closed her eyes as she wiggled her toes in the cool water.

"That's better."

Eve opened her eyes then glanced back toward the others before switching to a whisper. "It is going to be a long trip, Max. My feet will be killing me by the time we get there. I'll make it though, if for no other reason than to irritate Tyco."

Max grinned then nodded at her shoes sitting on the bank. "I am surprised you wore those."

Max seldom saw Eve wearing shoes back home. The thick, tough skin on her feet provided natural protection for everyday walking. She also had a thin, silky layer of fur on both the top and bottom of them, providing extra padding. Unfortunately for him, the fur also made her footsteps deadly quiet.

Eve crossed her arms. "I figured the trail would be really rocky. I didn't want to chance cutting my foot; however, the trail is worn enough that I really don't need them. In fact, they're making things worse."

"Well, we can fix that." Max picked up Eve's shoes. "I'll pack them on Starlight for now."

Max put the shoes in one of the saddlebags. Opening a different bag, he dug out their food. He returned in time to see Spook climb out of Eve's pocket and run down her arm where she had cupped water in her hands. Spook perched on Eve's wrist where she delicately drank the water.

Max shook his head, laughing. "You're very strange, you know."

"Yep, I know."

When the little mouse finished, Eve and Max sat down together. He divided the food and gave Eve her share along with Spook's cheese. They had barely finished when Tyco signaled for everyone to mount up and be on their way.

Two hours of daylight still remained when they arrived at the next camp. Smaller than the first, the entire camp was encompassed by a six-foot high stone wall. There stood another segment of wall that started out several feet away from the rest and ran out ten yards into the center of the Clanyre River. The trail led directly to an opening in the wall.

After passing through the entrance, a short stone overhang along the north side of the wall offered at least some protection from the sun and the occasional rain. On the south side stood a small guardhouse and hitching post for horses. A stack of wood prepared for a fire sat just off-center of the camp. The trail continued out a second opening on the west side. Max guessed the entire camp measured no more than seventy yards in diameter.

The group stopped by the overhang, the diggers and acolyte going a little farther down from the rest of them.

Max slid off Starlight and began unpacking for the night like the others. "Not much here."

Tyco looked up from laying out his bedroll. "This is a way point. Travelers spend the night then move on. Only the guards stay for any length of time."

Max looked around the camp. "I only see one guard. What if bandits attack?"

Tyco gave a short laugh. "Don't worry Max, there are three more in the guardhouse. That's plenty to handle most anything a bunch of untrained bandits can come up with. Any attack organized enough to be a threat will cause enough stir beforehand that the first camp would be able to send help. Farther in, where help is scarcer, you'll see twice as many."

Tyco finished unpacking. "Now, I would recommend refreshing yourself in the river. The Clanrye slips underground not much further west from here. This will be the last chance you get until we reach Moenia. Be sure to come back before dark; however, just in case."

A dip in the river sounded pretty good to Max. He turned to look for Eve only to see her already heading out the east side of the camp with Mr. Penna. Max ran after them, catching them short of the river's edge.

"Gee, thanks for waiting."

Eve grinned. "Sure, no problem. Well, see ya."

Eve turned and walked away leaving Max confused.

"What? See ya? Where are you going?"

Max started to follow her, but Mr. Penna grabbed hold of his arm.

"Sorry Maxwell, you cannot go with her. Do you see the wall stretching into the river? It is ladies only on the other side."

Max had noted the separate segment of wall running into the river earlier. His face reddened.

"Oh."

Mr. Penna let go of Max's arm. "Come, let us get cleaned up a bit. It will be four days before we have another chance."

Max followed Mr. Penna as he removed his outer clothes and waded into the river. The coolness of the water felt great after the day's long ride. Mr. Penna, always thinking ahead, handed Max a bar of soap. As refreshing as the bath was, Max kept worrying about Eve. She still had a lot of work to do on her swimming. To make matters worse, she did not return before they finished. Max started to wade over to the wall but was stopped once again by Mr. Penna.

"I am sure she is fine Maxwell. We saw the acolyte go over there ahead of us."

"But we don't know anything about her."

"Aside from us, Evangeline will not find a safer place to be than with the Children of the Immortals. So, it is back to camp with us."

The two gathered their things and headed back for the camp, Max looking over his shoulder the whole way.

# CHAPTER EIGHT

Eve left Mr. Penna and Max at the water's edge and headed for the other side of the dividing wall. She couldn't wait to feel the cool water on her toes again. She was used to the soft earth and grassy plains of Swiftwater, not the hard, rocky surface of the trail they traveled now. Her tough feet would adjust, but it would take a little time. Until then, she would have to take extra care of them.

Eve walked around the edge of the wall. Ten feet farther, next to the water, stood the acolyte. Her robe lay on the ground as she worked on removing the rest of her clothing. Eve, like Max, was curious about the woman. Now she could at least see the acolyte's features. Her hair was blond, ending right below her shoulder blades. She had a rounded face that carried only the slightest tan. She was slender and fit with fair skin. Eve guessed the woman to be in her early twenties.

Eve, not wanting to be caught staring, walked to the river where she let Spook out before removing her own clothes. Laying them in a pile, she carefully inched into the water, staying close to the wall for support. She stopped when the water reached her knees. A little scared, she very slowly sat down. After a few minutes she began to relax, enjoying the soothing water. A moment later she had an odd sensation of being watched. Turning her head to the right, she saw the acolyte looking back at her with an open mouth.

Eve's face flushed. "I...is something wrong?"

The woman shook her head as if clearing it. "I'm sorry; I just didn't expect to see you go out into the water."

Eve had known people would make fun of her fear of the water. That was why she had asked Max to help her learn to swim. Embarrassed, she took hold of the tip of her tail in both hands.

"I can go farther out. Well," Eve lowered her head, "when Max is with me, I can."

The woman waved her hands "No. No. I wasn't trying to make fun of you. It's that I have never seen a lacarnian, and I know several, step into the water before. It really surprised me to see you sitting down that far out."

The red faded from Eve's face. "I've worked really hard to get over my fear. When Max is with me I can go all they way to my chin, but this is as far as I could go by myself."

"Is Max the boy that was with you?"

Eve let go of her tail and smiled. "Yep."

"And he is actually helping you?"

Eve gave her a quizzical look. "Well, yeah. We've been friends since we were little."

The woman laughed. "I take it you are not from any of the large towns?"

Eve thought of their little village and laughed. "No, we're from Swiftwater. I bet it's about as small a place as you're going to find. Where are you from?"

The woman curtsied. "My apologies. My name is Melody. I was born in Moenia where The Children of the Immortals took me into their order when I was a little girl. I am actually returning there from a trip I took on their behalf. Who might you be?"

"I'm Evangeline." Eve let out a giggle. "But you can call me Eve."

"It is nice to meet you, Eve. If I may ask, what brings you out across the dead lands?"

"Tyco, the grumpy one bossing us around, used to be a

member of the Protectors. A messenger showed up in Swiftwater with orders that he is supposed to meet with them in Moenia. He asked Max to go along with him because Max wants to be a Protector like his father. I came to keep Max out of trouble."

Melody joined Eve in her laughter before asking. "Max's father isn't taking him?"

Eve frowned and shook her head. "He was killed by bandits when Max was six. That's why he's been so determined to join the Protectors. He wants to take his dad's place in helping others."

"I knew a lot of the Protectors. What was his father's name?"

"Peter Laskaris."

Melody's eyes widened. "Captain Laskaris?"

Now it was Eve's turn to be curious. "Yes. Have you heard of him?"

Melody seemed in deep thought. "Yes, Captain Laskaris was well known to the people west of the dead lands."

Melody let the thought drop and focused back on Eve.

"I'm surprised you wanted to go along with them to Moenia?"

Eve shrugged. "I didn't want to at first, but Max asked me to and, I'm worried about him. There's no telling what trouble he would get into without me."

Melody laughed. "Is that right? Like I said, I know several lacarna. I would be willing to bet you're the one that usually gets him into trouble."

Eve couldn't keep back the mischievous grin that always worried Max. "Maybe."

Melody almost doubled over with laugher. "I thought so. Now, I'd venture to guess the old man is Chiron Penna, but who's your furry little friend there?"

*How'd she know Mr. Penna's name? Furry friend?*

Eve looked behind her where Melody pointed. Spook had crept up to the water's edge where she sat methodically cleaning herself.

Eve giggled. "That's Spook."

Melody shook her head. "You are certainly different from any lacarna that I've ever met, but given who your friends are, I think I know why."

"What do you mean by that?"

Melody tapped her chin with her finger as she thought aloud. "Why don't you, Max and Mr. Penna come join the diggers and myself for dinner tonight? I'll explain more then."

Eve anxiously wanted to know more, but Melody clearly meant to keep that information to herself until later. Eve shrugged her shoulders.

"Okay."

Melody looked west. "The sun will start to set soon. We had better finish cleaning up and get back inside the camp walls."

The two of them finished bathing then re-dressed as the sun began to sink below the horizon. Together, they headed back into the camp.

## CHAPTER NINE

Max sat under the stone shelter, staring restlessly at the east gate of the camp. With the sun slipping below the horizon, he stood, determined to find Eve despite Mr. Penna's objection. He made it halfway to the entrance when Eve and the acolyte walked through. Seeing the worried expression on Max's face, Eve giggled.

"Hey, Maxy, off to save a damsel in distress?"

Feeling his face start to flush, Max ducked his head.

"No, no, I was getting hungry and didn't want to sit around waiting for you if you weren't coming. You know, in case you'd drowned or something."

"Max, you know I wouldn't go and do that. Who would keep you out of trouble?"

The acolyte stifled a laugh as she walked past Max towards the diggers. Eve returned with Max to Mr. Penna and Tyco. There she faced Mr. Penna, standing straight as she could trying to take on an air of dignity.

"We have been invited to dine with the diggers and Melody this evening. She would like to know more about us." Eve changed back to her normal, excitable self. "She's heard of your dad, Max; you too, Mr. Penna!"

Max's embarrassment about Eve vanished in an instant. "Really, what did she say?"

While the others were bathing, Tyco had pulled out a dagger

to sharpen to help pass the time. He paused at Eve's news.

"That woman is of the Children of the Immortals. They are an odd group. You should be careful who you choose to dine with. I would recommend staying over here."

Eve stuck her nose up. "I think you're right, Tyco. We should be careful of whom we eat with." Eve turned to Max and Mr. Penna. "Come on Max, Mr. Penna, let's get our food and head over." Eve looked back at Tyco. "I'm glad you don't want to go. You weren't invited anyways."

Tyco stared at Eve, a dour look on his face. Eve simply turned and headed for the center of the camp where the small stack of firewood now burned. Tyco grunted and returned to sharpening his dagger, a little more forcibly now.

Max looked expectantly at Mr. Penna. "Mr. Penna?"

Mr. Penna sighed. "I knew we would be recognized at some point. I had hoped it would not be so soon, but perhaps it being the Children is a good thing."

Max tried in desperation to contain his excitement. "Is that a yes or no?"

"Yes, Maxwell, let us join them."

Without any further hesitation, Max gathered their food and ran after Eve. Mr. Penna followed at his own, slow pace. Max caught up to Eve as she arrived at the fire where Melody and the diggers already sat. At their arrival, Melody stood, greeting Eve with a curtsy.

"Good evening, Evangeline."

Eve giggled, returning the curtsy. "Evening, Melody. I'd like you to meet Maxwell Laskaris and," Eve patted her foot impatiently, "when he gets here Mr., um, I mean, Chiron Penna. Max, this is Melody."

"Good evening, Ms. Melody. It is a pleasure to meet you."

Eve turned to Max in surprise. "Wow, Max, you do have manners!"

Max jabbed at Eve with his elbow, which she easily dodged. Melody started to laugh then cleared her throat.

"Good evening, Maxwell. I'm glad to meet you. You as well,

Mr. Penna."

Mr. Penna finally arrived, stepping next to Max. "Good evening, Ms...?"

"Oh, I forgot to tell Eve my full name. I am Melody Eliades." She gestured to the diggers Tyco mentioned. "With me are Zeth and Bastiaan."

The two diggers stood and shook hands with Max, Mr. Penna and Eve. When the introductions were over, they all sat down in a circle and Melody began the conversation.

"Maxwell, Eve tells me that you are Peter Laskaris's son."

"Yes, that's right." It was odd to hear a stranger mention his father.

Melody turned toward Mr. Penna. "And you used to accompany Mr. Laskaris, correct?"

"You are correct, Ms. Eliades. If I may, how is it that you know of us?"

"Of course, Mr. Penna. You see, I grew up in the care of the Children of the Immortals in Moenia. When I was twelve I remember a Protector coming to our sanctuary to speak with Metis, the leader of our order. Even then, I knew that the Children did not get along with the Protectors. I was curious as to what the man wanted so I hid behind the table on the second floor. When Metis met the man he spoke quietly to her then slipped her a small box. Metis nodded and the man returned outside. I ran over to a window in time to see him getting back on his horse. On another horse was an older gentleman who held a small child. I saw them leave the church grounds as one of the elders called me for my chores."

"I forgot about the Protector and his box until years later. While cleaning out one of the sanctuary's store rooms, I found the box. Remembering that day, curiosity got the better of me, and I tried to open it. The locks wouldn't budge, making me more determined to find out what it contained. I sought out Metis to see if she would tell me."

"Metis tried to shoo me away until I told her I knew where the box had come from. I thought she would be mad at me.

Instead, she sighed heavily, telling me it no longer mattered. She said the man who had left it, Peter Laskaris, had been a captain of the Protectors. The boy was his son and the older man, Chiron Penna, was a friend of them both. She then paused a moment as a few tears rolled down her face. Wiping them away, she said that bandits had killed all three and to put the box back where I had found it."

Melody smiled at Max. "Needless to say, Eve surprised me when she told me about you two. It's not often I run into people who are supposed to be dead."

Mr. Penna nodded slowly. "I have tried not to spread word of our survival. I knew that would end with this trip, I had only hoped we would at least make it to Moenia first."

"But, why?"

"The night the bandits murdered Peter they searched his home. I have always believed they were looking for Maxwell, though I have no reason as to why."

Max's eyes widened. "You mean, if Eve hadn't hid me, you think they would have killed me as well."

Mr. Penna bowed his head and nodded. He raised his head again, speaking to Melody.

"The day you recall, the one in which we left the box with your order, was our last day in Moenia. Peter had instructed me to pack the necessities for a long journey and to do it quickly. When all was ready we left the inner court of Moenia, stopping only at your church before leaving the city."

"Where were you going? What is so important about that box?"

Mr. Penna shook his head. "I do not know what lies inside the box. I had never seen it before that day. As to our destination, Hedgewood, originally. The night after we left the dead lands, bandits jumped us. We managed to escape, but they wounded Peter in the process. We changed our plans, heading for Pike to the southwest. When we were within sight of the town, Peter became reluctant to enter. He said the town was too close, that we had to go farther. I tried to convince him to stop, that he needed the immediate aid of a healer, but he would have none of it. Instead, he swung around the outside of town, heading down a narrow, poorly maintained road that led even farther off to the southwest. My hands already full with Max, I had little choice but to follow. Thankfully, just when I thought I was going to lose Peter, we came within sight of the small village of Swiftwater. The village's healer, a gifted woman, saved Peter, although he walked with a limp thereafter."

"Peter liked Swiftwater. He felt safe; we all did. Welcomed by the villagers with open arms, we decided to stay. For two years we enjoyed life to the fullest, then, late one night while I was camping outside of town, bandits attacked the town. By the time I returned, they were gone, and Peter was dead."

"One of the villagers told me the bandits had ransacked Peter's house before leaving, but took nothing with them. I asked of Maxwell and was told they did not find him in the house. The village started searching for him. We had little luck until the owner of the local café, Mrs. Tassi, noticed her daughter also missing." Mr. Penna winked at Eve. "She was a mischievous little girl whom Maxwell often played with."

Eve blushed and bowed her head as Mr. Penna continued. "Mrs. Tassi struck out for her daughter's favorite hiding places. She soon found the girl standing guard outside of a cabinet in the cafe's kitchen, Maxwell tucked inside, safe and sound."

"After that, I took on the responsibility of rearing Maxwell. Unsure of what we had run from and fearing another attack by the bandits, I did my best to keep our identity a secret from travelers. It appears, though, my time of secrecy has ended."

Melody spoke slowly, deep in thought. "So, that is what happened so many years ago. You have kept the truth hidden well, Mr. Penna, but," Melody nodded in Tyco's direction, "I imagine I'm not the only one from Moenia who knows that Maxwell is alive."

"No, I am sure you are not, my dear. That is why I have come along, even if I am too old to be of much aid anymore."

Eve jumped up. "That's ok Mr. Penna, I'm here. Right,

Maxy?"

Max buried his head in his hands, saying nothing. A tiny laugh slipped out of Melody.

"That story does explain the surprise I had at the river earlier tonight."

Mr. Penna gave Melody a questioning look. "Oh, what surprise would that be?"

Max leaned forward with concern. "Yeah, what happened? I knew I should have checked on Eve."

Eve sat down, "I was fine, I don't know what she's talking about."

Melody turned to Max with amusement in her eyes. "Most people take comfort in the fact that the lacarna are terrified of the water, Maxwell, and wouldn't dream of helping them learn to swim. The last thing I expected to see in this wasteland was a lacarna willingly wading into a river."

Max filled with pride. "You waded in by yourself, Eve? Wait, Melody, why would people not want the lacarna to swim?"

Melody sighed. "Very few places are like Swiftwater, Maxwell.

"What do you mean?"

"It's too late to explain centuries of history tonight, besides, you'll see for yourself soon enough. Just do me a favor, Maxwell, make your own decisions on what you feel is right, not what everyone else tries to tell you. You have an invaluable friendship; don't let anyone else change that. Now, how about dinner?"

Max's stomach growled. "Dinner sounds great. I'll help get things ready."

Eve stood up to help Max. "Me too. Out you go, Spook."

Spook peeked her head out of Eve's pocket, startling Melody.

"I had forgotten all about Spook. What's her story Eve?"

Eve lifted Spook out, sitting her on the ground. "I found her in the storeroom in the back of our café. I was supposed to get rid of her, but I couldn't, not after she helped me scare Max." Eve giggled. "That's why I named her Spook."

Melody laughed. "She scared you with a mouse, Maxwell?"

Max looked indignant. "She didn't scare me. She told me she had eaten it, I...thought it was disgusting. I didn't know she'd held it in her tail the whole time."

Eve doubled with laughter. "I don't know which I found funnier; the look you gave me when you thought I had eaten her or the one you gave me when you found out I hadn't."

Everyone joined Eve in her laughter, eventually even Max.

After dinner, the two groups separated; Max, Eve and Mr. Penna going back to their own spot with Tyco, who had already fallen asleep. Mr. Penna and Max soon fell fast asleep as well. Eve lingered a bit, her thoughts taking her back to the night of Peter's death.

*Is there someone out there that wants Max dead? Will I be able to stay with Max to protect him?*

Eve lay down knowing, despite her troubled mind, she needed to get her rest. As she closed her eyes she saw that Melody and the diggers were still talking energetically among themselves.

"Maxwell! Wake up!"

Max slowly opened his eyes to find Tyco looming over him.

"Come on Maxwell. We need to leave. Now!"

Max sat up. "What's going on?"

"We need to get moving, that's what is going on. Now get your stuff packed. Don't bother with breakfast, we don't have time."

Grumbling, Max got up to pack. Eve, yawning, came over to help.

"Do you know what's going on, Eve?"

Eve shook her head. "Nope, but Tyco's even got Mr. Penna annoyed."

Max paused to find Mr. Penna. He stood next to his mare stuffing his bedroll into the travel sack. Frowning, he addressed Tyco.

"What is your rush, Tyco? The sun will not rise for another

hour. The next camp will not take that long to reach."

Tyco sneered at Mr. Penna. "Your friends from yesterday have already left. We need to catch up to them."

Eve spread her arms wide as she let out a big yawn. "Yeah, they left about three hours ago."

Tyco stepped quickly over to Eve, grabbing her by the elbow. "Why didn't you wake me and tell me they were leaving?"

Eve twisted her elbow from Tyco's grasp. "Because, it was none of our business when they left."

Tyco's gaze bore into Eve. "If you had stayed away from them it would not have been our business. That isn't the case now." Tyco went back to his horse. "Come on, let's get going."

Max haphazardly finished packing and mounted Starlight. Tyco led them out of camp where he spurred Teak to a run. They moved at nothing less than a trot for the next two hours before stopping for a break. Tyco slid off Teak.

"You've got fifteen minutes to water the horses and eat something."

Everyone followed suit, leading the horses to the river. While Starlight drank, Max dug out some jerky, handing it to Eve. She swayed uneasily as she took it. Max grabbed her shoulder to steady her.

"Are you going to be okay?"

Eve nodded. "Yep, I just need to get something in my stomach then get a few stretches in."

"Are you sure? Maybe you should ride with me on Starlight."

"No, I don't want to make it harder for Starlight. I'll be fine, really. Keep some of that jerky out for me though. I'll need extra food if we keep moving at this pace."

With time running short, Max gave up the argument so they could eat. All too soon, Tyco shouted at them to get back on the horses and move out. Five hours later they reached the next camp. Quickly scanning the camp, Tyco spotted Melody and the diggers' horses tied at a railing next to the guardhouse. He made for the door.

Meanwhile, Max and Mr. Penna led their horses to a trough

to let them drink, then joined Eve who was quenching her own thirst from a water barrel. They were back with the horses when Tyco returned from the guardhouse. He got their attention before filling them in on what he had learned from the guards.

"The acolyte, along with the diggers, arrived here a little over two hours ago. They paid the guards to trade horses with them before making for the next camp. I have talked the guards into letting us do the same. We need to move our stuff over to the other horses immediately if we hope to catch up to them."

Max stood stunned as Tyco began unfastening his packs from Teak. "Tyco, we need at least a half hour to eat. Eve won't make it much farther without some decent food, and I'm not leaving Starlight in the middle of the dead lands."

Tyco whipped around. "We can come back for the horses later, Max. They'll be fine here." Tyco suddenly smiled oddly. "Better yet, Mr. Penna and Eve can stay here with Starlight and Teak to get their rest, then meet us later in Moenia."

Mr. Penna spoke in a calm voice. "What has you so upset, Tyco? Why are you so intent on catching up with Melody and the others?"

Tyco returned to working on removing the packs. "It is not so much as catching them as it is getting to Moenia before they do."

"Why? What is the danger?"

"I'm not sure exactly, but I know they're up to something. Children of the Immortals, or diggers for that matter, are simply not to be trusted."

Eve crossed her arms in disbelief. "What? That's crazy."

Max nodded. "Yeah, they seemed perfectly nice."

Tyco swung the packs off Teak "You have a lot to learn, Maxwell. It's a good thing I'm getting you to the Protectors when I am."

Mr. Penna let out a grunt. "That is up for debate, but I see you are determined to go. We will do as you suggest and follow tomorrow. Keep in mind; however, that Maxwell must join us at the city gate when we arrive. Evangeline will not be allowed to enter without her owner."

Max's jaw dropped. "What?"

Tyco ignored Max. "I can assure you when we receive word of your arrival I'll send Maxwell to the gate."

Mr. Penna studied Tyco's face. "I hope so, Tyco."

Eve nodded. "I'm okay with that; if it's for Max's safety."

Max balled his fists up in frustration. He did not like the others deciding what he was to do. "Wait a minute, I can't leave Eve behind! And what is this about her owner?"

Tyco spoke over his shoulder as he moved towards the guards' horses. "Not now, Maxwell. Hurry up and get your stuff off of Starlight and onto one of these other horses."

Max stood firm. "But?"

Mr. Penna crossed his arms and stood with his legs apart, a stance Max had seen often. "Just do it, Maxwell. Do not worry; we will catch up soon enough."

Max hung his head. "Yes, sir."

Max removed his things from Starlight, putting them on one of the fresh horses while Tyco rode to the west side of the camp. Finished, he mounted the horse, but Mr. Penna stopped him before he could join Tyco. Eve leaned against Mr. Penna, her head down.

"Maxwell, do you remember that bundle of biscuits that Mrs. Tassi gave you before we left Swiftwater?"

Max nodded.

"Good, in there you will find a piece of paper declaring you the owner of Evangeline. Whatever happens, do not lose it. Do you understand?"

Max stared blankly at Mr. Penna. Mr. Penna grabbed Max's knee, his voice stern.

"Do you understand, Maxwell? Do not lose that paper."

Max blinked, then nodded. "I...I won't lose them. But, I don't understand what you mean by..."

Mr. Penna's voice softened as he relaxed his grip. "I am sorry Maxwell, but you are about to learn a lot of things that are not very pleasant. The story I told you of the lacarna and the

Protectors was only the start. Just remember, your own experiences with Evangeline. Most importantly, be sure to be at the eastern gate in Moenia three days from now to meet us."

Mr. Penna let go of Max and slapped the backside of the horse causing it to rear up. It dropped back on all fours then broke into a dead run for the opening in the camp wall. As he exited the camp he glanced behind him. Eve waved pitifully at him, her face bearing the same worry and uncertainty that he felt. He saw something else too, something he couldn't identify. Noticing his stare, she stopped waving, turning to Mr. Penna with her head lowered.

## CHAPTER TEN

Two hours of hard riding had begun to wear on both Max and his horse. Even though he had already fallen several lengths behind Tyco, he slowed the horse to a walk. Ahead of him, Tyco turned his horse as quickly as he could and trotted back in his direction. Max's shoulders sagged.

*Now I've made him mad.*

Looking intently at the ground, Tyco stopped his horse 20 yards short of Max. When Max reached them he bent over to see what had captured Tyco's interest. In the dust he saw a confused mess of hoof prints all around the trail. Farther out, he spotted a large number of prints leading away towards the north.

Tyco raised his head. "It appears a group of bandits attacked our friends, causing them to split up. Most of the tracks lead north, but a few head towards the next camp. Whoever made for the camp will be riding even faster now. Come on, we need to keep moving if we intend to catch them."

Max sat up straight. "We're riding for the camp? What about whoever headed north?"

"Not our concern."

"Not our concern? But, there's nothing out there. They could be in serious trouble!"

"Max, if we don't reach Moenia before the other riders, we'll be the ones in trouble."

"I don't understand, Tyco. They didn't seem to mean us any harm. What's the danger?"

Tyco's hand tensed and relaxed repeatedly on the reins of the horse. "Maxwell, the Children of the Immortals are not friends to the Protectors. They are never to be trusted. Their early departure this morning can only mean that they have ill intentions. I don't want us to find out the hard way what those intentions are, so get moving."

Tyco turned the horse west and started down the trail. Max sat still, tracing the tracks north out of sight.

"Come, Maxwell!"

Tyco had stopped along the trail and now faced Max. "When we reach the camp we can send guards back this way to look for the others."

Max shifted uneasily on his horse. "It will be dark by the time they get here. They won't be able to follow the trail."

"Yet another reason for us to keep moving, Maxwell. If we go after them we will be caught out in the dark. We will all be lost. Now, for the last time, move!"

Max nudged the horse to move, but pulled on the right rein, steering the horse in a circle. *What do I do? Tyco knows a lot more than I do, and I don't want to be caught out here in the dark either. But, I don't want to leave the others out here, especially Melody.*

"Maxwell!"

*Wouldn't dad try to help them? That's what always happens in the stories Mr. Penna and the villagers tell about him. I know Eve would go. Eve! What will she say if it's Melody that's out there and I don't try and help. She'd never forgive me.*

Max sighed. *I hope this doesn't mess up my chances of getting into the Protectors.*

When the horse once again reached the tracks that led north, Max pulled him left, loosened the reins and kicked him forward. Behind and to the side he heard Tyco yell for him to stop. Max pushed the horse even faster, followed by a string of obscenities from Tyco that quickly faded from the growing distance.

The numerous footprints made the trail easy to follow allowing Max to keep the horse running as fast as he could. His mind racing with the possibilities of what might await him once he caught up.

Nearly an hour later, with the horse slowed to a weary trot, he entered into a narrow canyon. Rounding a corner, he found the bandits. Startled, Max jerked back on the reins, causing the horse to rear up. Max wrapped his arms around its neck to keep from sliding off. When the horse dropped back to all fours, he grabbed the reins and spun it around, leading it back behind the corner. Holding his breath, he stopped the horse and waited to see if anyone came after him.

A minute or two went by before Max convinced himself that the bandits had not seen him. He let his breath out in a gust.

*That was stupid.*

Max dismounted the horse, this time carefully sneaking up to the corner. With his nerves on end, he poked his head around. A hundred yards out, he counted the backs of at least fifteen bandits in a half circle facing towards the canyon wall. There, with her back pressed against the wall, stood Melody. Trapped, she was trying to inch her way towards a large crack to her left. Max scanned the rest of the area, but saw no sign of the diggers.

Turning his attention back to Melody, he tried to find what kept the bandits from attacking her. She kept one empty hand stretched out towards them and used the other to feel along the stone wall behind her. Yelling, one of the bandits threw a rock at her. To Max's surprise, it only made it a short distance before bouncing back, flying past the bandit who threw it.

Max focused in on the area a short distance in front of the bandits. He caught a shimmer in the air. Squinting as hard as he could, he made out a slight disturbance surrounding Melody ten feet out from her body. Max stood dumbstruck. He had never seen anything like it. As he watched in awe, Melody took a step sideways. The barrier flickered out for a brief second, prompting all of the bandits to throw rocks. Melody froze in place, the rocks bouncing off the renewed barrier. Max shook off the initial wonder at the spectacle, realizing he had to do something quickly before the barrier disappeared for good.

Max weighed his options. *I could creep up from behind, taking as many of the bandits out as I can before they notice me. Ahh, but I'm horrible at sneaking, and I can only take one, maybe two, before they catch on and overwhelm me. Although, that might give Melody enough time to reach the cave.*

*I guess I could charge in and try to reach Melody before the bandits could react. I could protect us as we made our way to that crack. It looks about four feet wide. There, at least, the bandits would have to fight me one at a time. But, the bandits would eventually wear me down, not to mention I've only practiced fighting with Tyco. I haven't actually done it.*

*Wait! I know, I can try the trick Eve and I have done on occasion.* Max studied the bandits surrounding Melody. "Yep, that will have to be it."

Max walked back to the horse, patting it on the shoulder. "I hope you're ready for this."

Max mounted the horse and led it back to the entrance of the canyon. Swinging the horse back around, he took a deep breath then let it out.

"Well, here goes."

Max tightened his hold on the reins and gave the horse a hard kick to the sides. Startled, the horse bolted forward. Rounding the corner, Max steered the horse straight for Melody. A smile appeared on Max's face.

*This is going to work.*

A heartbeat later the smile faded away. *The barrier! If I hit that...*

Max shouted at the top of his lungs. "Melody, the barrier!"

Melody jerked her head in his direction, along with all of the bandits. Dropping her hand, the barrier dissipated a split second before Max and the horse would have smashed into it. Ignoring the near miss, Max leaned left, reaching his hand down. Melody realized what Max had in mind and grabbed his wrist as he passed by. In that moment, Max realized two other pieces of his plan that he had overlooked. One, Eve was lighter and much more agile than Melody. Two, he and Eve had practiced several times before getting the maneuver correct.

Max swung Melody up with all the strength he had, but was pulled down a little as he did so. The horse, fast approaching the canyon wall, panicked when it felt Max slip. Attempting something between a stop and a hard right turn it slipped on the loose stone, falling sideways. Already loose in the saddle, both Max and Melody fell free of the horse as it went down, all three hitting the ground hard.

Max, full of adrenalin, leapt off the ground. He grabbed Melody's arm as she struggled to regain her footing, dragging her towards the crack in the wall. Inside, Max let go of Melody and reached for his swords, but grasped only air. Horrified, he realized the swords remained on the horse with the rest of his goods. Not stopping to think, he dashed out of the cave where the bandits had recovered from Max's surprise appearance.

The horse had managed to stand by the time Max reached it. He grabbed the hilt of one of his swords, sliding it out of its sheath. On the opposite side, a bandit slapped the horse's haunch. The horse reared, neighing in surprise, giving Max a head start towards the cave. The horse dropped to all fours and ran off, allowing the bandit to chase after Max. When Max reached the inside of the cave he spun, swinging his sword as he did so. The blade clanged against the descending sword of the bandit.

Melody yelled from behind Max. "Knock him back!"

Max put all his weight behind his sword and thrust hard, shoving the bandit back a foot. The bandit took another swing at Max. Max brought his sword up again to block the bandit's blade, but his sword stopped short, rebounding off the air. Max managed to hang on to the hilt as the sword reverberated from whatever it had hit. The bandit wasn't as lucky, his sword sailed out of his hand, nearly beheading a second bandit who had come to aid the first. Both bandits shouted obscenities at Max, who moved back with caution and stood beside Melody, his eyes never moving from the cave entrance.

"Where did that barrier come from?"

Melody stood, hand outstretched, shaking and short of breath. "I...created...it."

"How long can you keep it up?"

Melody breathed deeply in and out, trying to calm herself. "Since I only have to block...the entrance...I should be able to keep it up for several hours." The shaking slowly subsided. "But I'll need to keep my attention focused on it."

Max nodded as he began to feel pain all down the right side of his body. Max lifted his shirt a little to reveal minor cuts and bruises along his side. He didn't see any tears in his pants so he assumed it was the same for his leg. Concerned that Melody might have received injuries as well, he visually checked for any sign of blood or tears on her clothing.

"Are you hurt anywhere?"

"I think I twisted my ankle, other than that, just sore from the fall."

Max saw that she favored her left leg, but found no other signs of injury. "Do you need to sit down?"

Melody nodded. "Yes."

She started to sit, but lost her balance. Max wrapped an arm around her waist before she fell and helped ease her to the ground.

"Is anyone else coming, Max?"

"Tyco went on to the next camp. He said he would send guards back to look for us. I'm not sure they will be able to follow the tracks at night though."

Melody nodded at Max's sword. "How good are you with that thing?"

Max blushed, "Truthfully, I've never actually used it in a real fight, only practice."

Melody gave a weak smile. "That's more experience at fighting than I have."

Max studied the entrance. It was smaller than he had first thought, perhaps only about one and a half the width of a normal man.

"At least they can only come one at a time. I should be able to hold them off for a little while once the barrier is gone. Do you have any weapons?"

"No. I can only create the barrier. There isn't anything else alive out here to use. It's a wonder as dry as the air is that I can even use it."

Max wore a quizzical expression. "Huh?"

Melody gave a weak, amused smile. "You haven't met anyone from the Children of the Immortals before have you?"

Max shook his head. "Huh uh, I have no idea what you're talking about."

Melody sighed. "Well, now's not the time to go into it. Let's just say I'm not going to be able to offer much help."

"Got it."

Max turned to the back of the cave. "It looks like the cave continues back into the canyon. Maybe there is another way out."

Melody shook her head. "Without a torch we won't get very far. Besides, the few creatures that can survive in the dead lands make their homes in these caves, most of which make the bandits outside seem downright friendly. We will have to stay here and hope the guards reach us in time. I will hold the barrier up as long as I can. After that, it will be up to you."

Max nodded with little enthusiasm. He sat down next to Melody. There was nothing else to do now but wait. Melody kept her concentration on the barrier. For Max, time passed slower than during one of Mr. Penna's lectures.

## CHAPTER ELEVEN

A few hours had passed and Max had slipped into a trance-like state. The unexpected scream of a man shook him free.

"What was that?"

Melody's eyes were wide with shock. "I have no idea! Maybe one of the bandits?"

The cave echoed with another scream. "Noooo!"

The cry came from the bandit's camp outside the cave. Max stood and moved to the edge of Melody's barrier, next to the cave's entrance. From his limited view, he could see a few of the bandits had risen to their feet, weapons in hand. They milled around, looking just as confused as Max.

"Lacarath! Ahhh!"

The new scream arose from beyond the light of the torches. A wave of terror swept over the bandits, temporarily freezing them in place until a growl filled the canyon. The bandits dropped their weapons, scattering like bugs as they ran for their horses. Leaving everything behind, they rode off as fast as the horses would carry them. Behind Max, Melody gasped before crying out in a whisper.

"Max, the barrier!"

When the sun had set the bandits had lit torches, causing Melody's barrier to shimmer in their light. The dancing light resulted in Max's drifting into a trance. Now the shimmer flickered in and out of existence. Melody closed her eyes, concentrating; the barrier steadied.

"I don't think I can hold it much longer."

Max remained calm, scanning the bandits' camp. "We shouldn't need it. It looks like the bandits have left."

Melody began to panic, her voice cracking. "Didn't you hear the bandits? There is a lacarath out there."

Max smirked. "You mean the ferocious animals that prey on remote villages and feast on naughty children?" He cleared his throat, his smile gone. "They're just legends…right?"

Melody looked grim. "Lacarath are believed to be the predecessors of the lacarna, but I must admit, nobody has seen one in years. However, something sure scared those bandits away."

"Still, a lacarath?"

Melody's eyes went wide. "Nooo!"

The barrier flickered once, then, with a bright flash, disappeared. She swallowed hard.

"Can you see anything moving out there, Max?"

Max didn't move, but his voice shook. "Melody, if a lacarath did exist, what would it look like?"

Melody crawled over to Max where she followed his gaze out to the edge of the torchlight. Standing in the shadows with its side to them was a man-sized, four legged creature. Max pointed a shaking hand at the animal.

"Is that…?"

Melody pulled Max's hand down, cupping her other hand over his mouth. "Shhh!"

To their horror the animal turned its head in their direction. Both of them held their breath, hoping it hadn't seen them. After what seemed like an eternity, the animal turned its head forward again and walked out of the torchlight. Melody let out her breath. Max did the same.

"You really think that was a lacarath?"

"I guess I should have said nobody has proven they've seen a lacarath in years. We have heard rumors of sightings; however, in the more desolate places of Velrune. That thing out there sure fit the description of those sightings. I'll have to tell Bastiaan and…"

Melody's gaze drifted off into the darkness. "Bastiaan, Zeth, I hope you've had better luck."

When Max found Melody surrounded by the bandits, all thoughts of the diggers had left.

"The diggers! Melody, what happened to them? Did one of them head for the next camp? Where's the other one?"

Melody cupped her hand over Max's mouth again. "Not so loud Max, that thing may still be around." She dropped her hand. "Yes, Bastiaan rode for the next camp. Zeth headed north with me. When the bandits started to catch up with us, we separated. I made the mistake of riding into this canyon. I don't know where Zeth went."

Max kept his voice to a whisper this time. "Do you know if any of the bandits followed him?"

Melody shook her head. "I don't think so, but I am not sure."

Max gently touched Melody's shoulder. "I bet he's found his way back to the camp by now."

"I can only hope."

Max smiled. "He's probably better off than us. We either leave and chance getting eaten or stay here until the bandits return."

Melody shook her head. "I don't think any of the bandits will be back before daylight. They are just as afraid of the lacarath as we are."

"Then I guess we wait till daylight. Hopefully the guards from the next camp will find us."

The two sat in silence for close to an hour, listening for the slightest sound. Max was the first to hear the faint thudding of hoof beats. He tapped Melody's shoulder.

"Horses are coming."

The sound of hooves grew louder, echoing off the canyon walls. Max readied his sword and motioned Melody to step away from the entrance. Max took a few steps back to stay out of view, but stayed close enough that he could quickly defend the opening. The sound of the horses grew louder then stopped short of the cave. Max heard voices then a loud shout.

"Hello. Is anyone here?"

Max looked back at Melody, who shared his expression of hope. *Is it the guards from the next camp?*

As Max eased forward, a figure walked past the entrance and crouched next to the body of a bandit.

"It's a bandit, Sergeant, this is the right place."

"Hello, is anyone here? My name is Sergeant Kallis. I have come from the Protector's camp to the southwest. Lt. Biros sent me in search of his fellow traveling companions."

Max crept back to Melody. "I'll go and make sure they really are guards."

Melody gave a nervous nod. "Be careful, it could be a trick."

Max puffed out his chest and stepped out of the cave. "Over here."

The crouching man jumped at Max's appearance, his hand moving to the hilt of his sword. From Max's right came the voice of the Sergeant.

"Are you Maxwell?"

Turning, Max saw three other men on horseback. They wore the same light armor as the guards from the previous camps. A fourth man, bound and gagged, sat on another. A fifth horse carried no rider.

"Yes, I am Maxwell."

"I am Sergeant Kallis, Maxwell. We've been sent to find you and two others. It appears you have had a bit of trouble, but I can guarantee, with the exception of the one we captured, the bandits are long gone." The Sergeant nodded at Max's sword. "If you don't mind?"

Max lowered his weapon, embarrassed. "The sheath is still on the horse, wherever he went."

"That's okay, you kept the important part. Are the others with you?"

Melody stepped slowly out of the crack. "Only myself."

"Ahh, the acolyte. What of the digger?"

"We split up before entering the canyon. I don't know where he is. We had hoped he had made it to the camp."

The Sgt. shook his head. "Only one rider arrived. Bastiann, I believe. He was the first to alert us to the attack."

Melody clasped her hands together. "Was he hurt?"

"He would not let us aid him, so I do not know. He told us the location of the attack and that two of his companions had ridden north of the trail with several bandits in pursuit. He pleaded with us to come look for you. While I discussed our course of action with the other guards, the digger took off with one of our horses, not even bothering to take his belongings. Since we had his things, we let him go and prepared to find the rest of his party. We rode out of the camp as Lt. Biros arrived. He told us about you and stressed we bring you back at any cost. He then changed horses and went after the digger."

Melody sighed heavily. "Thank you, Sergeant Kallis, I'm glad to hear that at least one of my friends made it to camp. Thank you for coming after us."

Max reached up and shook Sgt. Kallis's hand, taking note of how his armor shined. The guards they had come across to this point had cared little for their appearance. Sgt. Kallis took pride in his position.

"Yeah, thanks. I was worried you wouldn't be able to follow the tracks at night."

"I hate to admit it, but we had all but given up at one point. Finding where you had left the main trail was easy, but we soon lost the light. It's slow going with torches, and I had decided to head back when we ran into him." Sergeant Kallis nodded his head in the direction of the bandit they had tied to the horse. "Or, more correctly, he ran into us. He came riding out of the dark screaming like a banshee, nearly running us over. Private Monroe had enough of his wits about him to chase the man down. We tried to get information from him, but he only babbled on about a lacarath attack at his camp. Since we couldn't get anything useful out of him we gagged him to stem the babbling. We took a gamble that he was one of the bandits the digger had spoken of and followed his tracks to here."

The man who had been crouching over the dead bandit joined the rest of them. "I don't know about a lacarath, sir, but some large creature did a number on these guys. I've never seen anything like it."

One of the other riders puffed out his chest. "No doubt our approach scared it off, right, Sergeant?"

Melody shook her head. "We caught a glimpse of it at the edge of the light. I doubt it left because it was frightened."

The man on the ground mounted his horse. "I'd have to agree with the acolyte, Sir. Judging by the claw marks on the bandit, such a creature would have little trouble dealing with us."

Sgt. Kallis scanned the canyon. "While I'll admit I would like to see a lacarath, I don't care to meet it at night or without something between it and me. Let's all make haste back to camp. Maxwell, you ride with me." Sgt. Kallis turned to the overconfident guard. "Monroe, you take the acolyte."

Max's brow furrowed. "Her name's Melody."

Sgt. Kallis ignored Max's comment, instead extending his hand to help Max onto the back of his horse. Monroe helped Melody onto his and without further delay they headed out of the canyon. Max looked back over his shoulder as they left.

"What about the dead bandits?"

The Sergeant didn't turn. "They deserve nothing from us, and that's what we're giving them."

Max had not expected such a callous answer from Sgt. Kallis. Even if the men were criminals, leaving their bodies exposed seemed wrong. He was too tired to argue the point; however. It was enough of a struggle to stay awake during the three hour ride to camp. Max dozed off several times before the greeting of the remaining guard in camp startled him.

"Sgt. Kallis, I see you found them."

"Yes. What of Lt. Biros or the digger, did they return?"

"No. Neither has returned."

"Did anyone else arrive at the camp?"

"No, no one else."

"Very well, dismissed!"

Sgt. Kallis helped Max swing off the horse before dismounting himself, the other guards following suit. "Lt. Biros instructed me to escort you to the next camp should he not return here. If he is not there, then we are to bring you on to Moenia. Get some rest. We leave first thing in the morning."

Max shook his head. "I'd like to wait a day. I still have friends at the previous camp. They will arrive tomorrow night."

"No good, I have my instructions. You will have to wait for them in Moenia."

Max swayed, light-headed from exhaustion. *I think I'll wait till morning to convince Sgt. Kallis. I can't think straight now.* Max hung his head. "Fine."

Sgt. Kallis nodded. "Good. Now, I will have someone bring you blankets. Stay next to the fire. You will want the extra warmth to help you recover."

Sgt. Kallis and the guards left for the guardhouse. Max walked with Melody to the fire where they sat next to one another. Melody sighed, close to tears.

"I hope Zeth and Bastiaan are safe."

Max felt a pang of guilt. *Here I am worried about leaving before Eve gets here. At least I know she's safe with Mr. Penna. Even without Mr. Penna, she could take care of herself. The diggers, on the other hand, are old and most likely aren't up to fighting.*

Max ignored his doubts and tried to cheer up Melody.

"I'm sure come daylight Zeth will find his way back. After all, aren't diggers great at tracking and discovering their surroundings? As far as Bastiaan goes, Tyco should be on his trail. If anything happens, Tyco should be there in short order to help."

"I'm not sure it's Tyco's intent to help any of us. For that matter, why did you two rush out of camp without Eve and Mr. Penna?"

Max shrugged his shoulders. "Tyco woke me this morning saying we had to get to Moenia as soon as possible, that you guys were up to something that could be harmful to me."

Melody snorted. "That's hardly the case."

"I didn't think so, but why did you leave in such a hurry?"

"Fair enough question. Last night we fell into discussing some recent information we had come across. Late in the evening we decided we needed to get this information back to my order as soon as possible, despite any risks."

"What information was so important?"

"Honestly, we're not really sure what the information means, so I don't want to share it yet."

Max's brow furrowed. "So, Tyco was right, you are up to something."

Melody's eyes widened in shock. "Of course not! Well, yes, but it's certainly nothing to harm you. We would never do such a thing."

Max relaxed. "I didn't think you would, but that's why Tyco was so intent on catching you guys."

Melody settled back down. "Sorry, Max, it has been a rough day."

"That's okay, I understand. I was there for part of it."

"Yes, you were." A warm smile filled Melody's face. "Thank you, Maxwell Laskaris."

Max blushed and turned away.

"Here are some blankets."

Max and Melody both jumped. Neither had noticed the guard carrying blankets arrive. The guard dropped the blankets next to Max then went back to wherever he had come from. They spread the blankets out near the fire, settling in for what remained of the night. The warmth of the fire soon putting them to sleep.

# CHAPTER TWELVE

"Evangeline, wake up."

Eve let out an aggravated moan. "Mmmm, go away."

"Evangeline, my dear, wake up," came the voice again, this time louder.

Eve felt something poke her lightly in the stomach. Startled, she sat bolt upright, swatting blindly in front of her. The poking stopped. She put her hands down and opened her eyes to the bright sunlight. Mr. Penna stood in front of her smiling and holding a two foot pole.

"It is not like you to sleep so late. The sun has already risen."

Eve, still not fully awake, only mumbled. "Sorry, Mr. Penna."

"Rough night I presume?"

Eve's tail found its way into her hands. "Y-Yeah. I was worried about Max and couldn't sleep."

"Is that it? I thought perhaps you stayed up all night gallivanting about or some such silly thing."

Eve tightened the grip on her tail, keeping quiet. Mr. Penna looked at her expectantly for several seconds then gave up.

"Well then, if that is what is troubling you, the sooner we get moving the sooner you will see him." He bent over and held his hand out to her. "Now then, let us get you some breakfast and be on our way."

"Kay."

Eve, finally awake, let go of her tail to take hold of Mr.

Penna's hand. He pulled her up with ease. On her feet, Eve pointed at the stick in Mr. Penna's hand.

"Please don't poke me like that again. You scared me. I might have hurt you."

Mr. Penna gave a hardy chuckle.

"I-I'm serious."

Mr. Penna laughed harder. "I am not poking fun at you, Evangeline. I know very well what you can do. This pole used to be twice as long."

Eve's eyes widened. "I'm sorry."

Mr. Penna scratched at his chin. "How does that old saying go? Oh yes. 'Let sleeping dogs lie or in time of need and dealing with a lacarnian," Mr. Penna held the pole vertical, "use a really long stick.'"

Eve now shared in Mr. Penna's laughter. "I don't remember hearing that last part before."

"That, my dear, is why I am the teacher. Now, enough of this silliness. Grab some breakfast and let us be on our way."

Eve had breakfast while Mr. Penna packed the horses, leaving for the next camp as soon as they finished. They maintained an easy pace for most of the day. Eve even let Spook out of her pocket so the mouse could play atop Starlight. Late in the afternoon they came across a large disturbance on the trail. Mr. Penna studied the area.

"It seems a bit of commotion took place here recently. A run in with bandits perhaps? A large number of hoof prints lead North. Evangeline, are you able to detect any scents with that keen nose of yours? I wonder if these tracks had anything to do with our friends."

"Maybe."

Eve walked around the tracks in an ever-expanding arc. *Should I tell Mr. Penna about last night? What if he gets mad at me, or worse, hates me for it? I can't tell him, not yet.*

After a few minutes she walked back over to Mr. Penna. "I can definitely smell Max and Tyco. I think I detected a hint of the diggers and Melody as well. Maybe two other groups. One in particular left a rather foul odor."

"Can you tell who went where?"

"Umm, Max and Melody, and at least one of the diggers, went north followed by the group with the foul odor. The other group, which smelled like the other guards we've met, went after them. The guards, Max and Melody returned and headed on to the next camp. Tyco never went north, he kept to the main trail."

Mr. Penna smiled oddly. "Is that so? That is quite a nose you have Evangeline."

Eve took her tail in her hands and looked down at her feet. *Uh oh, too much.*

She poked at a few pebbles with her toe. "Well, some of the scents were layered so I only assumed they left and came back. M-most of it I just kind of guessed at."

"Uh huh. Well, at least we do not have to worry about making any detours. Shall we be on our way then?"

Eve released her tail in relief. "Definitely!"

Without another word, Eve took off at a run to the west. Mr. Penna took Starlight's reins and followed after her. They reached the next camp in the early evening. Before Mr. Penna could stop her, Eve ran straight to and inside the guardhouse, speaking rapidly to the first guard she found.

"Did any other travelers come from the eastern camp yesterday or this morning?"

The guard responded crossly. "Where's your owner, lacarna?"

Eve started to get frustrated. "That's who I'm looking for. He got ahead of us and should have passed through here already. Have you seen anyone?"

The guard turned to another guard sitting in a corner. "Marcus, detain this lacarna. She is without her owner."

The guard in the corner stood and moved towards Eve to grab her arm. Eve jerked away in anger. "No, wait, that's who I'm trying to find."

Mr. Penna stepped into the guardhouse. "Good evening,

gentlemen. The lacarna is with me."

"Do you have her papers?"

"No. I am not her owner. We were separated. The rest of our party should have already come this way. In fact, we think some of the guards from here might have run across them on the trail. His name is Maxwell Laskaris. He may have been with an acolyte and some diggers. Possibly another man by the name of Tyco."

The guard relaxed. "Ah, you must be Mr. Penna. One of the diggers never showed, but the rest of your party has been through here. Lt. Biros left yesterday. The rest left early this morning. They mentioned that you would be coming along."

Eve calmed herself. "Then Max did arrive safely?"

The guard ignored her. Speaking only to Mr. Penna he relayed the events from the past couple of days. By the time he had finished, Eve had grown very anxious.

"Mr. Penna, if we leave tonight we can catch them before they leave the final camp in the morning."

The guard still did not face Eve. "I'm afraid I cannot let you or any traveler leave until morning. We are under strict orders from Sergeant Kallis."

Eve started to get angry again. "What do you mean you can't let us leave?"

Growing tired of her outbursts, the guard faced Eve. "The road is too dangerous. Between the bandit attack and the rumors of a lacarath it would be crazy to travel at night."

"I can smell the bandits long before they could ever see us and the lacarath attack happened far northeast of here."

The guard, losing his temper, moved towards Eve, but Mr. Penna stepped between them. "I can assure you we plan on following your directive to wait until morning."

"But, Mr. Penna."

Mr. Penna turned, his gaze boring into Eve. "No, Evangeline."

"But…"

Eve had seen Mr. Penna get mad at Max, but not this angry.

"That is enough Evangeline. Outside, now!"

Eve's jaw dropped. She took a step back. *He's never yelled at me before.*

She lowered her head and shuffled out of the guardhouse. Outside she did her best to fight back tears.

*I just want to get to Max.*

Mr. Penna came out of the guardhouse. Speaking gruffly, he pointed to a spot near the west opening of the camp.

"Take the horses over there, unpack our bedrolls and fix us supper."

Eve kept her head down, sniffled and mumbled. "Yes, Mr. Penna."

Eve led the horse to the spot Mr. Penna had indicated. She laid out the bedrolls and prepared a light supper. When she had everything finished Mr. Penna came over, collected his plate, and went back over to the guardhouse without saying a word to her.

Eve let Spook out while she ate. "What'd I do wrong, Spook? Does Mr. Penna really know what I did last night? Maybe I should go back home."

Once Eve finished supper she lay down on her bedroll and watched Spook play as she mulled over the past two days. She didn't notice Mr. Penna arrive until he was sitting across from her. He leaned in close, speaking in a low voice.

"I did not think those guards would ever tire. All but the night watchman are asleep now and he is not overly inclined to leave the guardhouse."

Mr. Penna paused a moment then reached out and softly stroked her face. "I am truly sorry I had to do that to you my dear, but I had little choice."

Tears started to form in the corner of Eve's eyes. "I just wanted to get to Max. I'm sorry, Mr. Penna."

Mr. Penna smiled tenderly at her. "Though I sounded harsh, I did not have any ill intent behind it. I am afraid you will soon find out that such treatment is expected in places like Moenia. Those guards had no intention of letting us go. If I did not act the part they would have been suspicious of us, which means they would have kept us under close watch. That would have made it a bit difficult to slip out without them knowing it."

*Slip out?* Eve choked back the tears, not sure she had heard him correctly. "What?"

"I am almost as anxious to reach Maxwell as you are my dear. Now I think we shall have our chance. I hope you can forgive me."

Eve dried her eyes. "So you only pretended to be mad at me?"

"My child, I would never dream of treating you in such a way. It pained my heart to even pretend to do so."

Eve gave a weak smile. "In that case, I forgive you." Her smiled faded. "I wonder if Max would have done that?"

Mr. Penna snorted. "Maxwell has the heart of the young and foolish. He would pretend nothing despite the consequences. To tell you the truth, I have a feeling that will never change. At least not when it concerns those he cares about."

Eve giggled. "I like that about him." Eve saw Mr. Penna smile the same way her mother did when she talked about Max like that.

*How is it they can tell so easily?*

Eve changed the subject. "So what do we do now?"

"We get the horses and leave as quietly as possible."

Eve looked at all the things she had unpacked; their bedrolls, plates, cups. "Do you think we can pack things up without them noticing?"

"No. That is why we are going to leave anything and everything that is not already packed. We will be at the final camp by morning; in Moenia by nightfall. We will not need this stuff anymore, at least not until we start back. We will worry about that when the time comes."

"So we just get on the horses and go?"

"Not you, I need you on foot leading. I cannot see all that well in the dark, or in daylight for that matter."

Eve laughed then covered her mouth before the night

watchman could hear her. When the fit passed she removed her hand.

"That's fine with me. Can you carry Spook though? I may have to stay close to the ground. I don't want her slipping out of my pocket in the dark."

Mr. Penna sighed. "I guess I owe you one for earlier, hand her over."

Eve gently took hold of Spook, who had worked her way up to Eve's shoulder. She placed her in Mr. Penna's hands, and he reluctantly deposited the mouse in his shirt pocket. He stared right at Eve.

"Are you ready?"

"Yep!"

Mr. Penna stood, gesturing to the open gate. "Then lead on."

Eve got up, glancing back at the guardhouse to make sure no one watched them. With no one in sight she slipped out the camp gate. Mr. Penna got on the mare and followed after Eve, being sure to stay within eyesight. Starlight, still tied to the mare's saddle, followed along.

An hour passed before the night watchman noticed that Eve and Mr. Penna had departed. He knew he would be in trouble with Sgt. Kallis when he returned, but not enough to run after the two in the dark. Instead he stayed in the camp and used his time to find a good excuse for their disappearance.

## CHAPTER THIRTEEN

The morning after the bandit attack, Max gave no resistance to leaving for the final camp. With little time to sleep, he was too exhausted to argue with Sgt. Kallis. Instead, he tried to use the day's travel to figure out the best way to convince the Sergeant to wait for Eve and Mr. Penna. Unfortunately, the several hours ride didn't help, leaving him at the last camp without a plan.

The following morning, with only his determination, Max stood by his horse refusing to budge until Eve could arrive. Behind him stood Melody, cringing at the impending argument. Sgt. Kallis towered over Max, no more than a foot in front of him.

"Maxwell, we are leaving now. Lieutenant Biros is expecting us in Moenia."

"He can surely wait one more day. Eve and Mr. Penna are only a day behind us."

The vein on Sergeant Kallis's forehead grew larger. "We can take care of that later. Now get on the horse!"

Melody raised her hand halfway. "I myself would like to wait another day to see if Zeth makes his way here. He is a good friend, and I don't want to give up on him."

Sergeant Kallis growled at her. "You stay out of this, acolyte."

Max leaned forward an inch. "We're staying here."

Sergeant Kallis reached out to grab Max. "Listen here, kid…"

Max grabbed the handle of his sword, sliding it partway out of the sheath one of the other guards had loaned him. He had taken to wearing it rather than packing it on the horse. He wouldn't be caught weaponless again.

Sergeant Kallis snickered. "Maxwell, my boy, you don't want to mess..." He tilted his head up to look past Max. "What the...?"

Max felt insulted that the Sergeant lost attention in his threat, until he heard what the Sergeant saw.

"Maaaxxxyyy."

Max re-sheathed his sword, a grin appearing on his face. Eve could distract anyone. He turned to face her, relaxing his body as he did so, waiting for the inevitable impact from her pounce. Eve ran straight for him, but to his surprise, she didn't leap into the air. Instead, she smacked right into him, wrapping her arms and legs around him in the process. However, the result was still the same; Max fell backwards, flat on the ground. He grinned from ear to ear.

"Hi, Eve."

Eve's face was buried in his chest, muffling her voice. "Hi, Maxy." She gave him a brief squeeze then popped her head up, cheerful as ever.

"Well, I guess you can leave now that I'm here. Let's go."

Max had an incredulous look on his face. "What? Don't you even want to know what happened after I left you guys?"

Eve hopped to her feet, waving a dismissive hand at Max. "Oh, I'm sure you got into some sort of trouble. How you got out of it without me I don't know, but you can tell me about it along the way. Besides, Mr. Grumpy behind you looks like he'll throw a tantrum if we don't get moving."

Max tried desperately not to laugh, but a snort still managed to escape. He made sure not to face the Sergeant as he got to his feet.

"Mr. Grumpy there would be Sergeant Kallis. He happened to rescue Melody and I the other night."

Eve turned her nose up. "Humph, must have gotten lucky. I

bet he had lots of help."

Max thought he heard the vein on Kallis's forehead pop. "Alright, that's enough! Get on your horses and get moving!"

Without another word, Sergeant Kallis and the two guards he had selected to escort Max and Melody mounted their horses and started out of the camp. Max walked over to where Mr. Penna, who seemed rather amused by the whole scene, held Starlight's reins. Max patted her on the side, receiving a gentle nip at his shoulder in return.

"I missed you too, Starlight."

Max swung himself onto the saddle while Eve took her place beside them. Mr. Penna turned to Melody, who was mounting her horse.

"You should have spent the last eleven years with the two of them."

Melody, who had kept quiet so as not to draw any more of Sergeant Kallis's anger, laughed joyfully. "I can only imagine. I needed the laugh though, as I take it that you haven't seen either Bastiann or Zeth."

Mr. Penna shook his head as he climbed onto the horse loaned to Max. "Perhaps they await you, safe and sound, in Moenia."

"I can only hope."

The four set out after Sergeant Kallis and the guards for the final leg of their trip. Earlier, Max had learned from one of the guards that the distance between the final camp and Moneia was half that of the other camps. Max's excitement at seeing the city came back in full force now that everyone was back together. To help distract himself, he recounted everything that had happened since he left Eve, finishing with the argument that had erupted between him and Sergeant Kallis. He waited anxiously for Eve's response only to be disappointed when she said nothing, but, instead, let out a big, long yawn. With Max starring at her, she realized her mistake.

"Sorry, I haven't slept since yesterday morning."

"Were you even listening?"

"Of course I was. It was very exciting".

Max snorted, shaking his head slowly. "You have always been a lot more adventurous than me."

Eve smiled. "Only because I had to get you out of trouble."

Max started to argue, but a concerned look came over Eve's face.

"What's wrong, Eve?"

"Well, you said the horse you were riding ran off, right?"

"Yes, that idiot of a bandit sent him running."

"And it had all your stuff on it?"

"Yeah, but I can replace everything before we leave Moenia again."

Eve stopped in her tracks. "So the horse never showed up at the camp?"

Max signaled Starlight to stop. "No, it never came to our camp."

Eve grabbed her tail, twisting it so hard Max thought she would break it. "Max, my papers, they were with all your things."

Max's stomach dropped. He had forgotten all about the papers. "Oh no!"

"What's wrong with you two?"

Eve and Max jumped, startled by Mr. Penna's voice. Neither had heard him or Melody catch up to them. Max dreaded telling Mr. Penna what had happened. Mr. Penna had, after all, specifically warned Max about losing the papers. Max knew; however, that if anyone could find a solution it would be Mr. Penna.

"Mr. Penna I don't have Eve's papers. They were on the horse I lost when I went after Melody."

Melody tensed. "That's going to be a big problem at the gate. They will want to do an inspection."

*An inspection, that doesn't sound good.* "I'm going back to find the horse."

Mr. Penna held up his hand. "Now wait a minute, Maxwell."

Max twisted the reins in his hands. "But, Mr. Penna, you

yourself said they won't let her through the gates without ownership papers."

"Settle down, Maxwell. You know as well as I that going back is not an option. Our escorts ahead have already noticed that we have stopped. They are not about to let us go back. Besides, I doubt the horse made it back to camp. There are a lot of things out there that would have long since made a meal out of it."

Eve gave her tail another twist, pulling a few strands of fur lose as she did so. "Then what are we going to do?"

"Well, as it happens, I had noticed when arriving this morning that you were missing your things. I assumed that included Eve's papers. I have since formulated a plan that should take care of any problems we may face."

Max and Eve leaned in toward Mr. Penna. "Well, what is it?"

Melody eyed Mr. Penna suspiciously. "Yes, what is it? Our order has tried several times to get undocumented lacarna in to the city with little luck. What do you have in mind?"

"I do not want to say yet. A better and more favorable idea might present itself before our arrival. Rest assured; however, we will get her in one way or another. For now, let us keep moving. Our escorts are growing impatient."

Mr. Penna maneuvered his horse past the others and continued down the trail. Melody bowed her head slightly.

"I'm sorry, Max, Eve. If we had not acted so foolishly by leaving in the middle of the night this would not have happened."

Max shook his head. "No, Melody. It's not your fault. I was reckless."

"It's okay Maxy. I'm glad you helped Melody." Eve gave a weak smile and shrugged her shoulders. "This is just what happens when I'm not there to keep you out of trouble."

Max rolled his eyes. "Let's go".

The three started down the trail once more. Melody stared in deep thought at the back of Mr. Penna a little farther ahead.

"I wonder what Mr. Penna has up his sleeve?"

Max shrugged his shoulders. "He's probably going to lecture

them on some pointless historical fact until they fall asleep. Then we can walk right by."

All three laughed, hoping for their own sake that wasn't his plan.

## CHAPTER FOURTEEN

They reached the western cliff of the dead lands in the mid-afternoon. Unlike the eastern side of the dead lands, here, a finely carved ramp, gated at the base, led straight through the wall into the center of Moenia. The city itself was surrounded by a ten foot high stone wall. At the sight of the city, Max, along with Eve, Melody and Mr. Penna, drew closer together into a tight clump.

Max sat in awe. "You don't simply walk right in to Moenia, do you?"

Melody grunted, "You don't simply walk out either."

At the gate, while Sergeant Kallis stated the party's names and their purpose for entering the city, Max took note of the guards. Unlike those in the camps, the four that stood at the gate remained alert and well-kept; ready for anything that might come. Max had the sense that if he had drawn his sword his life on Velrune would have come to a sudden end.

Their purpose announced, the officer in charge turned to Eve. "Who is this lacarnian's owner?"

Max hesitated at the sudden question giving Mr. Penna a chance to answer first.

"I am."

The guard held out his hand. "Her papers."

Mr. Penna didn't flinch. "I am afraid I do not have them on me. I was in such a rush when I left the city a few months ago that I left without them."

The guard eyed Mr. Penna with suspicion. "You should have been asked for her papers before leaving the city."

The other guards moved their hands towards the hilt of their weapons. Mr. Penna took note of the movement, but remained calm. Eve, on the other hand, grabbed Max's leg, squeezing.

"Unfortunately, you know as well as I do that many of the guards are all too happy to see a lacarnian leave the city, seldom bothering to check their papers. I am sure if you had been there when I left such a lapse in security would not have occurred, keeping me out of my current predicament."

The officer swelled with pride. Max chuckled to himself, Mr. Penna could flatter anyone. The officer relaxed, the other guards moved their hands away from their weapons.

"It is true that many of the guards are too lax with the rules, especially for people crossing the dead lands. I, on the other hand, take my post with all seriousness. I'm afraid I cannot let the lacarnian pass without the proper papers. She will need to remain here until you can retrieve them, or, failing that, she will have to be re-inspected."

Mr. Penna put his hand on his chin. "That could be a problem. She has assisted me for several years and is more likely to know where her papers are than I. It would take me a rather long time to find them by myself, especially when I have much more important matters to attend to. I have a better idea, why not send Sergeant Kallis with the lacarnian and I? He can verify the papers for you when she locates them."

Max almost laughed at the indignant look on the Sergeant's face. He felt Eve squeeze his leg even harder. Looking down, he could see she was trying to stifle her laughter. Sergeant Kallis didn't seem to notice.

"I will do no such thing. Lieutenant Tyco ordered me to bring the boy to the gate, and I have done so."

The officer grew angry. "Do not forget your place, Sergeant. I make the decisions concerning entry into Moenia. Furthermore, the Lieutenant passed through here earlier. He spoke of your arrival and left instructions for you to escort the boy to headquarters." The officer smiled smugly. "Since you will be going to the city, you can take this man and the lacarna with you and verify their information. If he cannot provide the proper papers then you can take her to headquarters when you deliver the boy. Is that clear?"

Sergeant Kallis's eyes burned with anger. "Yes, Sir!"

The officer turned to the gate. "Open the gates!"

The doors swung open, revealing two more guards on the other side. The officer motioned for Sergeant Kallis and the rest to enter into the city. Riding through the gates, Max hoped Mr. Penna had another trick up his sleeve once they reached his house.

A short distance along the ramp Max began to hear the noise of the city. At first it reminded him of the celebrations in Swiftwater when all three hundred of its residents would gather. By the time they reached the top; however, the noise level had doubled. Before them moved a tangled mass of lacarnians and humans. Max sat on his horse in amazement.

"What's going on?" Max's voice was drowned out by the noise of the crowd that reverberated off the walls of the many wooden buildings. He turned to Mr. Penna, raising his voice to a shout.

"Mr. Penna, what's going on?"

Mr. Penna turned, smiling. "We are outside the main market area of Moenia. See the horses and carts?"

Max looked to his left and saw not only that they were passing stables, but also numerous carts being loaded with an assortment of goods. He turned back to Mr. Penna.

"Is everyone leaving?"

Mr. Penna laughed. "No Maxwell, we are at the trading center of Moenia and the market is a short distance from here. Those goods are bound for outlying villages. This happens every week. Unfortunately, it means we will have to travel single file for a while to get through, so stay close, it is easy to get lost."

Mr. Penna moved in front of Max and behind Sergeant Kallis. Eve stayed right next to Starlight, unwilling to separate from Max. Melody brought up the rear, seeming completely comfortable with the chaos around them.

At first, the crowds of people gave them little notice, some not even willing to move out of the way. That changed as they left the trading area and its' stables. The people began to give them a wide berth, a few even watching them pass by with intense curiosity. Max felt uncomfortable at the attention. Melody shouted from behind him.

"Riding horses are rare Max and mostly owned by Protectors. Not only is Starlight a fine specimen to see, but she's also without Lord Avram's mark. Makes them wonder who you are."

Max nodded and tried his best to ignore the stares from the crowd, but in the end, he looked at them just as curiously. He had long since lost the memories of this city. His only known experience with the lacarna was Eve. Now, hundreds moved along the streets, both adults and children. Strangely, they were all female, and all wearing a collar similar to Eve's.

Before Max could take everything in, they moved to a quieter, more residential area of the city. The crowd thinned out to groups of two or three humans. The few lacarna that were on the streets skirted quickly past them.

Moving north, the houses began to get larger and fancier, going from all wooden structures to a mix of stone and wood. The road itself transitioned from dirt, to gravel, then to stone. Riding farther, they reached a section of the city separated by a four foot wall with a simple gate made of iron bars fashioned to block the road. It stood open at the moment, guarded by a pair of Protectors.

Sergeant Kallis nodded at the guards as they passed through the gate. On the other side, the street continued for several rows of immaculate stone homes with painted trims and intricate carvings. At the end of the street towered a twelve foot wall secured by a fortified gate. Atop the wall flew several pennants displaying the Protectors' emblem of a shield and sword.

"Maxy, this way."

Max snapped his attention back to Eve only to find she no longer stood at Starlight's side.

"Over here, Max."

She stood to his left at the entrance to an alley. Max turned Starlight, following Eve past several houses to where everyone else waited. Mr. Penna got off of his horse and approached the door of a home giving it a hard rap with his knuckles. A few moments passed without answer. Mr. Penna knocked again.

"Neysa, it is your master, Mr. Penna."

This time the door opened immediately. A lacarna wearing ragged clothing stepped part way out.

"Mr. Penna!"

Mr. Penna ignored the surprised expression on the lacarna's face.

"Neysa, it seems that I was in such a hurry to leave a few months ago that I forgot Evangeline's papers. Sergeant Kallis is here to verify that I am indeed her owner. Please take her and find them at once."

Max thought he saw a brief moment of confusion on Neysa's face before her eyes locked on Evangeline. Neysa swung open the door.

"Certainly, Mr. Penna." She stepped out and grabbed Eve's arm. "Evangeline, come and help me find your papers. We mustn't keep the Sergeant or Mr. Penna waiting."

Neysa dragged Eve into the house. Sergeant Kallis looked suspiciously down at Mr. Penna.

"It is a bit unusual for someone in the inner court to have a lacarnian, let alone two. What is it that you do, Mr. Penna?"

Mr. Penna cleared his throat. "I am an Inspector."

Melody let out a tiny gasp. Mr. Penna shifted nervously, but refused to acknowledge her.

"It is helpful to have one or two of them under my control. They can sometimes get information that I cannot."

Sergeant Kallis began to ask another question, but Melody interrupted him. "Were you really an Inspector?"

Mr. Penna stared hard at Melody. "Am, Ms. Eliades. I am an inspector, which reminds me. A few things you said during our trip have me concerned about your order's activities. I will be paying you a visit tomorrow."

Melody's face flushed red with anger. "What!"

Before any further discussion could take place, Neysa and Eve returned. Eve handed some papers over to Sergeant Kallis who hurriedly leafed through them.

"These seem to be in order. Next time do not forget them so as not to waste my or any other Protector's time." He handed the papers to Mr. Penna. "Come Maxwell, we are far enough behind schedule as it is. Lieutenant Biros is expecting you, and I need to return to my post."

Sergeant Kallis started back down the alley. "You're coming too, Ms. Eliades. You know as well as I that no member of the Children of the Immortals is allowed inside the court without an escort. I will drop you off at the gate where you can be on your way."

Melody hesitated. "I have questions for you, Mr. Penna. I…"

Mr. Penna handed the papers to Neysa. "We will discuss the issues tomorrow, Ms. Eliades. As for you, Maxwell, be here early in the morning. I want to show you the rest of the city. You need to get familiar with it if you are to one day join the Protectors."

Melody left to follow Sergeant Kallis. Max paused, a little confused by what had just happened, questions swirling around in his head. Mr. Penna nodded down the alley.

"Go on, Maxwell."

Eve started to wave goodbye but had her hand pulled down by Neysa.

"Bye, Maxy."

Max turned around, hoping Mr. Penna would straighten things out tomorrow. He reached Sergeant Kallis as he ushered Melody out of the gate. He then followed the Sergeant to the north end of the street, passing several well-dressed humans. No other lacarnians could be seen.

At the next gate, two heavily armored guards blocked their path. A third guard stepped out of a small structure next to the gate.

"State your names and business."

"I am Sgt. Alec Kallis. The boy is Maxwell Laskaris. We are to meet with Lieutenant Biros."

The guard nodded. "He is expecting you. Enter."

He signaled to a fourth guard that stood on top of the wall, above the gate. That guard, in turn, signaled to someone else on the other side. The wooden gate creaked open revealing an open courtyard. Passing through, Max saw a second iron gate above them that could be lowered for extra protection if needed.

Except for a stable, the courtyard was empty. On the far side, stretching at least three hundred feet wide and towering close to six stories in height in areas, stood the Protector headquarters. Max's heart raced as they left their horses at the stables and entered the building.

Inside, the entryway opened into a large, empty room. Max spotted Tyco speaking with another person under an archway leading off to another room. Hearing someone enter, Tyco glanced at the entryway where, upon seeing them, he finished his conversation and crossed the room.

"Sergeant Kallis, it is about time you brought Maxwell. I thought I had left you with an easy task."

The vein on Kallis's head started to throb again. "He is a stubborn boy and his friends did not make things any easier."

Tyco scoffed at the Sergeant. "A boy, a young lacarna girl, an old Professor, and a wannabe Immortal. Yes, a tough group for a well-trained Protector." Tyco sighed. "I suppose I should be glad you survived. Perhaps you should take some time off to recuperate."

"That's not necess…"

Tyco waved off-handedly. "Dismissed!"

Sergeant Kallis seethed. "Yes sir!" Turning, he stormed out of the building.

With the sergeant gone, Tyco relaxed, giving Max a warm

smile.

"So, Max, what do you think of Moenia?"

"It's huge! I can't wait until tomorrow for Mr. Penna to show me the rest of it."

Tyco straightened, throwing his shoulders back. "I don't know what he has in mind to show you, but I can easily say that you are in the best part of it. This is the headquarters of the Protectors, the most fortified structure in Moenia, containing valuables that you won't find anywhere else in Velrune."

Max's eyes widened. "Wow! Like what?"

Tyco chuckled. "Not now, Max, we have other business to attend to. Come, follow me."

Tyco led Max through several rooms and hallways before reaching a pair of large, lavishly decorated doors. A Protector standing guard opened one of the doors at Tyco's approach. They entered the doorway, stepping into a large room with a long, narrow table in its center. Four men rose from their seats at the table as the door closed behind Max.

Max swallowed hard. *These men are no ordinary Protectors. They can only be in their late twenties, but their armor is expensive and master crafted.*

He dared not guess the age of the fourth man who stood on the opposite side of the table. He seemed ancient with his white beard and hair and many wrinkles. He wore a magnificent robe instead of armor. It was this man who greeted them.

"Tyco, I see that you have brought Mr. Laskaris at last."

Tyco bowed. "Yes, my Lord."

The old man turned to Max. "Maxwell Laskaris, it is good to see you in person. Your father was a great man. His loss, and the reported loss of his son, deeply saddened us. When Tyco told us of your survival we dared not believe it, but here you are."

Max stood silent, unsure of how to respond. The old man detected his discomfort.

"How rude of me, I am Lord Avram, leader of the Protectors. Welcome, Maxwell Laskaris."

"Um, thanks, I'm excited to be here."

"I am sure you are, Maxwell. Lieutenant Biros has informed me that you wish to join the Protectors in order to follow in your father's footsteps. Is this true?"

*Is it true? It's all I have ever wanted since father died. I just wonder if I'm really good enough. Dad was so brave. I guess I still have a couple of years to train. I know I'll be ready then.*

Max gave a single nod. "Yes sir, I do."

Lord Avram smiled. "Very good. If you are half as talented as your father you will be a great asset to us. I assume Lieutenant Biros has told you that applicants must undergo intense training and pass a series of exams and rigorous physical tests before joining."

Max sighed as he thought of the long road ahead. *It may take more than a couple years. I'll ask Tyco to train with me more often once we get back home.*

Max puffed out his chest and looked Lord Avram directly in the eyes.

"I'll do whatever it takes, sir."

"I believe you will, my boy. That is why, after reading Lieutenant Biros' report of your training and natural abilities, along with our need for strong young men, I have decided to forgo the usual requirements. Maxwell Laskaris, you are granted entry into our ranks as a private."

Max nearly leapt out of his shoes. Lord Avram held up his hand.

"Provided, I might add, you successfully complete a mission for us."

"Anything, sir!"

"Very well. My captains Adrastos, Thanos and Leander have brought an issue before me that needs dealing with. Captain Adrastos, give Private Laskaris the parchment."

One of the other men, distinguished by his shaven head, rolled up a piece of parchment from the table and brought it over to Max. Max took the parchment as Lord Avram explained the mission.

"We've had reports of a gang of outlaws in Calix, a town several days west of Moenia, near the Obelia forest. There is always some type of disturbance in the outer villages, but in Calix it is growing to concerning proportions. I want you and another Protector to find who is running this gang and how many have joined. You will report your findings back to us. Is that clear?"

Max tried to contain his excitement, it didn't work. "Yes, sir!"

"Now that you are in our ranks, Private, you are to refer to me as Lord Avram."

"Yes, sir. I mean, yes, Lord Avram."

"You are dismissed. The parchment in your hands will give you further details. Oh, one more thing, Maxwell, should you hear any tales of a mysterious stone, report them to us as well."

"Yes, Lord Avram."

Max bowed to everyone in the room before Tyco guided him out. With the doors closed behind them, Tyco paused to talk to Max.

"So, what did you think?"

Max, overwhelmed by what had just happened, tried to come up with the words to express his excitement. Finally, he threw his hands in the air in excitement.

"I can't wait to get started."

"Good. I'll take you down to the armory to get you equipped for your mission. Eventually, you will want to have armor and weapons made specifically for you, but, for now, we'll see what we can find lying around. After that, I will take you to the sleeping quarters where you'll stay the night. It will do you good to spend time with the other Protectors."

"Are you staying here?"

"No, I have my own assignment. I'm leaving Moenia tonight, which means I will have to show you around the rest of headquarters another time. At least you will get to see the city tomorrow with Mr. Penna. Just make sure you meet the other Protector at the designated spot and time. It would not be good to be late for your first mission."

"I'll make sure I'm there early."

Tyco laughed. "I suppose there is a first time for everything."

Tyco walked down the hallway with Max in tow.

"Oh, one more thing, Maxwell. Lord Avram frowns on Protectors having close associations with the lacarna or the Children of the Immortals. I would say my farewells to Evangeline tomorrow."

Max stopped in his tracks. "Eve's my friend. She always goes with me."

Tyco stopped and turned. "Not anymore." He gave a reassuring smile. "Don't worry; you'll be gone for several weeks with this assignment. By the time you return you will have a better understanding of our rules."

Max nodded, but his heart wasn't in it. "I suppose."

As they started towards the armory once again, Max couldn't think of anything that would make him want to stay away from Eve. The Protectors would have to make an exception.

## CHAPTER FIFTEEN

Max had spent most of the night listening to the other Protectors tell of their adventures. When morning came, he was ready to start his own adventure, despite leaving the barracks still half asleep. On the way out of the courtyard, he stopped at the stables to check on Starlight. The trip had worn her out, but she would recover after enough rest.

Max left the compound and headed for Mr. Penna's. *I can't wait to tell Eve that I've joined the Protectors, and that we have a mission.*

When he arrived, Max knocked on Mr. Penna's door. To his surprise, Mr. Penna opened the door instead of Neysa.

"Ah, good morning, Maxwell. Ready to go?"

"I have been all night."

"Good, give me one moment, and I will be right out."

Mr. Penna disappeared back into the house, returning a minute or two later. He stepped outside, closing the door behind him.

"Alright, let us be on our way."

"Isn't Eve coming?"

Mr. Penna headed down the alleyway. "She left at first light."

Max followed Mr. Penna.

"Left? Where to?"

"I sent her with Neysa on some errands."

Max frowned. "Oh. I wanted to tell her that the Protectors

asked me to join them."

Mr. Penna stopped in his tracks. "So soon? Hmm, interesting." He resumed walking. "Do not worry, we are to meet them later in the day. I have a feeling she will have a few things to tell you as well."

The two spent the day winding their way through the city streets. Max felt as if he had stepped into another world. Swiftwater had few shops, everyone working with what they had or borrowed it from someone else. Only the rare traveling merchant brought anything unique. Here; however, a number of shops sold a variety of items from furniture to toys.

Once adjusted to the crowded streets and the menagerie of goods for sale, other things became apparent to Max. First, he could tell by the condition of the buildings and materials used that the city had been constructed over several different periods. Second, he noted the differences in the number of humans to lacarna. On the northern side of the city, humans abounded and kept a close watch on any stray lacarnians. Near the center market, the two races nearly evened out. As they continued past the market to the south, the population shifted in favor of the lacarna, so that by the time they reached the southernmost part of the city, few humans walked the street. The lacarnians watched him and Mr. Penna closely.

Having reached the southern tip of the city, they now stood in the archway of a stone wall that was centuries old. Plants had overtaken most of it so that little of the stone shown through. Beyond the archway grew a large garden filled with an unending variety of trees, flowers and plants. Strangely, several human men and women, dressed in plain white robes, tended the garden. Farther back stood a building that had become as overgrown as the archway.

Mr. Penna, whom Max now realized had intentionally paused here to give him the full effect of the place, strolled down the path into the building. Max took his time following, trying to take in as much of the garden as he could. More than once he tripped on a vine or root that had escaped its bounds and grown over the path.

Crossing the doorway of the building, Max stepped into a large open room containing several rows of tables and chairs. Vines sprouting flowers reached across the ceiling and down the corners. The walls themselves were mostly covered with moss with only bits and pieces of stonework showing.

Max chuckled. *I think the gardeners need to work in here.*

From his right, across the room, came a familiar, cheerful voice. "Maxy, over here."

To his right stood a small group of people conversing with one another. Max headed in their direction, looking for Eve as he went.

*I know that was her voice, but I don't...*

Someone waved at him. "Here, Maxy."

*Wait, that's Eve but she's wearing different clothes.*

Instead of her usual worn out pants and shirt, Eve now wore a pair of tight, leaf green shorts and a fitted shirt that stopped at her midriff. Focused on her, Max caught the leg of a chair with his foot, sending him tumbling to the floor.

"Ouch!"

Max rolled onto his back, rubbing his forehead. As the stars cleared, he found Eve bending over him. "Are you okay?"

Max groaned. "Yeah, but I'm not sure what happened."

Eve laughed. "Well, for starters, most people would have walked around the chair rather than straight into it."

Eve grabbed Max's hand and pulled, helping Max to his feet. "A chair? I didn't see it, I guess I was distracted."

Eve laughed. "I'll say, but by what?"

Max focused on Eve, taking note of her new clothing again. Blushing, he turned his head away to face one of the upper corners of the building. "The…uh…building. It looks really old."

Eve looked in the same direction. "It is, nearly 1,000 years." Eve faced Max again. "Now come on, Mr. Penna has already joined us."

Eve headed for the others, dragging Max along. "Oh, and

Max, watch out for the other chairs."

"Yeah, yeah."

Max let her pull him along as he studied the small bag strapped to Eve's back.

*What would she put in there?*

In answer to his silent question, Spook popped her head out the top of the bag, startling him.

*Well that answers that. I guess with her new clothes there isn't any other place for you to go.*

A moment later they joined the others who consisted of Melody, Mr. Penna, Neysa and another older lady who wore the same outfit as those out in the garden. They stood in a small circle facing each other. At Max's left stood Neysa who leaned over and whispered to him.

"I see you noticed Eve's new clothes."

Max felt the heat rise in his face and whispered back. "Uh, yeah, I didn't recognize her at first."

Eve turned. "I was wondering why you didn't pay any attention to us when you first came in. So, do you like them?"

Max's face felt like he'd been out in the sun too long. He too often forgot how well Eve could hear with those furry, pointed ears of hers.

"Yeah, Eve, they, uh, look great, but why the change?"

"Neysa said these would be a lot better for traveling in, especially without knowing what we would run into. I can definitely move a lot better in them."

To demonstrate her new found mobility, Eve bent backwards until her hands touched the floor. She then shoved her legs off the ground going up into a handstand. Max shook his head at the sight of her feet, she still wasn't wearing shoes.

Eve continued her arc, lowering her waist to move into a split when she came into contact with the ground. As if having exerted no effort at all she hopped up and grabbed Max's arm.

"I see you've got a few new things yourself."

In the armory Tyco had fitted him with gauntlets and a leather breastplate. Max had well-toned muscles, but not the build to support full armor. He would need to rely more on speed and flexibility. Along with the armor, Tyco had also given him two new short swords which he now carried sheathed on either side of his waist.

Max nodded with pride. "Tyco said if I was going to be a Protector I had better look the part."

Eve bounced up and down. "They let you join?"

Max saluted to no one in particular. "Private Maxwell Laskaris."

Eve hugged Max. "Congratulations!"

"Thanks, Eve. I even have my first mission. I have to go to a place called Calix."

"Great! When do we go?"

Max grew quiet. He scratched his head as he contemplated his conversation with Tyco.

"Well, actually, Tyco said it would be best if you didn't go with me."

Eve's smile disappeared. Max shifted from one foot to the other.

"Apparently there are rules about Protectors associating with lacarna."

Melody, who had been listening in, snickered. "Yeah, as in, they're not supposed to."

Max cleared his throat. "Yeah, that would be it."

Eve bowed her head. . "I thought this would happen, just not so soon." she said whimpering.

Max gently touched Eve's chin, lifting her head so he could see her eyes. "I didn't say you couldn't go. I mean, they surely make exceptions." Max turned to Melody. "Right?"

Melody shook her head. "The Protectors are not keen on making exceptions."

"But…"

Melody held up her hand. "Unless, of course, it benefits them."

Max beamed. "Oh, well, in that case, I'm sure I can find some benefit to having Eve along. Hey!" Max rubbed his arm where

Eve had punched him. "I mean, I can't count the number of great ways she will benefit me. Besides, it's not like I could actually stop her from coming along."

Eve hugged Max "That's more like it."

Mr. Penna chuckled. "You have much to learn, Maxwell, but at least you have a good idea of what is really important. You also have a good grasp of who is more dangerous to cross."

Eve let go of Max and looked disapprovingly at Mr. Penna. "Hey!"

The others joined in Mr. Penna's laughter. Once everyone settled back down Melody introduced the older lady that stood beside her.

"Max, this is Lady Metis, the head of our order. She has something for you."

Lady Metis, surveyed the group then took a wooden box, dyed deep red, from the table behind her, holding it for them to see.

"Lt. Laskaris gave me this box eleven years ago. I promised him I would keep it safe until he could return. Since he cannot return, as his heir, I offer it to you Maxwell Laskaris."

Max stared at the box with a mixture of curiosity and longing. His dad had left him few things from his past. Mr. Penna provided the only real resource about his father, but he spoke little beyond a few adventures, never giving any real details.

"What's in it?"

Lady Metis shook her head. "I do not know. He did not tell me. After hearing the reports of his death, I tried to open it, but could not. The locks are fastened shut with no place for a key."

Max took the box from Lady Metis. He studied the two latches, finding no place for any type of key or pin. Max rotated the box trying to find any type of release. Finding nothing, he tried to pull at one of the latches to no avail. Giving up he held it out to Mr. Penna.

"Do you know how to open it, Mr. Penna?"

"I am afraid not, Maxwell. I did not even know of its existence. I had my hands full with you when we arrived here so many years ago."

Max sighed. "A box I can't open isn't very helpful."

Lady Metis smiled softly. "It can be opened or your father would not have given it to me for safe keeping. It is an unusual box, so I imagine it will take an unusual method of opening it, if you do not wish to destroy what is inside. Take it with you to Calix. There are those in the outlands that are more familiar with such objects."

Max tucked the box under one arm. "I hope so. I would like to know what my father found so important that he locked it in such a box and kept it hidden from you, Mr. Penna."

"Your father kept few secrets from me, but he did keep them. I will look forward to your return so you can inform me of its contents."

"You're not going with us?"

"No, I am not. Neysa and I will be heading out on our own little adventure."

Max was surprised. Mr. Penna didn't like to travel much. "Where are you going?"

"I cannot say at this time, but I know it will be a long trip. In fact, I am sure you will return sooner than I, which makes it all the more important that I be off to prepare for it. As for you and Evangeline, Lady Metis, do you have room to put them up for the night?"

"Lacarnians are always welcome here. As for Maxwell, despite his new association with the Protectors, the young lad saved one of our own. We will honor that debt."

Max had not expected to leave Mr. Penna so soon. "We're not returning with you?"

"You have an early start tomorrow, Maxwell. You will need your rest. You will not get it with Neysa and me tonight. We have much to get ready. So, for now, this is where we part."

Mr. Penna reached out his hand to Max. Max felt a piece of him slip away. No one could replace his father, but Mr. Penna had tried and, at least from Max's perspective, had done a great job. This would be the first time the two had gone their separate ways. Max pushed Mr. Penna's hand aside, giving him a hug instead. Trying to keep his voice steady, he whispered in Mr. Penna's ear.

"I will make you and my father proud."

Mr. Penna returned the hug. "I have no doubt of that, my boy."

The two broke their embrace. Together the group walked out into the garden where they parted. At the archway, Mr. Penna turned to face them.

"We will meet again, Maxwell, be sure of that. I leave you now with one last piece of advice. Do not let the beliefs of others cloud what your own eyes and heart hold as the truth. If you are unsure of the truth, then do everything you can to find it. Until we meet again, Maxwell Laskaris."

Mr. Penna nodded then walked out of the archway. Lady Metis motioned Max and the others towards the church.

"The evening is moving along. I will have beds prepared for you. You will need your rest. I have a feeling that there is more to your mission than we may realize."

This got both Eve's and Max's attention. "What do you mean?"

"I am unsure of the meaning myself, but I have lived long enough to sense when things are about to change. We all may be in need of strength before long."

Back inside the building, Lady Metis went about her own business. Melody led Max and Eve to one of the tables where others had already begun the evening meal. As soon as they sat, a couple of young girls brought each of them a bowl of a wonderful smelling vegetable stew. While he waited for the stew to cool, he took a look around at the others that slowly filled the hall. Most all were female varying in age from children to the elderly. Eve's voice brought Max back to the meal.

"Mmm, this stew is really good, Melody."

"The vegetables are grown here so it is nice and fresh."

After the meal, Melody took Max and Eve to the sleeping

quarters in the back of the building where the two were given cots next to each other.

Max hadn't lain long before he grew restless. He could barely wait for tomorrow to come to set out on his first mission. On top of that, he had his father's box with its mysterious contents. His mind raced trying to guess at what it might contain. Next to him, Eve rolled onto her side.

"Can't sleep either, Maxy?"

"No, not at all."

Eve giggled. "Good, now I can tell you what I learned yesterday at Mr. Penna's. We've more in common than you think."

Max rolled over to face Eve as she started her story.

## CHAPTER SIXTEEN

Eve watched Max and Sgt. Kallis leave Melody at the gate and head north before Neysa pulled her into the house. Mr. Penna followed them in, closing the door behind him.

"Well, that was certainly interesting."

Eve and Neysa turned.

"Why do you have papers for me, Mr. Penna?"

"Chiros, why didn't you warn me you were coming home?"

Mr. Penna held up his hands. "Ladies, please, there is plenty of evening left for explanations. It has been a long trip and I would like to sit down to a nice meal first."

Neysa shrugged her shoulders. "You haven't changed much Chiros, but you're out of luck for a good meal. There isn't much to eat."

Eve looked around the house and saw only a single rickety chair next to a small wooden crate that sat in the middle of the floor. "Or places to sit."

Mr. Penna surveyed the room himself. "Hmm, I know I am getting forgetful, but I do recall having more furniture than this."

Neysa bowed her head. "I'm sorry, Chiros. I had to make do while you were away. I didn't always get the money you sent, nor could I get any legitimate work without you here to vouch for me."

Mr. Penna embraced Neysa's hand. "That is fine, my dear. I

am to blame for leaving you the way I did. In any event, if you have kept the vault safe, none of the other trappings matter."

"It's safe, or else we would not have found Evangeline's papers."

Eve bounced up and down, annoyed that Mr. Penna hadn't answered her question yet. "Why do you have papers for me?"

"All will be answered tonight."

Eve stomped her foot in frustration. "Oh, come on!"

Mr. Penna smiled. "I am going back down to the market. I need to give the mare to the stablehand. I will buy some food for us while I am there. In the meantime, you two get washed for the evening and relax a little. I have the feeling that our adventures are only starting."

Neysa joined Eve in her frustration. "What do you mean by that?"

Mr. Penna opened the door. "Tonight," he smiled and slipped outside.

"Uhgg, gone eleven years, and he hasn't changed at all. Come on, Evangeline, the bath is one thing I made sure to keep."

Eve followed Neysa, laughing. "You can call me Eve."

Two hours later, the three sat on the floor around the lone crate, food stacked between them. While they ate, Mr. Penna told Neysa all that had taken place since he and Peter had left Moenia so many years ago. Eve lost interest in the conversation. She let Spook out to run around the empty room, occasionally coming back to Eve to snag a piece of food out of her hand.

"Eve!"

Eve jumped, not realizing Mr. Penna had finished telling his story. Both he and Neysa looked at Eve with bemused expressions on their faces.

Neysa shook her head. "Even for our kind, Eve, having a pet mouse is a little strange."

Eve smiled mischievously. "Why, thank you."

"You're right, Chiros. She is definitely an odd one." Neysa's smile faded. "I hope it's enough for what is to come."

Eve grew concerned. "What's that supposed to mean?"

Mr. Penna sighed. "I suppose now it is time to answer some of your questions, Evangeline."

Eve bubbled over with excitement. "It's about time! Why do you have ownership papers for me? Do you really work for the Protectors? Why is…?"

Mr. Penna motioned for Eve to settle down. "Whoa, whoa. You are getting ahead of things Evangeline. The story starts long before you come into the picture."

Eve let out a deep sigh. "Fine."

She shifted herself into a more comfortable position, preparing for one of Mr. Penna's long stories.

Mr. Penna chuckled. "I will try and make it as short as possible. I promise." Taking a sip of tea, he began.

"Years ago I worked as an inspector. Things were different then. Most of the lacarna that came into the cities, having found a human partner, wanted to live in Moenia. Others simply found the city life more interesting, though not many."

"Any lacarnian that chose to live in the city had to have their claws removed. It is an old law meant to bring peace in the villages. Now it only gives the Protectors more power. In any event, the inspectors were tasked with verifying, and if necessary, removing the lacarna's claws along with keeping a written record of all whom they admitted."

Eve starred at Mr. Penna in shock. "That's what you did?"

Neysa put her finger to her lips. "Shhhh."

Eve huffed, but shut her mouth, allowing Mr. Penna to continue.

"Unlike your claws, Evangeline, the claws of those that came to the city were brittle and of little use. Few even had them. The collars are what they hated, and rightfully so."

"We placed the collars around their neck to show they were certified by us. A strange stone mined from the southern mountains was then split in two with half placed in the collar and half given to the lacarna's partner, or kept with us. This stone had the odd property of pulling itself together when its pieces came near each other. This gave us a way to validate who the lacarna belonged to."

Eve, about to burst, raised her hand.

"Yes, Evangeline?"

"I can't believe anyone would want to live in the city bad enough to give up their claws, even if they weren't that effective. And when did the collars change?"

Mr. Penna sighed. "You are as impatient as Maxwell. The collars I will get to. As for the lacarna, I often wondered what they left behind when they entered the city. I eventually got the chance to find out."

"The law provided a way for the Protectors to know how many lacarna lived in the city and the larger outlying villages, but not how many lived out in the woodlands. Lord Avram, the leader of the Protectors, feared the lacarna would one day start another war with the humans. In order to properly defend the city against such an event, he wanted a better idea of their numbers. To that extent, they decided to survey the surrounding woods."

"I was chosen to administer the survey. I believed their concerns unwarranted, but I could not pass on the chance to see the lacarna in their natural environment. To top it off, they assigned Lieutenant Laskaris, a friend of mine for several years, as my escort. I began to have dreams of a grand adventure."

Mr. Penna sighed as Eve raised her hand. "Yes."

"Why'd they pick you and Mr. Laskaris?"

"They picked me for my meticulous record-keeping. They chose Peter for his reputation. He had spent the last few years patrolling the outlying towns, settling any dispute between the lacarna and humans fairly. The lacarna grew to trust him despite their dislike for the Protectors. They knew that trust would take us to places few humans could go."

"We spent a couple of months traveling from village to village before we met a lacarnian messenger from a village on the edge of the Urania forest. Peter told her of the Protectors' concerns. She assured us that, as long as the humans left them alone, the lacarna had no intention of starting any conflict. To confirm this, she agreed to take us to her village, Xylia, where we could talk to her chief."

"I must admit, I was rather disappointed when we arrived at Xylia. I had expected the exotic, only to find a mostly normal village. A few homes were constructed out of limbs, vines, and such, but they had made several out of logs as well. Apparently, several humans lived in the village with the lacarna."

"The messenger brought us to the chief who also assured us that the lacarna had no intention of any violence against the humans. The fact that they had allowed several humans to join their village backed their claims in our eyes. At that point, Peter decided we had surveyed enough."

With Mr. Penna starring tiredly at her, Eve raised her hand. "Weren't you supposed to survey all the villages?"

Mr. Penna chuckled. "Peter played a little loose with the rules sometimes. Not in a criminal way, mind you, but he believed the Protectors had a tendency to go overboard at times. That is one of the reasons he got along so well with the lacarna. He found the very idea of them mounting an attack ridiculous."

Eve laughed. "That kinda sounds like Max."

Mr. Penna shook his head. "More than you know. I felt the same mind you, but I wanted to continue in hopes of learning more about the lacarnian culture. When I spoke of this to the Chief, he kindly invited us to spend as long as we wanted in the village. In fact, she pointed us to a rather excitable girl that had a great capacity for talking."

Neysa crossed her arms. "Hey now, you don't need to go adding the extra commentary. I had just moved out of the forest and never met outsiders."

Eve, in surprise, skipped raising her hand this time. "You mean you first met Neysa in that village?"

"Indeed. She was the first lacarnian either Peter or I had really sat down to spend time with. We spent an entire day with her as she told us, in detail, of her village deeper in the forest. Xylia had little in common with it."

Having never heard about the lacarnian villages, Eve's excitement got the better of her.

"What was different, Neysa? How did they live in the forest? Why did you leave?"

Neysa uncrossed her arms, smiling. "I left for the adventure. You see, the lacarna built the outer villages to give them a chance to interact with humans and learn more about them. In order to attract the humans to the villages they tried to adapt their lifestyle by building a small log inn and opening a trading shop containing plants and animals only found in the forest," Neysa giggled. "We even wore clothing."

Eve's eyes grew wide. "You mean you didn't in forest villages?"

Neysa rocked back in her chair, laughing. "Not a thing. lacarnian's are almost all female and humans weren't allowed in. We didn't see the point. After all, clothing is too restrictive, don't you think?"

Eve pulled at her shirt. "Well, yeah. It itches too, but I've never had the option to go without them."

Mr. Penna shook his head. "Neysa is distracting you with silly little details."

Neysa crossed her arms. "Fine, you continue then."

"You see, Evangeline, the bodies of the lacarna living in the forest were different from the others."

Eve tilted her head. "Different? How?"

"The lacarna that lived in the forest had tougher skin, hair that was thicker, closer to fur, and their arms and legs were more evenly proportioned to their body. Tell me, Evangeline, did you notice any differences between you and the lacarna in the city?"

Eve thought for a moment then looked directly into Mr. Penna's eyes. "Y…yes, most looked more like humans that had grown ears and a tail and not as much like a cat that had become more human." She paused for several seconds. "Mr. Penna, are you saying I'm from the forest?" Eve shook her head. "You don't know that for sure, do you?"

Mr. Penna smiled. "The information Neysa provided fascinated me. I wanted to go see one of the forest villages for myself and record how they lived. Neysa; however, said few humans were ever allowed to enter them. At the end of the day, I headed off to the hut the Chief had provided us, thrilled with all the information, but disappointed that I could not go deeper into the forest."

Eve planted her hands on her hips. "Hey! You didn't answer my question."

Mr. Penna held up his hand to stop Eve. "No, I did not. We have not gotten that far in the story yet."

Eve crossed her arms. "Hmph!"

Mr. Penna lowered his hand. "The next morning, Neysa woke Peter and I before the sun had even risen. She could barely contain herself, enthusiastically telling us that she had received permission to lead us to her home village. I could not believe my luck."

"We left immediately and arrived at her village early the next day. When I saw it, I stood speechless. I could never have imagined such a place. It had no houses, huts, or other crafted structures, at least that I could see. Then, Neysa pointed to the trees. Far off the ground, the branches and leaves formed small, natural shelters. She told us that the lacarna lived in the open, only taking shelter during storms."

"Neysa then led us straight to the center of the village, something that made me rather nervous. I asked Neysa if we should barge in without any warning, to which she informed me, in a rather smug fashion, that we in no way traveled quietly enough to surprise the village."

Neysa broke out in laughter. "I couldn't believe the noise you two made. They probably heard us when we started out the morning before."

Mr. Penna cleared his throat. "The Chief of the village greeted us, with Neysa informing her about our wish to see how the lacarna lived. The Chief gave her approval, even inviting us to stay a few days. She said that as long as we did not interfere we could talk to whomever we wanted to, whenever we wanted.

"We stayed two days before the Chief politely insisted that we leave, apologizing for the short stay. We did not argue or ask why, as she had already given us a great privilege. We thanked her, along with the other lacarnians we had spent time with, and prepared to leave the next day.

"Neysa had us up and ready to go early in the morning. We reached the edge of the village clearing when we noticed the arrival of another party. I remember them well, as I have not seen another sight like it. First, there was an adult male lacarnian, a rarity among their race. With him was an adult female who held the hand of a very young lacarnian girl that stood between them. Finally, a few feet behind the lacarnians, stood a human girl of about nine or ten.

"I was curious as to who they were and turned to Neysa to ask if she knew. I found her as fascinated by the sight as I. At the sound of my voice, she jumped, told us we needed to leave immediately and ushered us out.

"From there, Peter and I returned to Moenia where we filed our report on the information we had gathered. I went back to processing lacarnians and Peter left for patrol duty."

Mr. Penna stretched his arms and legs. "It is time for a break."

"Ahh, Mr. Penna, you haven't gotten to me yet."

"I will in due time, Evangeline, but for now, please help Neysa and I clean up this mess."

"Okay.

Eve jumped to her feet to help Neysa. *I'm starting to understand Max's frustration with Mr. Penna. He really does draw things out as much as possible.*

Together, they cleared away the mess left over from the meal. Spook, having already done her part by eating the crumbs, climbed onto Eve's head for a nap.

## CHAPTER SEVENTEEN

Neysa stacked several blankets in a corner of the room. She, along with Mr. Penna, positioned themselves on the blankets so that their backs leaned against the wall. Eve flopped down, stomach first, facing them, on her own stack.

"Okay, Mr. Penna, every thing's put away. This time you can't stop until after you get to my part."

Mr. Penna's eyes twinkled. "Do not worry, Evangeline. I will finish my story this time."

Mr. Penna paused a moment as if to remember where he had left off, then started in with the rest of his story.

"Several months after our return to Moenia, I saw a surge in the number of lacarna that entered into the city. With them came stories of bandits that had chased them out of the human villages, forcing them into the protection of the capital. Not only did this tax our inspection and registry system, but it became a challenge to find places for them to stay. At first, we found empty houses for them, putting five or six in each. When those ran out, we invited human citizens to come and hire them as help with the condition they also board them. Unfortunately, the process was not well thought out. Before long, it turned into an auction house."

Mr. Penna shook his head. A slight tremor shot through his body.

"I despised the auction house, but knew of little I could do.

The bandit attacks gave us little choice, or so I first believed. Then, one day, Neysa came into the processing center. When I saw her, I wondered why the bandits would bother with a lacarnian village on the outskirts of the forest. I wanted to talk to her and find out what happened, but one of the other inspectors got to her before I could, sending her to the holding area to await her turn in the auction.

"That night I had trouble sleeping as I wondered why Neysa was in Moenia. The next morning I informed my superior I could not be at my post due to an illness. I then slipped off to the auction house.

"I knew what went on at the auction house, but I had never been there myself. It broke my heart to actually see lacarnians sold to the highest bidder with no regards to age or family members. When they brought Neysa out, a chill ran down my spine. I decided immediately to buy her, despite the disapproval I would receive from the Protectors. I owed her that much for the kindness she had shown Peter and me.

"The deal done, I took Neysa straight home and questioned her. She told me that bandits had indeed attacked the village. She noted a few strange things though. First, they were very well armed, odd for thieves who spend most of their time in hiding. Second, they took nothing, instead burning the village to the ground. Third, guards from the Protectors arrived to escort the lacarnians to Moenia, even those that wanted to rejoin the villages in the forest.

"My talk with Neysa made me suspicious. From that point on, I paid very close attention to the lacarnians I processed. To my growing concern, more and more of them had the appearance of those that lived near or in the forest. Mystified as to why bandits would attack the forest lacarna who held nothing valuable, I began to keep a separate log of those I processed, hoping I might find something to piece the puzzle together.

"Then, one day, the Protectors escorted an unusual group of lacarna into the city. The physical features, typical of the forest lacarna, were much more pronounced. Some appeared more beast than human, almost as if a panther decided one day it would walk on two legs instead of four. Upon inspection, I also found them to have fully functional claws that could easily strip flesh from bone, far from the fragile, worthless ones I was used to seeing.

"Having not seen lacarnians such as these before, I could only conclude that they must have come from deep within the forest. A little girl I saw standing in line confirmed my conclusion. I recognized her in an instant as the lacarnian girl I had seen in the forest village. Sadly, the two adults from that day were not anywhere in sight.

"The stories of bandit attacks no longer made sense. A group of bandits could never penetrate so deeply into the forest. If somehow they did, the lacarna could easily drive them off. No, it would have taken a large, organized force to drive them out.

"Whatever the truth, I knew these forest lacarnians could not stay in the city. They could never adjust to such life, and I feared the humans would mistreat them for their beastlike appearance. Without thinking it through, I falsified the records of any I processed, marking them as clawless and having come from human villages. I hoped if I made them less of a threat I would have an easier time getting them out of the city, though I knew not how. In case I formed a plan, I made duplicates of their papers for my own possession, keeping their true identity in my personal logs.

"That night, the image of the little lacarnian girl haunted my sleep. I woke the next morning with the determination to get her out of the city one way or another, even though it would draw suspicion on me for buying yet another lacarnian.

I left for the auction house and arrived to find the place filled with people, making it difficult to move around. At some point, I found myself stuck behind a young couple discussing their anger with the treatment of the lacarna. Curious, I introduced myself and asked why they had come. They informed me they came to the city to adopt a child as they could not bear any of their own. The orphanage; however, had only a few children, none of which the caretakers would allow the couple to take. The two lived in a tiny village across the dead lands, a place the caretakers deemed too dangerous for the children. On their way out of the city they saw the crowd at the auction house and slipped in to see the commotion.

"With the auction starting, I took a chance at the opportunity before me. I mentioned to the couple that, on occasion, a lacarnian child would be sold and the Protectors had no rules as to who could buy them. I assured them that such a child would thrive in the outlands, more so than any human child.

"The idea of purchasing a child in an auction appalled them. For a moment, I thought the lady would hit me for making such a suggestion. Their reaction left me no doubt that they would treat a lacarnian with the care and respect your people deserved.

"Desperate not to let them go, I explained how they could give a child a much better life in their village. I told them of the mistreatment the lacarna often faced in Moenia. I even offered to give them the money to make the purchase.

"No matter my tactic, I could not convince them. The man pushed me aside to leave, but his wife stopped him. The auctioneers had brought out the little girl. I could almost see their hearts break at the sight of her. The poor thing was ragged and scared. When the bidding started, I offered my money pouch to them. They hesitated at first, but, as they watched, some brute of a man took the high bid. With one last nudge from me, the man grabbed my pouch and bid until he won.

"After the sale, I went straight home and began writing letters to every acquaintance I had outside of Moenia. I told them of the auctions and of what I knew of the lacarna people. I offered to help finance any that would come. I also made counterfeit ownership papers of those I found homes for, in case I misjudged someone's character.

"Less than a month later, Peter, clearly on edge, appeared at my home late at night. He stated that in two days he would take his son and leave Moenia for good. He asked if I would join him. In answer, I told him everything I had done, arguing that I could not leave with so many lacarnians to help. Upon hearing my tale, he said, with no uncertainty, that I must leave. He warned that, because of our friendship, the Protectors would be watching me closely. If they found out what I was doing, they would arrest me.

"I could see the fear and worry in Peter's face. Though the decision tore at me, in the end I could not let my safety add to his troubles. We left two days later."

A look of joy filled Mr. Penna's face. "I have long held that the Creators left this world centuries ago; yet I cannot believe that mere coincidence brought us to the same village where the couple had taken the little lacarnian girl."

Mr. Penna starred directly into Eve's eyes. "That, my little lacarnian, is why I have your pape-"

Eve launched herself at Mr. Penna, wrapping her arms around his neck. "Thank you!"

Mr. Penna returned Eve's hug. "You do not need to thank me, but you are welcome, nonetheless."

Eve sat back down. "Did your friends come? Did they take anyone else from the auctions?"

Mr. Penna nodded. "Yes, and I believe it is time to track them down. The Protectors have put their plans into motion. I only hope that I have not waited too long."

Neysa wiped a few stray tears from her eyes. "What do you mean?"

"I am not certain of anything, but more and more pieces seem to be coming together; Peter leaving suddenly eleven years ago, the bandit attacks, Tyco's arrival at the village, his sudden desire to bring Maxwell here and the disappearance of the diggers when Tyco realized they had found out about Maxwell. I think all these things are somehow related to those lacarnians brought to the city years ago."

"So what's the plan, Chiros?"

"Tomorrow, I will take Maxwell around the city as promised, ending at Melody's church. I will return here tomorrow night to prepare. Neysa, I want us to leave the following morning."

Eve crossed her arms. "Max and I can't come?"

Mr. Penna shook his head. "The Protectors have their own plans for Maxwell. I assume you will be going with him."

"If they let me. Tyco wasn't thrilled I came this far."

"I am sure they will not be happy with your presence; I am sure that means you will only be that much more determined to go."

Eve tucked her head down sheepishly. "Maybe."

Mr. Penna chuckled. "I thought as much. That is why I want Neysa to take you shopping tomorrow. You will need to be prepared for whatever lies ahead."

Mr. Penna stood. "When you two have finished shopping, head over to the church. I have a feeling Melody will have more information for us. For now, go get some rest."

"Yes, Chiros." Neysa got to her feet. "Come along, Eve."

Eve jumped to her feet, giving Mr. Penna another hug before following Neysa. "Right behind you."

Early the next morning, Eve and Neysa left for the market. "Now, Eve, be sure to stay next to me. They know to leave me well alone, but an unfamiliar face would be fair game."

"Who are 'They'?"

"Protectors, their cronies and general slime. On the south side of the city you'll be fine. Until then, stay close."

The two made their way south out of the gate, the guards eyeing them suspiciously as they did so. They received the same stares by many other humans along their route to the center of Moenia. As the streets grew more and more crowded, Neysa stuck out her hand.

"Take hold, I don't want to lose you."

Eve crossed her arms, pouting. "I'm not a child, I won't get lost."

Neysa smiled. "I have no doubt of your abilities to take care of yourself outside of these walls, but the city is far different than your little village. Now, take my hand before someone grabs you."

Eve took note of all of the humans around them, one even bumping her as he passed. *I guess it wouldn't hurt, just in case.* She took Neysa's hand without any further resistance.

The market offered a wholly new experience for Eve, one she was quickly ready to be done with. The streets were so crowed they had to push people out of the way to get anywhere. Every now and again she saw a human harassing some of the younger lacarnians. Eve gripped Neysa's hand tighter.

The booths Eve first saw had lacarnians working at them, but they were carefully watched by humans who sat in the back, eying all the customers. Few lacarna stopped at these booths, instead heading for the booths on the south side of the market. Here, either the humans worked with the lacarna or lacarnians ran the booths entirely. Neysa had them stop at several of these booths, insisting Eve needed clothing more appropriate for traveling. A final, small booth on the very outskirts of the market, finally provided a few things that both Neysa and she agreed on. None too soon for Eve, they left the market, walking farther south.

"So what did you think of the market, Eve?"

"Awful. I hated the crowd, the noise and the smell."

Neysa laughed. "That pretty much sums things up. Now you know how lucky you had it growing up in a small village. Don't worry, you'll like the next place a lot better."

"Oh? Where are we going?"

"We're going to the Church of the Immortals where we'll meet up with Melody and, later, Mr. Penna and Max."

"The Church of the Immortals? What's it like?"

Neysa thought for a moment then shook her head. "I can't really explain it. You will just have to wait." Then Neysa giggled. "Oh, and you can let go of my hand now if you want."

Eve blushed, letting go. *Oops, I forgot I'm not with mother. I'm not used to so many humans. I hope Neysa is right about the next place. I can't let Max see me like this.*

Farther south, the two stepped through an ancient archway separating the city from a beautiful garden. Several humans, dressed like Melody, along with lacarnians, tended a wide variety of plants and flowers. An overwhelming feeling of peace washed over Eve.

*What is this place?*

Smiling, Eve turned to Neysa. "Can I?"

Neysa laughed, "We have a little time. Go on little one."

Eve ran down one of the garden's paths to explore the plants, passing an elderly lady headed towards Neysa along the way.

## CHAPTER EIGHTEEN

Max slowly awakened from a deep sleep, unsure of his surroundings. He sat up and let the room come into focus.

*Oh yeah, we stayed with the Children of the Immortals.* Max yawned. *Boy, Eve's story lasted a long time, but wow. No wonder Mr. Penna always treated her so nice.*

Max turned to wake Eve, but she was gone and her bed made. *Where did she go? Why is it so light in here? Uh oh.*

Max swung his feet over the edge of his bed and then into his boots. *Well, at least I stayed dressed.*

Max hopped off the bed, grabbed his things and ran for the door. At the entryway, he nearly collided with Melody.

"It's about time, Max. We're running late."

"I know, I know. I'm ready though." Max lifted his arms and spun around. "See, already dressed."

Melody scoffed. "More like you never changed in the first place. You look like you were wadded up and thrown in a corner. Oh well, no time now."

Melody grabbed Max by the arm, pulling him through the meeting hall and out into the garden. "Eve, I've got him."

"Okay!"

Max heard Eve's reply, but did not see her until a second later when she popped out of a big patch of purple flowers by the far wall. Spotting Max and Melody, she bounded over to them with a big grin on her face.

"I like this place."

Melody brushed a few flower petals off Eve's head. "It likes you too, more than most lacarnians."

Max's eyebrows arched. "What do you mean by that?"

"It has to do with what I told you back in the cave."

"The cave?"

Melody sighed. "I'll explain again later. For now, we need to hurry to the west gate."

"We? I think Eve and I can find it ourselves. You don't need to go along."

Melody simply winked as she led them to the archway that marked the boundary of the garden. A pair of backpacks and a small waist pack leaned against the wall next to the arch. Eve grabbed the waist pack and pointed at one of the backpacks.

"That one's yours Max. I figured you would sleep in, so I packed it for you."

Max lifted the backpack, finding it heavier than he expected. "What all did you put in here?"

"Only the things you might need…" She trailed off waiting until Max slipped on the pack. "…and some of my stuff as well, since I only have the waist pack." She smiled devilishly. "Maybe that'll help you learn to get out of bed on time."

Melody interrupted Max before he had a chance to argue. "Come on you two, we're late."

Max didn't move, noticing Melody put on the other backpack. "Where are you going, Melody?"

"With you, of course."

"With us? Why?"

"Lady Metis has a message for an artifact collector in Calix. Since you two are going that way, she instructed me to join you. Safety in numbers, after all."

Max's shoulders sagged. "Once again, I don't really have a choice, do I?"

"Afraid not, Max."

Max sighed, resigned to his fate. "Fine."

Together they headed for Moenia's west gate. Unlike the east gate, at least a dozen Protectors stood guard around it. Between the open gate doors paced the largest man Max had ever seen. He stood over six feet tall and his bulky frame easily supported the heavy plate armor he wore. The man spotted their approach, stopping to glare at them.

"A mangy cat, an acolyte and a kid. You three must be the ones Lord Avram sent me to babysit."

Max bristled. "Eve is not a mangy cat."

"All lacarnians are kid. You'll learn."

"She's been my closest friend since childhood, that isn't going to change."

Eve leaned against Max. "It's okay, Maxy. Muscles here has his own opinion." She smiled sweetly at the large man. "You know how little I care about those."

The man turned to Melody. "What's your story? It's already bad enough having the fur ball along, now I have to deal with one of the Children as well."

Melody crossed her arms, but smiled similarly to Eve. "The name's Melody. Max here helped me out of a bind a few days back. I have business in Calix, so I thought I would go along and return the favor."

The man shook his head. "I don't know why I agreed to this. You guys didn't even get here on time. Now we'll have to move faster today to make up for it."

Max offered a handshake. "Maxwell Laskaris. I can assure you we'll be able to keep up."

The man glanced down at Max's hand then back at Max. "Lysander Harris. Now move out."

Lysander turned and started down the road that would lead them to Calix. The others followed after him.

Melody let out a sigh. "Well, this going be fun."

Over the next couple of days they followed the road through the plains and villages. Max and Eve entertained Melody with stories of their adventures in Swiftwater as kids. She, in turn, told them more about the Children of the Immortals. Lysander separated himself from them, but always remained within close hearing distance. On the third night, while sitting around a small campfire, Melody talked about the garden in front of the church. Max thought back to the morning they had left.

"Hey, Melody, what did you mean when you said 'the garden liked Eve'?"

"To explain that, Max, I need to explain about our power. Every living thing is made of a spirit energy that you can't see: the trees, the flowers and even the tiniest of things that float in the air. It is the control of these spirits that gives the Children of Immortals their power. A power the Immortals themselves taught us. Hence, our order's name."

Max thought hard. "So, that barrier back in the cave, you formed that by controlling the spirits in the stuff that floats in the air?"

Melody nodded. "That's right. Different people have an affinity towards different living things. I work with the tiny insects and plant life found in the air. Others can control larger plants of different varieties."

"What can they do?"

"Some can strengthen the healing abilities found in plants used for salves. Others can increase a plant's growth rate, making it possible to harvest fruit and nuts sooner."

Max stared in amazement. "I've never even heard of this before. Mr. Penna never mentioned it, or the healer in our village."

Eve shook her head, just as fascinated as Max. "This is new to me too."

"It may be new to you, but as a lacarnian, you have the natural ability to control all plant life. That is why the flowers grew around you the way they did back in the garden. We've heard of a few Children of the Immortals having such ability, but not for ages."

Max studied his sheathed sword. "Can the spirits be used in a harmful way? I mean, I've trained to defend myself against people, not plants."

Melody nodded. "Yes they can, like anything else. For example, Eve wears the worst application of the spirits."

Both Max and Eve sat confused. "Huh?"

Lysander grunted from his seat several feet away. "The collars are only harmful for those that are in disobedience of the law."

A fire sparked in Melody's eyes. "What about the humans that use them to abuse the lacarna. You don't call that harmful?"

"Those that misuse the collars are dealt with appropriately."

Max looked back and forth between the two. "What are you talking about?"

Melody huffed. "The Controller Stones in the collars."

"Stones? I thought the spirits only inhabited living things."

"The stones aren't alive, Max, but something inside them is. Haven't you ever wondered how they shocked the wearer? Or did you even care?"

Max's brow furrowed. "Shock? What shock?"

Melody got to her feet, turning away from Max. "Here I thought when you rushed in to help me that you were different, Maxwell."

Eve jumped up. "Melody, he doesn't know about the collars!"

Melody faced Eve. "How could he not…"

"Because I'm the only lacarnian Max has ever known since he was little, and I've never worn my collar while at Swiftwater. The day we left was the first time Max even knew I had it." Eve shuffled her feet. "I told him it was the fashion in Moenia."

Melody eyes widened. "How could you go all those years without wearing your collar? Why didn't you tell Max the truth?"

Eve grabbed her tail. "I didn't know how to explain things to Max. Until Tyco arrived two years ago, the only Protector to ever bother to come to Swiftwater was Max's father." Eve shrugged her shoulders. "Nobody cares about the rules out there, especially my parents."

The flame died out in Melody. "Then, who has your

Controller Stone?"

"Mr. Penna had it for the trip over." Eve smiled. "Then, last night when he hugged Max, he slipped it into Max's pants pocket."

Max felt around in his pockets until his hand came across a small, smooth object. He pulled it out. The half-stone matched the color of the one in Eve's collar.

"What does it do?"

Lysander spoke again. "Assurance. It keeps a human alive in case the lacarnian he has taken in turns wild."

Melody stepped past Eve, taking the stone from Max's hand. "Half of the stone goes into the collar, the other half is held by the lacarnian's master. At the time of ownership, the lacarnian's master is taught to use the spirits in the stone to send a shock to the other half. The collar itself is designed to focus the shock into the neck of the lacarnian and prevent them from sending a shock back to their owner." Melody slammed the stone back into Max's hand. "I wish I knew who first showed the Protectors how to use the stone that way. I have a few choice words to give them."

Max blinked in disbelief. "Why would anyone want to shock someone?"

Lysander remained nonchalant. "Like I said, to keep the lacarna from turning on us humans."

Max stared at the stone. "I'd never want to do that to Eve." He held his hand out to Eve. "Why don't you carry it?"

She shook her head. "I can't. When both halves of the stone are held by the same person, the halves emit the shock and won't stop until they're separated again. Please keep it, Max. You and Mr. Penna are the only two besides mother that I trust to carry it."

Max studied Eve for a moment before closing his fingers around the stone. "Okay, but the next time you pounce on me, I'm using it."

Eve burst out laughing. "Deal."

Now Melody acted sheepish. "I'm sorry I yelled at you, Max.

I had no idea you'd never heard any of this before."

Max stuck the stone back into his pocket. "That's okay, I understand why you got so upset."

Lysander shook his head in disgust. "Kid, you have a lot to learn. This junk isn't going to fly inside the Protectors. What village did you grow up in again?"

"Swiftwater, on the other side of the dead lands."

Lysander snickered. "That explains it. You've been too sheltered to know what the lacarna are capable of."

Melody's eyes bore into Lysander. "Do you even know yourself, or do you only know the lies Lord Avram spreads among the Protectors?"

Lysander narrowed his eyes, but didn't respond.

"Why did you even accept this mission?"

"I needed a distraction." Lysander stood and began walking way.

Melody started to follow. "From what, torturing the lacarna in the city?"

"I believe in the law, to seeing the guilty punished, not torturing the innocent. Even if they are beasts.

"Then what?"

"If it will keep you quiet, I lost my daughter not long ago."

Melody stopped in tracks. "Oh."

Eve bowed her head. "I'm sorry."

Lysander paused and turned to take in Eve for the first time. "I don't need sympathy from a fur ball. Get to sleep, all of you."

They watched as he walked out of the light of their campfire.

The next morning, Lysander kept even more distance between them, only allowing them to draw near when they reached Calix. Standing outside of the entrance, they pushed their previous disagreements aside to ready themselves. This is where the mission really began.

## CHAPTER NINETEEN

Lysander pointed at a small tavern not far inside the town. "We'll start there. Any and all gossip can be found at the local tavern in every town. We can also get food and drink to refresh ourselves."

Max immediately headed for the tavern. "Then let's go."

The weather-beaten tavern kept most of the elements out, but offered little else. The well-worn tables bore numerous carvings left by the many customers over the years. The chairs, strewn about in a haphazard fashion, gave an unnerving creak when sat upon. Lysander stopped in the center of the room.

"Okay, Maxwell, we will spread out. Just strike a conversation with people as they take a seat."

Max nodded. "Okay." He took a seat at one of the tables and faced the door.

Lysander shook his head. "Max, you need to be a little more casual about this or else you'll scare everyone away."

"Oh, sorry." Max changed to a seat where he could watch the rest of the tavern. Lysander and Melody sat at stools in front of the bar. Eve shot off to a table in the back corner where another young lacarnian girl sat.

Over the next couple of hours, people came and went. Several talked with either Melody or Lysander, but most left Max to himself. No one wanted to talk to a kid in a tavern, so he spent most of the time watching Melody and Lysander. After a while, that became boring, and he lost interest in the task at hand. His eyes wandered over to where Eve sat at the table in the corner. She had started a lively conversation with the other girl right from the start.

Max sighed, pulled out his father's box from his backpack and fiddled with it. A few minutes later, Max heard the door to the tavern open once again. He looked to see who he could drive off this time. The door closed behind...nobody? Max scanned the room, he recognized all of the faces in the tavern. None had left.

*Strange, maybe the boredom is getting to me.*

Max couldn't put aside the feeling, though, that someone had opened the door. He stood and walked towards it. Drawing near, his heart began to race. He threw open the door and stepped outside.

The street flowed with people, their feet stirring up dust from the dry ground. Max sniffed at the air. He had smelt something out of place: the scent of wildflowers. He turned to his right and the scent got a little stronger. Not far up the street, he glimpsed a purple parasol so dark it was almost black, before it disappeared in the crowd. Max knew without a doubt that it was the owner of the parasol that had opened the door. He hurried after it.

Max had a difficult time keeping the parasol in sight as he navigated the crowed street. It appeared and disappeared several times during his pursuit, always the same distance ahead of him. When he could not see the parasol, he followed the fragrance of the wildflowers.

Max finally came to a stop near the other end of town. The parasol had not reappeared at its usual interval, nor did he smell the wildflowers anymore.

*Maybe I passed her, or worse yet, she's put away the parasol.*

Max decided to head back when a soft breeze came from the side alley. The smell of wildflowers almost overpowered him. He weaved through several people, popping out in the alley. He frowned, empty. He looked back into the street, unsure he had come the right way.

*No, I know the breeze came from here.*

Turning back to the alley, the sight of a small child, no older than eleven, startled him. She stood at the far end, about seventy feet away.

*How did I miss her?* Max checked both sides of the alley. *No crates or barrels for her to have hidden behind, and there's a fence behind her.*

Max focused back on the girl, only to be immediately enamored by her appearance. In a town of people wearing worn clothes, dirty from a hard day's work, she stood out like a sore thumb. She had long silver hair that flowed the length of her back and ended at her knees. She wore a blood red dress. The cuffs, collar and trimming were black. The hemline fell just above the ground so that only her shoes stuck out from under it. The shoes themselves, despite the dusty street, where black and shined to perfection. In her gloved hands, she held the purple parasol he had followed. It tilted slightly behind her, casting a shadow over her face. Her eyes, blue like the sky, shone from the shadow.

Max's surroundings faded away as he floated into the vastness of the girl's eyes. From around him, he heard the soft voice of a child.

"Boy, where did you get that box?"

"Box?"

"Yes, boy. The box in your hands."

A vague memory came to Max, a memory of sitting at a table fiddling with a box. He concentrated hard to raise his arms. In his hands, he held the same box.

"This? It was my father's."

The voice drew closer. "Oh? Well, I like it very much. May I have it?"

Max struggled to find his voice. "No, I haven't found out what's inside of it yet."

"Really, why not?"

"The latch is stuck."

The voice was right next to him. "Perhaps I can open it. Hand it to me."

Max started to hold out the box, but pulled it back to himself. "N-no, what if you don't give it back?"

The voice became stern. "A locked box will do you no good. Give it to me."

Max felt a tingling sensation all over his body. The blue sky started to turn gray as his body sank towards the ground. He clutched the box tightly to his chest.

"No, you can't have it."

"I have no time for this. Give me my box!"

The anger in the voice re-awakened Max's senses. In the distance he heard another voice.

"Maxy, where are you?"

*Eve!*

The alleyway snapped back into focus. "Eve, over here, in the…"

Max felt a tug at the box. He looked back just as the little girl yanked on it again.

"How did you…?"

The girl let go of the box and let a small knife slip out of her sleeve and into her hand.

"Let go I said!"

She stabbed at his left hand. Max twisted his body enough that the blade missed its target, instead striking his bracer and bouncing off. She swung again, this time the blade slid across the top of his hand. A streak of blood welled up in the long cut. Startled by the pain, Max backhanded the girl, hitting her square in the face. She rocked back on her heels, lost her balance, and fell. Max yelled towards the street.

"Eve! I'm over here!"

Dust whirled behind him. When he turned back, the girl had disappeared. Eve, Melody, and Lysander ran up behind him. Melody fought to catch her breath.

"Here you are. Why did you wander off like that?"

Max stared dumbfounded at the empty alley. "I…I followed

someone."

Melody scanned the alley. "Who?"

Max shook his head in an attempt to clear it. "I don't know, a strange little girl holding a parasol, but...she disappeared."

Melody stared accusingly at Lysander. "Lysander, did you slip Max some beer at the tavern?"

Lysander tossed his hands in the air. "Hey, I had nothing to do with this! Maybe the alcohol fumes got him."

Eve's ears twitched. "No, there was another person here."

Everyone watched as Eve stepped farther into the alley. She sniffed at the air, her ears erect and alert.

"I smell flowers, but it's not from a perfume."

Max pointed at Eve. "Yes! That's what helped me follow her!"

"It's very strange though. It's new, yet very old at the same time."

Melody gave her a curious look. "What do you mean?"

"Well, you know how babies and old people smell differently?"

Everyone nodded.

"It's like that, only all at the same time."

Eve sniffed again and made an odd face. "Then there is this hint of decay or sickness, like a pile of old, rotten leaves."

"I think the furball is getting her smells mixed with all the farmers around here."

Max nodded. "Yeah, I only saw one person, and she was definitely a child."

Eve glared at Max. "Have I ever been wrong?"

Max cringed. "No, no, sorry."

Eve shook her head. "No, it's all from the same person. I...I think I've smelled it before, but I can't remember where."

Melody sighed, putting her hands on her hips. "Well, at least we know Max isn't drunk on fumes, or anything else."

Eve nodded at Max. "The cut on his hand was enough proof for me."

Max lifted his hand. "Huh...oh."

A trickle of blood flowed down the back of his hand, dripping off of his fingertips. Everything had happened so quickly, he had forgotten about the cut. Now that things had settled down, the pain returned. He grimaced.

"I blocked the first strike, but she got a second in before I knocked her down."

Melody seemed doubtful of his sobriety again. "She attacked you?"

Lysander's eyes grew cold, frightening Max. "You knocked down a little girl!"

"Sh…She wanted the box. When I wouldn't give it to her, she stabbed me with a knife."

"How did she get the jump on you, private?"

"I don't really know. One moment she was standing at the far end of the alley, the next she had grabbed hold of the box. When she stabbed me, I just reacted by swinging my arm out." Max pointed at the ground. "She fell right there. I turned to yell for you guys, and when I looked back, she had vanished."

Eve got on her knees to sniff at the ground. "The scent is stronger. I know I've smelt it before."

Eve sneezed, sending dust everywhere. Melody brushed her cloak off while she thought.

"I wonder why she wanted the box. She could not have known where it came from."

"Lord Avram sent Max and I here to check our reports of a camp of troublemakers. They're probably thieves, and she's one of them."

Max shook his head. "She didn't look like any thief." Max held up the box. "Besides, there is nothing fancy about this box to attract attention."

Eve pointed at one of the latches on the box. "Max, the lock!"

Max took a closer look. The left pin had slid out of its locked position, letting the latch flip open.

"How?"

Melody reached for the box. "May I take a closer look, Max?"

Max handed the box to Melody. She examined it for a moment then took a handkerchief from her pocket and wiped the left lock clean. The pin slid back in place.

Max was horrified. "Melody!"

Melody returned the box to Max. He tried pulling the pin, but it wouldn't budge. "What did you do?"

Melody showed him her handkerchief. "I wiped the blood off of it."

"Why?"

"To test a theory. I've heard of a device called a 'Blood Box'. The locks of this device only react to the blood of the person who initially locked it. Try it."

Max let a drop of blood from his hand touch the pin on the lock. It slid open. He tried the other lock, but nothing happened.

"Another person must have locked the other side, Max. Supposedly that was a common practice between two parties who traded with one another. Since only fresh blood works, both parties had to be present to reopen the box. The downside; however, is that one person could kill the other, and they had his fresh blood." Melody put her cloth away.

"I've never come across this box before. Why would my blood unlock one side?"

"Blood from direct family members worked as well. Your father must have helped lock that box. Maybe the second person is a Protector."

"Maybe, I guess I'll ask when we return. Melody, are you sure there is no other way to unlock it?"

"Not that I know of."

Eve bounced up and down. "Hey, maybe the Collector will know."

Max looked at her blankly. "Who?"

Lysander nodded at Eve. "While you were out getting into fights with little girls, the furball actually found some usefully information."

"Yep! The girl I talked to told me about a camp outside of town."

"It must be the group of thieves and other rabble that headquarters told us about." Lysander smirked. "They probably thought Evangeline belonged with them."

Max heard a low growl start in Eve's chest. Having been on the receiving end of it once or twice, he knew where it might lead. He tried to get her back to his early question.

"So who is this Collector, Eve?"

Eve's eyes drilled into Lysander. "He is an old man in town who collects all sorts of junk. Apparently, he knows how to find the camp."

"He is also who Lady Metis sent me to give a message to, so, we need to head there anyway."

Max put the box into his backpack. "That's great! Even better if he knows another way to open dad's box. Let's go."

Eve relaxed, smiling. "Kay". She took off out of the alley and down the street with the others in tow. "They said his place is pretty hard to miss."

## CHAPTER TWENTY

Max stood and marveled at the mass of statues, furniture, wagons, pieces of various scrap and other assorted items surrounding a rundown building.

"Pretty hard to miss is an understatement."

Paying no attention to the collection, Eve entered the home. Pulling his attention away from the sight, Max entered in behind her. Inside, he found the same clutter with every sort of trinket imaginable lining row after row of shelves.

Melody stepped into the doorway behind Max. "Wow! Careful, Lysander, it's a tight squeeze."

Max moved forward to let Melody and Lysander in. He heard Lysander mumble something before a commotion of scrapes and rattles shook the shelves to Max's right. Melody shot her hands out in time to catch a rock carving that fell from an upper shelf.

Melody gasped. "Lysander!"

Max heard an unintelligible curse from Lysander.

Melody stifled a laugh. "Maybe you should wait outside."

"Agreed."

After some more rattling, Max heard the door close behind them.

Melody let out a deep breath. "That was close. I don't know what this thing is, but I'm sure I don't have the money to replace it." She placed the carving back on the shelf. "See, Max, bigger isn't always better."

"Yeah, imagine all those missions inside of small sundry shops I wouldn't be able to do."

Melody laughed and pointed ahead of Max. "Go find Eve."

Max walked down the aisle, fascinated by the various items on the shelves. Passing an intersecting aisle, he saw nothing but more rows of shelves.

*Where did that girl go? Oh well, she can't be too hard to...*

Eve popped out of the side aisle between Melody and himself. "Hurry up guys."

Melody jumped and bumped a shelf, causing several small figurines to teeter dangerously along its edge. "Eve!"

Eve snapped her tail along the shelf to steady the figurines. "This way already."

Spinning around, she walked back down the aisle she'd come from. Max tried not to laugh, but had little luck.

"Finally, she spooked someone besides me."

He thought Melody would smack him. "That wasn't funny!"

"Hey, at least she didn't pounce on you, and, yes, it really was funny."

Melody swung at Max's head. He ducked, jogging after Eve, leaving Melody fuming behind him.

"Where did she even come from?"

Max snickered. "If I could answer that, maybe I wouldn't get pounced on so often."

He had almost started after Eve too late. Walking hurriedly down one aisle after another, he'd barely see the tip of her tail before it whipped around another corner. After making several more turns, he rounded a corner and stopped abruptly in front of a desk. Behind the desk sat an old man painting a figurine similar to the ones Melody almost knocked off. Eve stood next to Max, elbows on the desk, watching the old man paint. A moment later, Melody rounded the corner, smacking into the back of Max.

"Sorry, Max."

"No problem."

Eve started to laugh, but saw Max blush. She squeezed between him and Melody.

"You should be more careful, Melody."

"Eve, it wasn't her fault."

Melody gave a strange smile. "It's okay, Max. Eve, I'll be more careful in the future. You don't have to worry about me."

Eve eyed Melody. "Kay."

Max looked back and forth between them. "What was that about, Eve? What's with that weird smile, Melody?"

"I'll explain later...maybe." Melody laughed. "For now, we shouldn't be so rude to our host."

Max knew he would not get an answer now, so he turned his attention back to the old man. The figurine sat completed on the desk. The old man sat starring at them, arms crossed. Max cleared his throat.

"Uhh, excuse me?"

The man didn't move. Max leaned over the counter, afraid the old man had stopped breathing.

"Uhh, hi, are you okay?"

Eve pushed Max to the side. "Oh, move over."

She bent over, plopped her elbows back on the desk and placed her head between her hands.

"Hiya, I'm Evangeline."

The old man cracked a smile. "Good afternoon, Evangeline. Welcome to my humble shop."

Eve scanned the nearby shelves. "It's very odd. I like it."

The man nodded. "Thank you. I doubt you will find any other place like it in all of Velrune. Look around, if you don't find anything you like, let me know. I am sure I can get it for you."

Eve focused back on the old man. "How about information?"

"I have a wide variety of that as well." The old man's lips drew tight as he gave Max a cold stare. "However, I reserve that commodity for special customers only."

Max returned the stare. "The law states that you give any information regarding illegal activity to the Protectors."

The old man didn't bat an eye. "Who said I knew anything about illegal activity? Besides, if you haven't noticed by now, few in this town care for your law."

Eve straightened, putting on her most innocent face; the one Max recalled having lulled him into more than one of her adventures. "Maxy is my friend and I'm sure he won't report anything back to the Protectors."

The old man remained firm. "Perhaps there is hope for him if a lacarnian can call him a friend, but he is no friend of mine."

Eve's tail swished back and forth in frustration. "But..."

"It's okay, Eve, I'll go outside. Someone should check on Lysander anyway."

"Wise choice, young man, and take the young lady with you." The man nodded at Melody.

"Me, I'm hardly in league with the Protectors. Besides, I have a message for you from Lady Metis."

"You may not be in league with the Protectors, but I believe the Church of the Immortals to be misguided. I do not trust anyone from their order with the truth. Hand me the message from your lady and leave."

"What do you mean you do not trust us with the truth?"

The old man shook his head. "I have nothing else to say."

Melody reached in her robe and pulled out a sealed letter which she tossed on the desk.

"Fine. Come, Maxwell."

Melody did an about face and headed for the door, or at least that is where she tried to head. Max had his doubts.

"Are you sure you remember the way out of here?"

"I think we turn left at the bonsai tree then right at the wooden fish."

Max laughed. *This place could certainly carry such an assortment.*

"That wasn't a joke, Max."

Sure enough, Max spotted a bonsai tree that was in desperate need of trimming. Melody took a left then a right at a beautifully painted carving of a fish. Back outside, they found Lysander sitting impatiently among a stack of assorted chairs.

He stood upon seeing them.

"So, what did you find out?"

"Nothing. He wouldn't talk to Melody or me, only Eve."

Lysander shook his head. "What is it with this town? They are awfully friendly with the fur balls."

Melody rolled her eyes. "Gee, I can't imagine why he didn't want to talk to a member of the Protectors."

Lysander groaned. "Here we go again with how the Protectors treat the lacarna. You need to be careful about making judgments without knowing all the facts. You have let that girl Max calls a friend cloud your mind."

"I may not know everything that has happened in the past, but at the present there are a lot of people that don't like how the Protectors handle things."

"Someone is always going to get upset about what we do, lacarnians or humans." Lysander walked away from them. "I'll be in the tavern, come and get me when the fur ball is back."

Max watched him go. "I don't understand. My father protected everyone equally, but that's not what I'm seeing from the other Protectors."

Melody put her hand on Max's shoulder. "Maybe they have changed since then, Max. Or, maybe this is how they've always been, and your dad was the odd one out."

The door opened and closed behind them. Turning, they saw Eve walking towards them. She noticed their sour mood.

"What's wrong?"

Max sighed. "Apparently, you're clouding our minds."

Eve smiled mischievously. "You're just now figuring that out, or did Melody tell you?"

Max shook his head. "More like Lysander."

"Ahh, he's on to me. I guess I'll have to work my wiles on him too."

Max snickered. "Good luck with that."

Eve looked around. "Where did he go?"

"He headed for the tavern."

Eve shrugged her shoulders. "Oh well, we can't do anything

until tonight."

Max and Melody leaned towards Eve. "You found something out?"

"Yep. Here."

Eve handed both of them a small, black brooch in the shape of a cat. "We'll need to wear these or we won't be able to find the path that leads from the edge of town to the camp. They only work at night though."

Max and Melody examined the brooches then handed them back to Eve. Max spread his arms.

"Well, what do we do for the next few hours? I don't think the tavern is a good idea."

Eve sighed. "Can't we just leave him there until after we find the camp?"

Max hesitated for a second and then shook his head. "No."

Melody brightened with an idea. "How about we grab a bite to eat?"

Eve bounded up and down. "Great! I'm starved and so is Spook."

Max heard a squeak from the satchel on Eve's back. Maybe Eve had clouded his mind. He could have sworn the mouse just agreed to their plan of action. Max stepped back, raising his hand towards the busy street.

"Ok, Eve, you've got the nose, which way for the best food."

Eve sniffed at the air. "Mmmm, this way."

She started down the street, her nose held high in the air.

## CHAPTER TWENTY-ONE

Eve jumped to her feet. "Here they come."

Melody stopped pacing. "Good, now get down from there."

"Okay, Okay."

Eve walked down the sloped roof of the house. At the edge, she leapt off, landing on the ground next to an agitated Melody.

"So much for being subtle, Eve"

"There's no one around, or I'd have smelled them."

"Maybe, but that's what's bothering me. Why isn't there anyone here?"

Eve shrugged her shoulders. "I guess that's why the people at the camp are using this as their entry point into town."

Max and Lysander approached the narrow walkway between the two deserted houses. "Eve? Melody?"

Eve waved at them. "Here, Maxy."

Melody knocked Eve's hand down. "Eve, shhh!"

Max followed the voices until he found the two girls. "This is it, huh?"

"Yep!"

Melody cringed. "Shhh!"

Lysander snickered then resumed his normal composure. "Don't worry, it turns out this place is more known than people first let on. For example, there is a path behind here that leads into the forest, right?"

Melody nodded in surprise. "That's right. I take it you found someone in the tavern actually willing to talk to you?"

"A couple. They said several people have tried to find the camp. A few even tried the path behind these houses, but they never got far in the woods before coming back out here where they started. None could say how they got turned around."

Melody crossed her arms. "And how much had they been drinking at the time?"

Lysander cleared his throat. "A bit."

"And how about you?"

Lysander stood straight and serious. "None. I never drink when I am on duty."

Lysander relaxed, taking a few wandering steps forward between the houses. "I don't see how we will fare any better though."

Eve spun around, facing away from them. "Easy, we have something they didn't. Melody, can you get the brooches?"

Melody reached her hand into the satchel on Eve's back. A squeak of protest erupted from it. Melody yanked her hand out, eliciting a giggle from Eve.

"Careful of Spook."

The little mouse climbed out of the satchel and onto Eve's shoulder. Melody rolled her eyes then reached into the satchel, pulling out the brooches. She handed one to each of them as Eve continued.

"Don't put them on yet. Let's follow the path to the edge of the woods first."

They left the houses, following the path until it ended at the forest's edge. Lysander spread out his arms.

"Okay, dead end. Now what?"

Melody closed her eyes. "Hmm, the spirits in the forest are acting strangely; like they are being controlled."

Eve pinned her broach to her shirt. "Ooh?"

Everyone else hurriedly put there broaches on as well. A path through the forest appeared in front of them. Eve cleared her throat and faced them. "Now then, here are the rules."

Max's shoulders slumped. "Rules? You didn't mention

anything about rules earlier."

Eve smiled. "Oops."

Max groaned. Melody patted his shoulder.

"I'm sure it will be fine, Max."

Max shook his head. "Eve doesn't forget things. She just conveniently leaves out the details. All the trouble she gets me into starts out this way. The happier she is, the worse the adventure."

Melody laughed. "Come on, Max, it can't be that bad."

Eve ignored the two, clearing her throat a second time. "There are multiple paths in the forest. The old man told me which ones to take, so that shouldn't cause us a problem. The important thing to remember is that, once we're in, we only have ten minutes to reach the camp before the brooches break."

"I knew it. Let me guess, if the brooches break, we lose the path, ending up back here."

Eve nodded. "That, or worse."

Melody's smile disappeared. She dropped her hand from Max's shoulder.

"Worse?"

Eve grinned from ear to ear. "We could be forever lost, fall into a pit, eaten…"

Max waved his hand, not wanting to hear anymore. "Told ya."

This time Melody let out a groan. Eve's grin faded a little.

"It won't be that bad, Melody, but we will have to move pretty fast to make it."

Lysander stepped close to Eve and stared down at her. "Just remember, we don't move as fast as you."

Max moved to their side. "Easy, Lysander, if Eve wanted to get rid of you, she'd find a more direct method. Trust me. But, if you're that worried, you can go in front of me."

Lysander thought a moment then shook his head. "No, I'll take the rear. There is a chance I can't make it no matter what the pace. I'll have to trust you, Max, to do your job if that happens."

Max nodded. "Of course."

Melody, resigned to whatever fate lay before her, joined the other three. "I'll follow Eve. I'm pretty light on my feet."

Spook squeaked as she climbed onto Eve's head and lay between her ears. Eve petted the mouse.

"I guess you want a good seat, huh? At least someone, besides me, is having fun."

Eve brought her attention back to the others as she bounced up and down. "Okay then, is everyone ready?"

At everyone's acknowledgment, Eve entered the forest, not giving them a chance to change their minds. The others filed in behind and ran after her. They had not gone far before other trails began to split off in different directions. Eve changed paths several times within the first few minutes, causing Max to give up trying to keep track of where they were going. He focused on following Melody, letting the trees and path blur by.

Suddenly, Melody switched to a full run. Max struggled to keep pace.

*We must be running out of time.*

Behind him, Lysander's footsteps fell farther and farther behind. As Max neared his limit, he burst into a clearing. Caught off guard, it took him a moment to realize Melody had stopped. He slid to a halt just short of running into her. His relief at avoiding the collision faded instantly. He spun as Lysander barreled out of the forest at full speed with his head down. Max tried to wave him off.

"Lysander!"

Lysander lifted his head, his eyes growing wide at seeing Max. It was too late. Lysander plowed into Max, shoving him into Melody and knocking them to the ground.

"Owww!"

*That was Eve's voice!* "Eve!"

"I'm under Melody."

Lysander jumped up. "I'm sorry, here."

Lysander extended a hand to Max and helped him off of Melody. He helped Melody up next, with Max reaching for Eve.

Max took hold of her arm, but she jerked it back.

"Ouch! That hurts!"

Max knelt beside her. "What's wrong?"

Eve's teeth were clenched tight. "I think my arm is broken."

"I'm sorry, Evangeline. I was about to lose sight of Max so I focused solely on running. I heard Max yell, but I couldn't stop in time."

The apology caught all three by surprise. Eve gave him a weak smile.

"I…it's okay, but I'm not leading next time."

Max rolled his eyes and focused on Eve's arm. "Is there anything you can do for her, Melody?"

Melody shook her head. "I'm not that skilled. If I had the right things, I could set the bone, but that's it."

"I'll manage, Max. I heal quickly. Besides, I need to find Spook. She got knocked off my head."

"Your friend is over here by the fire."

The collision had distracted them from their surroundings. Startled by the unknown voice, they took in the clearing, seeing a campfire about hundred and twenty feet in front of them. A dozen lacarnian women and a few humans sat around it, staring at them. One of the lacarnian women stood.

"Bring her over here."

Lysander eyed those around the camp. "Careful, Maxwell, this must be the camp that headquarters told us about."

"If they meant us harm, wouldn't they have attacked us by now?"

Melody bent over and picked up a piece of a brooch from the ground. "It's not like we can go anywhere else. Our time is up."

Lysander nodded. "So be it, but stay behind me."

Melody rolled her eyes, but complied. Max carefully gathered Eve in his arms and followed Lysander and Melody to the edge of the campfire. The lacarnian woman brushed by Lysander and pointed Max to a stump.

"Sit her there so we can have a better look."

Max lowered Eve onto the stump and then sat on one next to

her. Spook scurried over from the fire and climbed onto Eve's shoulder. Another lacarnian, much older than the rest, approached Eve.

"Let's have a look at you, my child."

The woman took Eve's arm and slowly moved it in different directions, making Eve wince, before gently putting it back down.

"It is definitely broken. No worries child, Miss Alexandra will fix it in no time."

Melody stepped around Eve to better see the old woman.

"Fix it? Is there a member of the Children here?"

The old woman shuffled back to her seat. "No, no. Miss Alexandra belongs to no such order."

"Then who is she?"

The woman smiled fondly. "She is the one who watches out for us."

Lysander, ignoring the conversation, bent down next to Max. "Did you notice none of the lacarnians are wearing collars?"

The smile vanished from the old woman's face. "Of course we are not! Miss Alexandra finds those things as dreadful as we do."

The woman's reaction startled Max. Beside him, Lysander tensed, readying for a fight. Before the situation could escalate, another lacarnian stepped between them.

"Miss Alexandra will see you now."

Eve gasped. "You're the one I talked to at the tavern!"

"I'm often there watching for those that would do well in our camp. I thought she might like you," the girl looked with disdain at the rest of them, "but I did not expect Miss Alexandra to invite everyone. Now come."

The girl left the campsite in the direction she had come. Max helped Eve stand and they, along with Melody and Lysander, followed her. Past the small camp lay a narrow stone path lined with torches on either side that ignited as they neared, only to extinguish a few feet behind them. The path led to a copse of trees in the middle of the meadow that hid within it a smaller version of Melody's church. Here, the vines and trees intertwined so much with the structure that they could see little of the original stone.

The girl opened the door to the building. "Enter."

Max, followed by the others, stepped inside the doorway. The girl, staying outside, closed the door behind them. Torches glowed from either side of the doorway, lighting the entrance, but leaving the front of the building in shadows. There, Max could make out a single table, next to which stood a small figure. The hair on Max's neck rose as the figure reached out her hand.

"Evangeline, come to me."

The stern, but childlike voice sounded familiar. Max took hold of Eve's good arm.

"I'm not sure about this, Eve."

Melody touched Eve on the shoulder. "Same here, the spirits in this room are incredibly active. It could be dangerous."

Max took a step forward. "Why don't you come to us?"

The small, but firm voice responded. "Because this is my home where I do as I please."

Eve gently brushed Max's hand off of her arm. "It's okay, Max. I don't know why, but I feel very safe here."

"Eve is correct. I mean her no harm. I only wish to heal her."

Lysander moved next to Max. "And the rest of us?"

"I will not harm you, for the time being."

"How reassuring."

Eve squeezed between Max and Lysander. "Really, it's okay."

She crossed the floor into the shadows. The figure spoke to her for a moment then had Eve lay on the table. Max tensed at the sight, but Melody took hold of his arm.

"Wait, Max."

Max waited nervously as the figure placed a small, thin object on Eve's arm. The figure then held her hand closely over it. To Max's surprise the object sank into Eve's arm. A moment later Eve sat up, moving her arm about freely. She hopped off the table and ran back to Max.

"She fixed it!"

Melody grabbed Eve's arm and examined it, astonished. "But how? It takes skilled use and understanding of the spirits to heal bones that quickly."

"Nonsense, acolyte, I used a basic technique."

Melody let go of Eve's arm and faced the figure. "Basic technique? I have only seen the Revered Mother of our order heal a broken bone in that manner."

A long sigh escaped the figure. "Has that much knowledge really been lost?"

"Knowledge, what do you mean? Who are you?"

"My apologies, I am Alexandra."

"I didn't mean your name. Those in the camp told us that. Who are you that you can manipulate the spirits so willingly?"

"You should not be so rude, acolyte. I suppose; however, that we need to get to the business at hand. First, some more light would be nice."

Torches at the darkened end of the building flared to life, fully lighting the figure. Max's mouth dropped open.

"You're the girl from the alley!"

Max drew his sword, ready to defend himself and the others. Alexandra spread out her arms, the open palms of her hands facing them.

"That will not be necessary, Maxwell. I have no intention of attacking you again."

"How can I be sure? I don't even know why you attacked me the first time, or how? One moment you stood at the far end of the alley, the next you had a hold of my box. And, how do you know my name?"

"Unfortunately, in the alley I did not know who you were. I mistook you for a thief. You see, I had a box similar to yours taken from me. When I saw you with that box at the tavern I thought it mine. I jumped to conclusions and overreacted. I apologize for my rashness."

Alexandra walked to within a few feet of Max and curtsied. "Now that I know who you are I certainly mean you no harm."

Free of the shadows, Max studied Alexandra's appearance.

Her face was the soft, round face of a child's. Her hands, like her face, were unusually pale; together they gave her the appearance of a fragile porcelain doll much like the ones a villager in Swiftwater made from the river's clay. Max feared that if he touched her she would shatter. He sheathed his sword.

"What about the rest? How did you get from one end of the alley to the other without me noticing?"

Melody fixed her gaze on Alexandra. "If she can heal a bone with that much ease, I imagine there are a lot of things she can do; mesmerizing you long enough to attack being only one of them."

"But she can't be over, what, eleven years old?"

"I am nine, actually. To your credit, you did much better than most in resisting me." Alexandra gingerly rubbed the side of her face. "I certainly did not expect you to backhand me."

Max shuffled his feet. "You did attack me."

"I am not looking for an apology. You fought back as, you should have. I misjudged your abilities."

Max straightened. "What about my name?"

"Ahh, yes, Maxwell Laskaris, son of Lieutenant Peter Laskaris."

"How do you know that? You're not old enough to have met my father."

"I have many resources. I also know about the rest of you: Lysander, Melody and Evangeline."

Lysander crossed his arms. "I assume, by resources, you mean that rabble out by the fire who are in violation of the law by not wearing collars. We also have reports of theft and other trouble in town. Where are your parents, Maxwell and I need to speak with them concerning all of this."

Alexandra's pale cheeks flared red. "The lacarnians are not pets! I will not have them wearing collars as if they were. As for the trouble in town, that has nothing to do with us. Those in my camp pay for what they bring here and are strictly prohibited from fighting or doing any harm." Alexandra took a deep breath. "As for my parents, they are long dead. I run this camp."

"Do you expect me to believe a little brat is running this place?"

The fire in Alexandra's cheeks rekindled. Her hands tightened into fists. "You are here by my invitation, or you would not have made it through the forest."

Max stepped between the two. "Why did you invite us here?"

Alexandra turned from Lysander. "I need your help."

Lysander crossed his arms. "Why would we do that?"

"Because I have information about things you all want, things like the Lifestone."

Lysander snickered. "Lifestone? That's a myth."

"Perhaps, but the head of the Protectors has quite an interest in it nonetheless. If the Lifestone isn't enough, I also know of a person who can open your box, Maxwell."

"Really? Where?"

"The forest of Urania."

Melody shook her head. "Urania's a forest that was once the home of all lacarna. Now, though, it has grown so thick that none can navigate it. That, and no one knows what dangerous creatures still live inside of it. You can't go in there, Max."

"But, if there is someone there who can get this box open..."

Alexandra nodded. "There is and it is the same place I need to go. I know the path through the forest, but I am too weak to go alone. I had hoped both the possibility of opening your father's box, Maxwell, and getting information about the Lifestone would be payment enough for your escort."

Eve clapped her hands together. "Sounds like fun to me. I'll go."

Max shook his head. "A mysterious and dangerous forest; why am I not surprised, Eve? I'll go too. I have to get this box opened and find out what my dad felt was so important."

"Melody threw her arms up. "Me too, I can't pass on the chance to see Urania, few in my order could."

Alexandra stepped past them and opened the door. "Very well, then. I have supplies waiting for us at the camp."

Lysander blocked Max's path. "Hold it, Maxwell. Lord Avram sent us here to investigate the trouble with the town then report back, no extra field trips."

"He also mentioned to keep an ear out about a mysterious stone. What other stone could he have meant other than the Lifestone?"

Eve smiled at Lysander. "Max has ya there. Besides, you're outnumbered."

Alexandra looked at Lysander. "Well, Protector?"

"If you are lying, I will put everyone in this camp in prison, including you, regardless whether their crimes are valid or not."

"Fair enough. Now, go back down to the camp. There you will find new backpacks for each of you, pre-packed with the necessary items. I will follow in short order."

The four walked back to the camp where the lacarna were waiting for them, backpacks in hand. As the lacarna helped them with the packs, Melody took the chance to speak with the young girl helping her.

"Tell me, how long has this camp been here?"

"I don't know, since before I came."

"Then, how long have you been here?"

The girl thought for a moment then shrugged her shoulders. "I guess I don't know that either."

"How do you not know that?"

The girl grew frightened and moved away from Melody. The old woman who had examined Eve came over.

"Time is a hard thing to keep track of here. Nothing ever changes except the members of the camp."

"But, you go in to town for supplies."

"Only a few go, and they only speak to Miss Alexandra of what they see."

"It sounds like you are prisoners here."

"Nonsense! She may choose who can enter, but, when we are ready to move on, she allows us to do so. While here, we are free to live as we please with the Miss asking little in return."

"So you never question her on what happens outside of this

meadow?"

"No, Alexandra has a kind soul and keeps our best interests in mind, but she does not like to be bothered."

"You said she asks little in return. What does she ask for?"

"That is not your concern."

The old woman left Melody's side, returning to her seat by the fire. Lysander stepped behind Melody.

"Were you, like me, trying to figure out how a nine year old girl organized a camp that feels as though it has existed for years?"

"It certainly doesn't add up very well."

"You said what she did for Eve took a lot of skill. How much?"

"Far more than any little girl should have. As I said, only the Revered Mother could heal broken bones."

"What about this glade? The old woman said Alexandra controlled who entered it."

"I've read of a few people in the history of our order who had the ability to do such a thing, but only for a short time. There are; however, tales of feats similar to this from a time before our order, from another group of people."

"Who?"

Max spoke from behind Lysander. "The Immortals, right?"

Lysander jumped and stepped aside. "Where did you come from? I thought we were alone."

Eve slipped around from behind Max, pointing to her ears. "I could hear you guys from the forest if I wanted to, and, by the way, so could they."

Eve nodded at the lacarna watching them. The four grew nervous from the cold stares. To their relief, Alexandra arrived and broke the tension.

"Are you ready?"

The four turned to find Alexandra facing them, wearing her own small backpack. They replied with eagerness.

"Yes!"

"Then let us be on our way."

Alexandra walked towards the spot where they first entered the camp, stopping at the edge of the meadow. She faced the camp and addressed the old lacarnian woman.

"Remember, Lycoris, my agreement with the spirits will end when I leave. In a few days the camp will no longer be hidden."

"We will be careful, Miss Alexandra. In the meantime, we will await your word."

Alexandra turned towards Max and the others.

"Come."

Alexandra stepped into the forest. Eve, not the least bothered by the entire incident, followed her without question. Max shared a glance of concern with Melody and Lysander before going in himself.

Eve had filled him in on Lysander and Melody's discussion as she listened in. *I wonder if Alexandra could really be an Immortal.*

Max laughed to himself. That was too much to believe.

*At the very least, I hope she's telling the truth about knowing a person who can open this box.*

Behind him, he heard Melody and Lysander step into the forest.

## CHAPTER TWENTY-TWO

Alexandra led them along a narrow path for only a short distance before abandoning it to forge her own path between the trees. While she and Eve moved effortlessly past tree limbs and roots, Max struggled to keep from tripping.

*Maybe she really does control this forest.*

Luckily, following Eve's bright red tail kept him from hitting anything too big. Behind him, Melody followed with less trouble, but a string of curses flowed from Lysander as he walked into everything from roots to tree trunks. A particularly loud thud made Max cringe.

"Blasted trees! Couldn't that brat at least follow the trail back to town first?"

Alexandra's small voice came from the front. "No."

Distracted, Max failed to duck a small limb that whipped back after Eve pushed by it. *I didn't think she was paying attention to us.*

Lysander raised his voice. "No? No! All I get is no!"

"I need not explain myself to you, Protector. However, it it will shut you up, I will say that the town has too many curious eyes and ears. Now, stay quiet, or I will send you back to town by yourself, never to see me again. You no longer have the brooches after all."

Except for the occasional curse caused by a run-in with a limb or root, everyone remained silent until they exited the forest an hour later. Max breathed a sigh of relief when he saw open ground again.

"Thank goodness that's over with."

Lysander stumbled out last, rubbing his forehead. "I've been in brawls that hurt less."

Max broke out laughing. Lysander had twigs, leaves and other brush sticking out from all sorts of places. Standing in the moonlight, he looked like a forest monster from a child's story.

Max swore he saw a smile flash across Alexandra's face when she spoke to Lysander. "You will recover; we are still too close to town. When we stop at dawn, you can complain all you want."

From the forest they headed out across several small hills before reaching the plains where the walking became easier. When dawn arrived, they were well ready for a break. Alexandra came to a stop and faced them.

"We will rest here for a few hours. At late morning, we will move again until early afternoon. Then, we will stop until after the sun sets."

Lysander plucked a lingering twig from his hair. "That's not much rest."

"We need to keep moving. I have no doubt the Protectors are trying to follow us. I intend to keep ahead of them."

"You are very determined to avoid the Protectors. What do they want with you?"

"It is not so much me they are after, but where I am taking you and what lies there."

"I intend to make a full report anyway, so what's the difference?"

"Time. If I have time, I might be able to change your mind."

"Doubtful."

"The truth can be a powerful thing, even for the likes of you, Lysander."

"What truth?"

"You will have to wait to find out. Now," she extended her hand, "hand me my tent."

Lysander stared at Alexandra blankly. "Tent, I don't have your tent."

Alexandra had a smug look on her face. "Yes, you do. I had them put it in your backpack. You are, after all, the biggest one here."

Lysander took a step forward. "If your tent is in my backpack, then what are you carrying?"

Alexandra didn't flinch. "Things too important for a klutz, such as you, to carry. Now, give me my tent."

Lysander crossed his arms. "And if I don't?"

Alexandra gave a slight flick of her wrist sending the tall grass around Lysander wrapping around his feet and ankles. Another flick and the grass jerked him to the ground, face first, where more grass swarmed over his body, binding him in place. She bent over Lysander, opened his backpack and pulled out a piece of black canvas and four short poles.

"I do not recommend saying no to me."

Alexandra moved a little ways away from the others and extended the poles to three feet in length. She then placed each one on the ground, the grass winding around them as she did so. She then stretched the black canvas over them, the sides falling level with the ground. With her makeshift tent completed, she crawled under, leaving Max fascinated.

"Wow, Melody, is that why the garden at your Church has grown so much?"

Melody shook her head. "No, no one at the Church has that kind of control over the spirits. All we do is provide a rich, caring environment where the spirits can be happy. I have never seen anyone control plants with that much ease."

The grass binding Lysander released, allowing him to stand.

"It may be a neat trick, but someone needs to teach that little brat to respect her elders."

Melody gave a nervous laugh. "Good luck with that."

Eve smirked. "If she is an Immortal, like you guys were saying, wouldn't she be your elder, Lysander?"

Max slid off his backpack and sat on the grass. "About that, I thought all the Immortals had disappeared?"

Melody sat next to Max, kicking off her shoes and laying back on the soft grass. "All except the cursed ones, the Spirit Leeches."

Lysander shook his head. "Even those were hunted down by the Protectors. One hasn't been seen in years."

Lysander sat down across from Max and Melody. Swinging his backpack around, he began to shuffle through it.

"I wonder what else of hers they stuck in here."

Eve flopped down on the other side of Max. "But what if she is one?"

Lysander looked up. "Then Max and I will arrest her and take her to headquarters for judgment."

Max gave Lysander a blank look. "Why would we do that?"

"The Spirit Leeches are criminals. They prey on the innocent, draining them of their spirit energy, killing them."

"But, who are they?"

"They are Immortals who betrayed their own kind and were cursed for their crime."

Max waved his hands." Whoa, wait a second. She's only nine. How could she have betrayed anyone?"

Melody nodded. "I must admit, there is nothing recorded from our order concerning Spirit Leeches of such a young age, but I can't explain the power she has either."

Lysander glanced at Alexandra's tent. "And that has me worried. Your order knows more about this stuff than anyone, and you don't even know what to make of her. What I do know, for sure, is that she's dangerous. Stay alert, Max."

Eve huffed. "You guys are being too dramatic. Leave her alone. Relax and enjoy the scenery.

Max rolled his eyes. "And you're having too much fun, Eve."

Eve laughed merrily, causing the others to put the topic aside for the moment. Sitting up, she rummaged around in her backpack.

"Hmm, guess we don't get a tent. Ooo, they packed cheese for Spook."

Eve took out a small piece of cheese. Spook, hearing her name, popped out of her satchel, spied the cheese and quickly climbed over Eve to snatch it. This time, Max and Melody broke out laughing. Lysander shook his head and resumed shuffling through his pack.

"Seems I get all the heavy equipment: rope, spade…what the?" Lysander pulled out a dark purple colored parasol.

Max pointed at the parasol. "Hey, that's the parasol Alexandra carried when I saw her in town."

Lysander grunted. "Well at least one of us will look fashionable. What am I, her servant?"

Eve stood and walked over to Lysander. "Give it here, I'll keep it."

Looking at Alexandra's tent, Max shook his head. "I don't think it has anything to do with fashion. Didn't you notice how pale she is? She must burn easy in the sunlight."

Lysander handed over the parasol. "That is a condition commonly found in Spirit Leeches. Careful how friendly you become with her."

Eve sat back down in her spot. "Spirit Leech or not, she's a peach compared to you."

Lysander's face grew red. "We better get some rest while we can. We move again in a few hours."

While they knew Lysander was simply trying to stop the conversation, they still took the advice. It had been a long night. They each found the softest patch of ground they could and laid down for a nap.

Four hours later, Eve awoke to find Alexandra standing over her, parasol in hand. "It is time to go. I can only move while the sun is overhead, once it starts to sink we will have to stop until nightfall."

Eve popped up from the ground. "How did you sneak up on me?"

The slightest of smiles touched the corners of Alexandra's lips. "I grew up around the lacarna so I know their abilities. Do not worry though, you will learn how to detect my presence." She turned to walk away. "Oh, thank you for getting my parasol."

Eve shrugged her shoulders. "Welcome. Max recognized it when Lysander pulled it out of his pack. He thought you might need it in the sun."

Alexandra paused. "Hmm."

Max stood from where he had been sleeping, Eve and Alexandra's conversation having awoken him. "Hey, Alex, I..."

Alexandra spun around, her eyes burning with fire. "My name is Alexandra!" She spun away, "Now move," and started walking.

Max, startled by Alexandra's reaction, forgot his question. Lysander stepped beside him.

"Told you to be careful."

Max grabbed his chest. "When did you get up?"

Lysander pointed to Max's other side. "Same time as Melody."

Melody waved at Max. "Hi."

Max shook his head. "Eve's right, I really need to pay more attention. In any event, Alexandra's not waiting for us."

Alexandra had already put close to 150 feet between them with Eve trailing a short distance behind her. Max, Melody and Lysander grabbed their backpacks and rushed after them.

Two hours later, when Alexandra's parcel could no longer adequately block the sun's light, they stopped to rest once again. When the sun set, they moved again, this time going until the next day's sunrise. Max stuck close to Lysander the first night, trying to get more information about the Spirit Leeches.

"Hey, Lysander, Mr. Penna never mentioned the Spirit Leeches in his lectures."

"That doesn't surprise me. Not too many people know about them anymore, and the rest of us would like to forget about them."

"Why? Does it have something to do with what you said about them betraying their own kind? What happened?"

Lysander took a deep breath. "What I've been told, Max, is this. During the lacarnian war against the humans, some of the

Immortals sided with the lacarna rather than trying to find a fair way to end the conflict. After the war, the other Immortals held them accountable for their actions. They punished them by inflicting them with a disease that would slowly eat away at their spirit energy, eventually killing them."

Max shook his head. "But the disease didn't kill them all, did it?"

"No, some found they could draw out the life spirit of others to temporarily counter the disease's effect."

"Draw out their spirit energy? You said that earlier too. I don't understand what you mean."

Lysander looked back to Melody who walked a few steps behind them. "I think you can explain this part better than me."

Melody nodded. "Max, do you remember what I told you about the spirits? How they are in all living things? Well, that goes for us too. It's kind of like this: If we get a cut, we bleed; the more we bleed, the weaker we get; if we bleed too much, we die. It works the same with our spirit energy. As we lose our spirit energy we grow weak, we lose too much, we die. The Spirit Leeches act like a cut, creating a place for the spirit energy to flow out. The good news is, like our blood, our spirit energy replenishes overtime, or at least for normal humans it does. The disease the Spirit Leeches have eats away the energy faster than it can replenish."

Max thought about this for a moment before speaking. "So, the Spirit Leeches can draw out the energy of others to replace their own?"

"Correct, but, like their own energy, the energy they stole from another being also depletes over time. They must find one victim after the next to keep replacing their energy in order to stay alive."

"Okay, I think I got it, except for one thing. How do they draw out the spirit energy of others?"

"I'm not sure. I doubt it's easy. The simple things I can do, like create the barrier, takes a lot of skill and concentration."

Lysander shook his head. "From what I've seen, it's simple

enough. They simply lay their hands on the person and take it."

Max's eyes went wide. "You've actually seen it happen?"

Max's question drew both Melody and Eve closer to them, both curious as to what Lysander might have seen. Lysander bowed his head, taking a moment to think before answering.

"When I was a child, my parents and I were returning to Moenia from a picnic with another couple and their children. We lost track of time, returning after the sun had set. We made it within a half-mile of the city gates when a Spirit Leech, hidden behind a few rocks, jumped us. She grabbed the other man's wife, yanking her to the ground. Right before us, the Spirit Leech began draining the poor woman of her very life. I could see the color fade from the woman's face. Seconds later, my father and the woman's husband attacked the Spirit Leech, but it fought them off and ran."

"We rushed to the city, informing the Protectors at the gate of the incident. Luckily, the woman survived, thanks to the quick response by her husband and my father. Three days later a patrol found and captured the Spirit Leech."

"What did they do with the Spirit Leech?" asked Max.

"They tried and executed it."

"Even though the woman recovered?"

"That thing would have finished her off if it had the chance."

"How do you know?"

"Because, the curse not only affected their bodies, but their minds as well. They're mad, not caring what they hurt."

Eve butted in. "Well then, Alexandra must not be one, she seems perfectly fine to me."

Lysander laughed. "Fine! She's supposedly nine, but she acts like an adult beyond any of our years. Then there are her powers that even Melody can't explain."

"Okay, but she hasn't tried to hurt any of us. She even healed my arm."

"Her behavior is different from what I have heard of the Spirit Leeches. However, I have a hard time believing she is an Immortal. Either way, she must really need something from us to come out in the open like this."

Melody crossed her arms, angry. "I realize it must have been terrifying to witness such an attack when you were so young, but you can't apply one person's actions to everyone like them. That is the same attitude the Protectors have always had and why our Order has never gotten along with them."

"That attitude is what has kept us alive and in control."

"It's also what keeps you from having an open mind, about the Spirit Leeches, our order, and the lacarna. Perhaps you should give us a chance sometime instead of blindly following your beloved Lord Avram and his lies."

Lysander stopped and faced Melody. "Careful of what you say, acolyte."

Melody huffed, but said nothing else. Lysander turned and started walking again. Max, Melody and Eve gave him a little distance before following.

Melody mumbled under her breath, "Stupid, close-minded Protectors."

Eve smiled slightly, but seemed thoughtful. "What do you think about her, Max?"

Max shrugged his shoulders. "Something is wrong with her, that's for certain. I also have a feeling she's not telling us all the reasons she's taking us to this forest either."

"I don't think she'd hurt us though, Maxy, even if she is a Spirit Leech. I mean, how many of them have the Protectors actually run into?"

"I don't know, and I'm not sure if it would matter. They seem to make their laws on what they think is the truth about people without really getting to know them first." Max shook his head. "I believed being a Protector would be easy; that they did everything that was right and fair. Now it seems that what they think is fair is not how everyone else feels, including me."

Eve sighed. "I wish Mr. Penna had come with us."

"Why? You know all he'd do is give us some vague answer that would make no sense and then tell us to figure it out ourselves. You, on the other hand, have no problem telling me what you think. You also judge people pretty well, if you trust her, I do too."

"B...but, Maxy, what if I'm wrong?"

Max laughed. "Then, once again, you'll have to get me out of trouble."

Eve, laughing, punched Max in the shoulder. "Sure, you join the Protectors, and I do all the work."

Even Melody laughed now, forgetting her frustration with Lysander.

No one brought the topic up again for the rest of the trip to the forest. After two nights on the move, the lack of sleep began to wear them down. They skipped any conversation requiring much thought, focusing instead on following Alexandra.

## CHAPTER TWENTY-THREE

Five days after leaving Alexandra's camp, they reached the Urania Forest, arriving late in the evening. Alexandra stopped short of entering the forest.

"We will rest here until morning. It is not wise to travel through Urania at night."

Lysander gave one look at the thickness of the forest vegetation and slumped his shoulders. "How far in do we have to go?"

"To the center, next to the mountain's edge. It will take a day and half."

"Is that where I can find out how to open my father's box?"

Lysander snickered. "And where the Lifestone is?"

Alexandra let out a yawn, the first they had seen from her. "Yes, yes, now go to sleep."

Skipping her tent, she found a spot free of rocks or other lumps and lay down. The others, glad for the rest, did likewise. They fell asleep quickly, but an hour later Eve woke with a start.

*What was that?*

Ears swiveling, she listened for signs of movement. All was still, with only the slow, rhythmic breathing of the others disturbing the night.

*I know I heard a voice. Wait, I don't hear Alexandra.*

Eve rose onto her elbows and verified the sleeping forms around her. No Alexandra. The voice came again, a faint whisper from the forest.

"Come back, please, come back."

Eve felt the pain in the voice. A strong desire to enter the woods washed over her. Standing without making the slightest of sounds, she crept to the edge of the forest. There she spotted Alexandra, her back towards her, sitting on a fallen tree. Not wanting to wake the others, Eve quietly sat down next to her, keeping her voice to a whisper.

"I, I think the forest called to me?"

Alexandra didn't move as she gazed longingly into the woods. "I am not surprised."

Eve waited for more, but, after several minutes, she gave up. "I feel it pulling at me, like the flowers at the church's garden in Moenia, only much, much stronger. It almost seems, familiar. Like a person I met a long time ago, but can't quite remember."

Alexandra smiled joyfully, an act even Eve believed her incapable of.

"All lacarnians have a special connection to the spirits of their birth place." Her smile faded away. "Except for those born in the villages among the dust and stone. They have nothing to bond with. They lose so much before they even have a chance."

Eve caught her breath. *All lacarnians have a connection to the spirits of where they're born?*

"Wait, Alexandra, are you saying this is where I was born?"

Alexandra cautiously put her hand on top of Eve's. The warmth of her hand surprised Eve as a joyous sensation flowed through her. A memory of lying on her back in a forest thicket formed in her mind. In it she could feel the same force that had called to her this night. All of a sudden, Alexandra stood over her, laughing with abandon. Eve gasped and the memory faded.

"This was my home and yours. Alexandra, we've met before."

A single tear fell down Alexandra's cheek, only noticeable because of the moonlight that reflected in it. "Yes, at one time, it was your home. I was only a guest."

Behind them came Melody's soft voice. "You were only a

guest during Eve's time here, but long ago it was once yours, wasn't it?"

Alexandra sighed, her face revealing a deep sorrow. Eve, her hand still under Alexandra's, could feel her pain too.

"Yes, a very, very long time ago. Before..."

Melody sat on the other side of Alexandra, staring off into the forest as well. "I've heard of only the Immortals having the power to control the spirits the way you can."

Alexandra shook her head. "I have no more power than you, or even Lysander for that matter. I have only had time to better understand the spirits."

Eve shook off the faded memory. "Wait, Melody, are you saying Alexandra is an Immortal? I thought you said they all disappeared. Well, except the Spirit Leeches, but Lysander said even they are all gone now."

Melody shook her head. "No one really knew what really happened to the Immortals, and the Spirit Leeches would want to stay in hiding to avoid the Protectors. I honestly can't say that neither still exist. Alexandra?"

Alexandra nodded. "As far as I know, there are only two of us left from those long ago days. In your terms, one of us is an Immortal, the other, a Spirit Leech."

Eve flipped her hand over and grasped Alexandra's. "You're the Immortal, right? I mean, you sound nothing like how Lysander described the Spirit Leeches. You haven't tried to harm us. You're not mad."

Alexandra remained quiet. Melody took her eyes away from the forest to look at Alexandra before speaking to Eve.

"The Immortals were not really immortal. They only seemed so from their much longer lifespan, and their abilities made them seem like gods. That is why they were given that name. In the end, they still grew old and died. On the other hand, the Spirit Leeches, at the time they became cursed, stopped aging."

Alexandra sighed, giving Eve's hand a brief squeeze. "At one time I never wanted to grow up. Now I dream that one day I might. Ironic, is it not?"

None of the three spoke, instead drifting into their own thoughts as the night passed. After a time, Eve realized she still held Alexandra's hand and gently let go.

"Alexandra, will we really find someone in there that can open Max's box?"

"Yes."

"And, you're not planning to hurt us?"

"No, Evangeline, that is not my intention."

Eve gave a curt nod. "Kay, then I'll help you get what you need. I just hope Lysander doesn't find out about you before then."

"He already knows."

Eve seemed doubtful. "Are you sure? He's not the brightest?"

"There is more to Lysander than you think. Like many, he does not show his true self. Besides, finding the Spirit Leeches is a core part of a Protector's training and the highest mandate of Lord Avram."

"Then why did he agree to come here rather than arrest you at the camp?"

Melody joined the conversation. "Because he's waiting, Eve. Haven't you noticed how Alexandra's face has paled and thinned over the past several days? She's slowed down too. Remember Lysander's story, the curse weakens an individual over time. If she does not draw energy soon, she will be too weak to fight."

"I don't know, Melody. I don't think Lysander would make the mistake of giving her the chance of attacking him before she grew too weak. Not that I'm saying you would, Alexandra."

Alexandra smiled weakly. "It is alright, Eve. I know you meant nothing by it. As for Lysander, he has his own reasons for agreeing to come. I can also assure all of you that, while I have drawn from those willing to give, I have not attacked anyone in ages. I have learned to control myself and, in order for what I seek to come true, I need things to remain that way."

Melody looked at her questioningly. "What is it that you seek, Alexandra?"

"To set things right. In order for me to explain further, we must reach the village in the forest. I only hope you believe when you see what is hidden there."

Melody stood. "In that case, you need your rest, we all do."

Alexandra stood. "Agreed."

The three walked back to the sound of Lysander and Max snoring. Finding their own spots, they fell back to sleep.

A gentle shaking awoke Max.

"Come on, Maxy. It's morning."

"What, no morning attack? You're slipping, Eve."

Eve grinned. "Don't get used to it."

Max stood and joined the others in packing their things. When they were ready, Lysander stood in front of the trees, blocking their path.

"What is it you really want in there, Alexandra?"

"You will have to wait to find out."

"That's not encouraging. So far you've done nothing to allow us to trust you. Why should we risk following you?"

"I have already given you reasons to follow me. As for trust, I have not killed any of you. Does that not count for something?"

Eve stepped next to Alexandra. "I trust her." Eve turned to Max for support. "Melody and I talked with her last night, Max. I believed her when she said she would not hurt us, and that there is a way to open your dad's box."

Lysander smirked. "You're just a kid, Evangeline. You're easily manipulated."

Eve scowled at Lysander. Alexandra laid her closed parasol on the ground. "Fine, if I must do this now then I will. Lysander, you hold that Maxwell's father was a good man, one to be trusted, do you not?"

"Yes, of course, most everyone in the Protectors does."

Alexandra turned to Max. "Pull out your father's box."

Max hesitated at first, but, under the cold stare of Alexandra, decided it best to do as she said. He took the box out of his backpack and held it in front of him. In one smooth motion,

Alexandra slipped a small dagger out of her sleeve and made a shallow cut across the palm of her hand.

"Lysander, the Protectors trusted Peter, I know that. Well, Peter trusted me."

Blood trickled from the cut on Alexandra's hand as she walked over to Max and placed her palm on the second latch of the box. It slid open.

"Sit the box down and give me your hand."

Max followed Alexandra's instruction. She took his hand and carefully poked one of his fingers with the dagger.

"Open the other latch."

Max placed his finger on the other latch; it slid open.

"Open it, Maxwell."

Max, filled with nervous excitement, lifted the lid. The excitement faded, replaced with confusion. Eve grabbed her tail in concern.

"What is it, Max?"

Alexandra turned to Eve. "Four pieces of bark."

"What?"

Max pulled out a piece of bark an inch wide and three inches long. "Bark. Four pieces of bark."

"Maxwell, your father and I, together, put those pieces in the box and sealed it. That is the reason I give you and Lysander to trust me."

"But, what are they for?"

"Follow me, and you will find out."

"Wait, you said you're nine. How could you have locked the box? Your parents, maybe, but not you."

Lysander stomped over to Alexandra, grabbed her hand and turned it, palm up. The cut on her palm had healed, but the surrounding skin had lost all color.

"As I thought, a Spirit Leech."

Alexandra pulled her hand back. "Yes, I will not blatantly deny it, though I had hoped that you would not find out until we reached our destination."

"That is because you are an outlaw, and it is my duty to bring you to headquarters."

Max put the piece of bark back into the box and tucked it back into his pack. "No, not yet."

Lysander growled. "Maxwell, don't forget you are a Protector."

"My father helped her for a reason. I need to know why. Don't you?"

"You don't know what happened. She might have tricked or forced him to help her."

Max remained steadfast. "Do you believe my father to have been so weak or gullible?"

Lysander thought for a moment before speaking in a resigned tone. "No, I do not."

"I intend to find out what my father thought so important. We can arrest her afterwards."

"We don't know what we are heading towards, Maxwell, or what she might do."

"Then I guess we'd better be prepared for anything. Alexandra, take us in."

Alexandra gave a simple nod. "You are becoming your father, Maxwell. I hope it is time for what is coming."

Alexandra walked past Lysander and entered the forest. The others followed.

# CHAPTER TWENTY-FOUR

Max felt as though he had stepped into a dream. The numerous trees bulged five feet in width or more. The branches, no more than seven feet off the ground, grew as thick as Max. Together, they weaved a canopy so thick that the sunlight could not penetrate it, giving the illusion they were in a cave.

Despite the lack of sunlight, they still had fifteen to twenty feet of vision. Everything in the forest gave off a slight glow that brightened and dimmed as Alexandra and Eve passed.

At first, Max marveled at the strangeness of the forest, but, as they walked farther in, he became aware of a heavy sadness hanging about them. It seemed to come from the very plants and trees that surrounded them.

Over time, the sadness and lack of sunlight slowly numbed them to the surrounding forest and each other. When Alexandra fell, everyone stared blankly at her as she lay on the ground, trying to put together what had happened. Eve shook off the stupor first, hurrying over to her.

"Sorry, Alexandra. I don't know what happened to me."

Eve extended a hand to Alexandra and pulled her to her feet.

"That is alright. I know what this place can do."

Alexandra swayed a little, prompting Eve to steady her. "We have walked well into the night. I guess I need to rest."

Max scanned the branches above. "You mean we've spent a whole day in here? How can you tell?"

Alexandra swayed again. This time, Eve forced her to sit on a large root protruding from the ground.

"The tops of the trees are open to the sky, they know the time of day."

Melody checked Alexandra for any injuries. "You can talk to the spirits that easily?"

"I lived here for many years; we got to know one another rather well. You could learn to speak to them too, Melody."

"I don't know about that."

Max touched his palm to one of the trees. "They're sad, aren't they?"

Lysander set his backpack on the ground. "What? Are you going crazy on me, Max?"

Alexandra managed a weak smile. "Yes, they are, Maxwell. Soon you will know why." She let out a big yawn. "For now, sleep."

Alexandra slid off the root to lie down next to it. She immediately fell asleep. Eve chose to climb one of the trees, disappearing from sight. In his mind, Max could see her stretching out on one of the limbs above.

"You've been dying to do that since we came in here, haven't you, Eve."

A few leaves rustled above. "Yep!"

*I can't believe she can sleep like that without falling.*

Max stopped trying to spot her between the branches and sat down next to a tree. To his right, Lysander stared nervously up. Max stifled a laugh.

"She likes high places, it has nothing to do with watching you, Lysander."

Lysander glanced at Max then sat down with his back against a tree to his left. Melody found her own tree to lean against not far from Alexandra. Max took a deep breath to relax and fell fast asleep.

Some time later, Max awoke to the sight of Lysander standing over the still sleeping Alexandra with his hand resting on the hilt of his sword. Remaining still so as not to alert Lysander, he scanned the area for the others. Melody lay next to the tree she had sat by, still sleeping. As for Eve, her body was hidden, only the reflection of her eyes shown, standing out from the other fauna as she lay in the branches several feet directly above Alexandra. Max waited to see what would happen, prepared to dart into the middle of them all if necessary.

Lysander stepped back a few feet before giving a loud, shrill whistle that startled everyone. Max even saw a few of the leaves shake where Eve lay hidden.

"Wake up!"

Melody sat bolt upright. "What's going on?"

"I want to get moving. If Alexandra refuses to tell us what exactly is going on, then I prefer to get to our destination and find out."

Alexandra sat up slowly, trying to wipe the sleep from her eyes with little luck. She struggled to stand, using the tree trunk for support.

"We are almost there. Perhaps I could begin to fill you in on the details along the way."

"Then let's move." Lysander turned his head upwards. "Come on down cat, I know you're up there."

A slight rustle came from above before Eve dropped down directly behind Lysander. He paid her no attention, instead turning back to Alexandra.

"Lead on."

Alexandra took a few cautious steps to check her balance, then headed farther into the forest. Everyone stayed close to her as she finally spoke of why she had brought them there.

"What do you know of this place?"

Melody was quick to answer. "It is said that the lacarna first came into existence in Urania and, within it, once laid their largest village." Melody became very excited. "Also, in the mountains at the back of the village, lies a cave with the history of Velrune etched on its walls. However, no one from our order has been able to confirm any of this."

"So you doubt these stories, Melody?"

"Well, there is another tale, known only by a few, about the lacarna having come from a place beyond the mountains."

"It is amazing the variety of tales one may hear over time. It becomes hard to tell which is true and which is not, or if the truth is a combination of them all."

Max groaned, Alexandra sounded a lot like Mr. Penna. "So, which is it?"

"You will soon find out. The village is our destination."

Eve brightened. "Are there still lacarnians there, maybe someone who knew my parents?"

Alexandra shook her head. "No, it is empty now."

"Oh. What happened?"

"Bandits drove them and the few humans living there out into the plains."

Lysander nodded slowly. "I remember that happening, I had joined the Protectors not long before. The surge of wild, uncivilized lacarnians entering all at once caused a lot of strain in our security."

Eve shook her head in frustration. "That doesn't make sense. Mrs. Tassi has always told me that the lacarna are the strongest creatures on Velrune. I mean, isn't that why the Protectors are so afraid of us? How could bandits ever run them out of their home?"

"Because, the lacarnians did not want to incite another war, Evangeline. Instead, they held to their original agreement to the Creators to obey the Protectors at all cost."

Max scratched his head in thought, nearly tripping over a root. "How would they possibly disobey the Protectors by fighting against bandits?"

"Because the Protectors sent the bandits into the forest."

Max stopped dead in his tracks. "What?"

Lysander stopped next to Max, placing his hand on Max's shoulder. "I told you not to trust her Maxwell. The Spirit Leeches are mad. The Protectors have never had anything to do with the bandits. Besides, chasing the lacarna out of the woods and into the cities only made it more difficult for us to protect the humans."

Melody stopped with the rest of them. "No, it didn't. Moving the lacarna into the city guaranteed they would get fitted with a controller stone, thus enslaving them."

Lysander stepped toe to toe with Melody, his bulky frame dwarfing hers. "It is not our mission to enslave anyone, only to protect the humans."

Max moved to Melody's side. "I thought it was the Protectors' mission to protect both the humans and lacarnians!"

Melody snickered, not taking her eyes from Lysander. "So the story goes."

Lysander shoved between the two, stomping over to where Alexandra had stopped to watch the argument.

"Why are you telling these lies, Spirit Leech?"

"Lies? I speak of what I saw with my own eyes!"

Lysander took a step back in shock. Alexandra moved with him, craning her neck to stare directly in his face.

"Why do you look so stunned? If am a Spirit Leech, would it not make sense that I lived here with the lacarna? After all, I betrayed the other Immortals for them, did I not? There certainly wasn't any other place safe for me. So, I was here the day a human told us the Protectors had paid bandits to chase the lacarna out. I was here when they came too, crouched in the shadows where the chief had hidden me. If it is lies you are worried about, look to your precious Lord Avram. As for me, I will give you the truth. It is my only hope of setting things right."

Alexandra whipped around, striking off farther into the forest, her pace quickened by her anger. Eve stuck her tongue out at Lysander and followed after her. Max and Melody gave him a wide birth and followed Eve. After several seconds, Max tapped Melody on her arm. He kept his voice to a whisper so Alexandra wouldn't hear him.

"Exactly how long ago did the Spirit Leeches betray the other Immortals?"

"Four hundred years."

"Wow, I can't imagine living that long."

"She's older than that, Max. The Immortals age slower than we do. She's nine by their definition of time, not ours." Melody stopped. "I have really met an Immortal. Do you know how many in my order would give everything they have for a chance like this? She's a living piece of history."

Lysander caught back up, brushing by Melody. "She's a criminal who is unlikely to tell you the truth. Keep moving."

Max matched Lysander's stride. "That's something I don't understand. You said that the Spirit Leeches were cursed because they turned against the other Immortals in the war, right?"

"Yes, and it's why, when we are done here, we must arrest her."

"But, Alexandra is a little girl. How could she have willing betrayed anyone?"

"Who knows what part she played, but she admits she's a Spirit Leech. She must have been involved somehow."

"I don't know. Something's not right. Maybe the Immortals made a mistake."

"At the moment it doesn't matter, Max. We need to pay attention to our current situation. If she has lived for as long as she says, she's bound to have learned a few tricks."

"You mean like disappearing?"

Max and Lysander came to an abrupt stop, with Melody running into the back of Lysander.

"Why did you two stop so suddenly?"

Max suppressed a laugh. "Alexandra disappeared."

"What!"

Melody shoved herself between the two. Ahead of them stood Eve in front of a wall of tangled vines. Moving close, they saw that it stretched upward into the branches and to the left and right beyond sight.

Max looked around. "Eve, where did Alexandra go?"

Eve blushed. "I don't know. I was trying to listen to you guys, then next thing I know, she's gone, and I'm in front of this."

Eve spread her arms at the wall. Max pushed his hand against the vines forming the wall, they barely budged.

"She didn't go that way."

Eve sniffed at the air then examined the ground. "But her tracks lead right to it."

Lysander examined the wall himself. "I thought lacarnians were excellent trackers?"

"We are, but there's no scent left. Everything stops at this wall." Eve pushed against the vines with one hand. "And like Max said, it's solid." Eve looked back the way they had come. "Maybe I missed something."

To Max's horror a hand slipped through the wall, latching on to Eve's wrist. "Eve!"

Eve jumped at the touch and tried to pull away. The hand tightened its' grip. A small voice came from the other side of the wall as the hand tugged at Eve.

"Come on already."

Everyone froze. "Alexandra?"

Eve stopped resisting, letting the hand pull her towards the vines. Melody shook off the shock and grabbed Eve's tail just as the vine wall closed around the rest of her body.

"Quick, grab hold!"

Max took hold of Melody's free arm and stretched his other hand out for Lysander. He quickly took hold of it, and in one long chain, Alexandra pulled them through. Once on the other side, they let go of one another.

"Sorry about grabbing your tail, Eve."

Eve held her tail in her hands, rubbing the spot Melody had taken hold of. "It's okay."

Max doubled over laughing. "I don't think I've ever seen you jump like that, Eve."

Eve shot a look at Max; a look he'd only see a few times. Remembering what happened afterwards, he immediately stopped laughing. Lysander shoved past him and stood before Alexandra.

"Where are we?"

A beautiful smiled formed on her pale face. "My and Eve's home."

## CHAPTER TWENTY-FIVE

In the recesses of his mind, Max registered Alexandra's statement, but he would ask about that later. For now, he stood speechless as he took in his surroundings, starting with the vine wall Alexandra had pulled them through. On this side, he could see that it actually formed a large dome, the top reaching the height of the trees where it allowed in a moderate amount of light.

Here, the trees grew nearly twenty feet apart. Between them grew a myriad of plants and flowers whose colors had turned a sickly brown. Above, in the sagging branches of the trees, the vines and leaves formed numerous alcoves, many large enough to hold five or six people. A heavy sadness draped over all of it, marring what should have been a beautiful scene.

Max's gaze eventually fell on Alexandra who had waited patiently for them to absorb their surroundings. She managed a tired curtsy.

"Welcome to Urania." She smiled at Eve. "Welcome home, Evangeline."

Eve took a tentative step forward. A joy-filled smile appeared on her face. She spun, laughing in pure merriment.

"I can feel them! They're like old friends."

Max watched in amazement as the plants around Eve straightened and blossomed, their colors shining bright. When she walked to one of the nearby trees, the branches that had sagged a moment before lifted themselves, sprouting new leaves. A tiny giggle escaped from Alexandra.

"The forest is glad to see you, Evangeline."

Melody pointed in awe at Alexandra's feet. "And you."

Like Eve, the flowers had sprung back to life around Alexandra. Max looked at the ground by his own feet, but nothing had changed. The same held true for Lysander, however a few had revived for Melody who slowly spun to see them.

"What is this?"

Alexandra spread her hands. "This is the power your order believed the Immortals to have."

Lysander had the same expression of wonder on his face as the rest of them. "But, you haven't done anything, have you?"

"Not a thing. The spirits are acting on their own. They are happy to have company once again."

Melody bent down to examine the flowers at her feet. "I don't understand. I have always been taught that we need to impose our will over the spirits in order for them to act."

"That is why the spirits no longer respond to you and the other Children like they did for us. You do not control them; instead you speak with them as equals and take care of one another. What your order has achieved has come about only because a few spirits felt compassionate enough to help you."

"Is that why that old man, the collector, said we are misguided?"

Alexandra took Melody's hand and indicated for her to stand. "Do not feel ashamed. We did not grasp this at first either, but the lacarna taught us. The spirits and the lacarna have always had a special bond. That is why they flourish around Evangeline. She may not remember them, but they know her quite well."

Lysander stared in awe at the flowers. "I've never seen anything like this."

Alexandra's smile disappeared. "Few humans have, though they could if they wanted. The Children have nothing special over any other human, merely a basic understanding of the spirits. If taught properly, all could learn to work with them."

Melody held up her hand. "Wait a second, back up. It is the belief of my church that the Immortals, once called the Creators, made Velrune. If that's the case, why would the lacarna need to teach you how to communicate with the spirits?"

"Because we are not the Creators. In fact, we are nothing more than humans. In other words, I am the same as you."

Lysander's head jerked away from the flowers to face Alexandra. "Blasphemy! You've gone mad. Even the Protectors believe the Immortals created Velrune and all that is in it."

"Ironically, it is the Protectors that have caused so much confusion about our past. If you do not believe me, come, and I will show you proof." Alexandra turned and began walking across the empty village. "Evangeline, come!"

Eve dropped down out of the branches behind Max, startling him. Focused on the conversation, he had not seen her leave.

"Where did you go?"

Eve pointed to one of the alcoves three quarters up a tree to their left. "I think I lived in that one."

Alexandra looked back to follow Eve's finger then smiled. "That you did, but we can reminisce later. Come."

Alexandra led them across the dome floor, along the way passing a building similar to the one at Alexandra's camp. Its presence here surprised Max.

"Why is there a Church of the Immortals here?"

Alexandra kept walking, talking back over her shoulder. "Several Immortals lived here at one time. They preferred more than branches and leaves for their homes."

A moment later, they reached the other side of the dome. Before them stood a dark opening in the vine wall. Alexandra paused.

"This is the entrance to a cave in the western mountains. Be careful entering, it will be quite dark until I can get the torches lit."

Alexandra stepped through the opening with the others

following. Inside, the light from the domed area quickly faded, leaving them in complete darkness. Max put his hand on the wall as he walked to keep his direction. After roughly a hundred feet, Max felt the wall drop away. He immediately stopped, afraid he would run into either a person or a wall. A few seconds later, a torch flared in front of them, displaying Alexandra and the edges of the circular room they stood in. Other torches lit, their flames growing slowly, allowing time for everyone's eyes to adjust. Beside him, Melody sucked in her breath. "The paintings! This is the cave isn't it? The one with the history of Velrune."

Lysander took in the numerous drawings on the walls of the cave. "Or at least the lacarna's biased version of it."

Alexandra shook her head. "The lacarna never bothered to record their history."

"Then who?"

Eve walked over to the wall and crouched in front of him. Studying a small painting, she reached out to touch it. Melody started towards her.

"Eve, I don't think we should touch anything."

"Even if it's mine?"

Melody and Max moved behind Eve, who had her hand placed flat against the wall.

"I thought I remembered, but…"

Eve removed her hand, revealing the yellow handprint of a child.

Alexandra came and squatted next to Eve. She put her hand on a green print next to the yellow one. It was a perfect fit.

"Unlike me, Eve, you have grown since we made these." A pleasant giggle escaped Alexandra. "We got in such trouble."

She stood. "To answer your question, Lysander, the humans who lived here with the lacarna recorded these. Sit and I will read them to you, just as I did for Maxwell's father."

"My father came here?"

Ignoring Max, Alexandra walked to the edge of the wall next to the tunnel. Pointing to the top she began explaining the paintings.

"Our human ancestors' first memories were of waking in the plains. They recorded their number as sixty."

Alexandra read the paintings downward in a strip then moved to the top right. Everyone else took a seat in the middle of the room to listen.

"Seeking shelter, they entered a nearby forest where they came across a group of large cats. To their amazement, one stood, changing to a form similar to theirs. It spoke, welcoming them to the forest. Frightened by the shape-changing beast, most of the humans fled the forest. A few, however, followed the beasts to their home in the woods.

"The large cats befriended the humans that followed, showing them how to live in the forest. Over time, the cats even shared their knowledge of the spirits, teaching the humans how to communicate with them. The humans named the cats lacarnians, which simply meant friend of the spirits.

"At first, the humans in the forest shared what they learned from the lacarna with the humans that remained in the plains. But, as the plains humans grew in number, they became more and more concerned with their own affairs, losing contact with those in the forest. Each group went their own way, with the forest humans living more like the lacarna, some even mating with them.

"Then, one day, the plains humans cut down trees at the forest edge, angering the lacarna. The forest humans spoke on behalf of the lacarna, but, when the plains humans found out that their brethren had mated with the beasts, they were disgusted. Angered at the forest human's acts, they sought to kill their offspring. The lacarnians came to the defense of the forest humans, driving them off and slaying many in the process.

"The two factions remained apart for the next several generations, until a terrible sickness befell the plains humans. The lacarnians, at the request of the forest humans, went to their aid. They brought forth their greatest treasure, the Lifestone. It was a clear, blue stone that they claimed had the power to create life. Using the stone, the plains humans were cured of their sickness, but at a great cost. You see, for the stone to work, it needs to feed. In this case, it fed on the long lifespan of the humans.

"The plains humans were thankful, but became afraid of what their now shortened future held for them and their children. To ease their fears, some of the forest humans ventured out and built gathering places amongst the larger populations of the plains humans. At these places, the forest humans recorded the knowledge and family history of the plains humans for generations."

Melody interrupted. "Our church in Moenia has an archive room below the main structure filled with scrolls of family trees. Those are the records of the plains humans, aren't they?"

Alexandra nodded. "The Church of the Immortals was formed by the forest humans, though it did not receive that name until later. Moenia was the first and largest."

Lysander shook his head. "This is nonsense. I've never heard this story before."

"Few have. You see, the forest humans missed living with the lacarna and most moved back. They tried to encourage the plains humans to join them, but few came.

"Communication between the two once again diminished. After several generations, the plains humans had regained their numbers and spread out far and wide. In doing so, and without record keepers, the knowledge of their past became lost to them. They forgot that the forest humans and the few that remaining in the churches were once the same as them. They now saw a people who did not seem to age and recovered from all injuries. In all appearance, they were immortal and added to that was their mysterious ability to commune with the spirits. All of this is what led the plains humans to believe the forest humans were the Creators of Velrune itself, a far cry from the truth."

Max stopped Alexandra. "Why didn't they try to correct the misunderstanding?"

"The few that remained in the cities could not overcome the beliefs of so many people."

"Didn't those that moved back to the forest try to help?"

"By this time, there were not many humans in the forest either."

"Why? What happened to them? Didn't they have children?"

Eve laughed and nodded at Alexandra. "Obviously they did."

Max's face flushed. "Oh."

Alexandra smiled. "Actually, Eve, Maxwell presents a valid question. I was a rarity due to both of my parents being human. Most of the forest humans mated with the lacarna producing, well, children like Eve. To those outside of the forest, children like Eve were not considered human."

"In the end, three groups existed. The plains humans, who became known generically as humans. They were the largest group, as they had made a point to reproduce to counteract their much shorter lifespan. The second group consisted of the lacarna who were evolving into a half-human half-cat race. Finally, there were the few original forest humans who were now mistakenly called the Immortals."

Alexandra swayed. Eve sprung from her seated position, catching her before she could fall. Together they sat down. Max scooted over to them.

"What's wrong Alexandra? You're very pale."

Lysander sighed. "It is the curse I told you of, Max. A Spirit Leech weakens over time as her spirit energy is depleted. Alexandra has gotten very weak in the time since we left her camp."

"Is it true then? The cursed ones, the Spirit Leeches, really live off the spirit energy of others."

"Unfortunately, Maxwell, yes, we do."

"But, Lysander says the Spirit Leeches are all mad. You don't seem insane to me."

"I admit that some could not handle what happened to them. For them I cannot disagree with the Protectors actions. However, they did not discriminate between the mad and the peaceful."

Lysander's raised voice echoed off the cave walls. "You call taking another's spirit energy being peaceful?"

"There were people who understood our plight, willingly giving of their energy. We made sure to take only what we needed to survive, leaving them exhausted, but otherwise unharmed."

Melody tapped her chin, thinking. "When I talked to the people in your camp, they said you asked little of them. What you asked was to draw their energy, wasn't it?"

Alexandra nodded.

Lysander stood, pacing back and forth. "They should be tried as well for assisting you. Why would they help someone that betrayed her own people?"

"Another corrupted story, one that comes later. Please, let me finish the one written here first."

Alexandra pointed at the final strip of paintings. "Eventually, the humans once again tried to take trees from the forest. It was only a few at first. The lacarna easily chased them away. Later, the humans became more determined, sending several hundred to gather trees in hopes of intimidating the lacarna. The lacarna easily overpowered them, killing most outright. A second large-scale battle broke out, lasting several days. At the end, one hundred and twelve lacarnians died while several thousand humans lost their lives."

"The humans' loss would have been even greater had the Immortals, once the forest humans, not stepped in to mediate an agreement. The lacarnians saw the human need for shelter and agreed to allow humans to harvest trees they designated. Furthermore, to help settle future issues, the Immortals formed an authoritative group consisting of both lacarnians and humans. They named this group the Protectors. An Immortal was chosen to be the head and ultimate judge of the Protectors."

Alexandra paused, her eyes slowly closing. Eve gently shook her.

"Alexandra."

Alexandra's eyes fluttered back open. "It must be getting

late."

Melody stood, dusting herself off. "You should get some rest."

Max stood too, giving a big yawn. "I wouldn't mind a little sleep myself. Are there any beds in the structure outside?"

"At one time there were."

Melody moved towards the tunnel. "Max and I will go see. Eve, stay here with Alexandra."

Lysander headed towards the cave passage as well. "I'm coming too. I've heard all I can take for now."

The three left the cave and walked to the building. Lysander stayed outside while Max and Melody went in to investigate. The building had the same layout as the one at Alexandra's camp. In the back room, they found a few beds made from vines that intertwined with the building.

"If we get some of those large leaves from the trees, we can use them as bedding. I know I could easily take a nap on them."

Melody laughed. "Something tells me you could easily take a nap anywhere. Come on, let's go get Eve and Alexandra."

They stepped back outside where Max noticed Lysander missing. "Hey, where did Lysander go?"

"Who knows? If we're lucky he got lost."

"He's not that bad, at least compared to some of the others I've met recently."

Melody crossed her arms. "I suppose not. I mean, he does seem to be listening. That's more than a lot of them do."

Max heard light footsteps from the side of the building. Eve and Alexandra rounded the corner, surprising Melody.

"Oh! Max and I were getting ready to come for you two."

"That is all right. I am feeling a little better."

Max saw that a little color had returned to Alexandra's face - not that she had much to begin with. On the other hand, Eve seemed a little pale.

"Let us go inside, there is more I would like to tell you before we rest." Alexandra looked around. "Where is Lysander?"

"That's what Melody and I were wondering. He left before

we came back out."

Eve giggled. "Maybe he had to go pee, in which case we should let him be."

Max rolled his eyes. "Eve."

"What? We all have to go eventually."

Melody rubbed her head. "I'm going inside."

Max happily followed, with Eve and Alexandra coming after him. Each found a log in the main room to sit on and removed their backpacks. Spook climbed out of Eve's satchel, scurrying over to Alexandra and up onto her shoulder. The two had become friends during their trip. Everyone had settled when Lysander walked in.

"Did I miss anything?"

Max looked over his shoulder. "Where did you go?"

"I wanted a better look at this place, that's all."

Alexandra stared at Lysander. "Is that all?"

Lysander returned the stare as he sat down. "Yes."

Alexandra focused on the others. "Everything else I have to tell you comes from my own experience or from what my parents told me directly."

Lysander crossed his arms and leaned back. "And why should we believe what you have to say?"

"Because it is the truth. In time, you will see that. I only hope that it is soon enough."

Alexandra took a deep breath then let it out. "My tale begins after the appointment of a new judge to the Protectors. I was eight."

# CHAPTER TWENTY-SIX

"Alex, why don't you go play with Emma while we talk with Cassiopeia?"

"Ahh, daddy, I want to hear about Cassy's adventures."

"Later, Alex. Now run along."

I held Emma, my doll, close to my chest as I slid off of my father's knee. I walked over to a corner of the building where I had been enjoying a nice pretend lunch before Cass, a lacarnian woman, arrived. I served Emma a bowel of berries while I listened to my father question Cassiopeia.

"We did not expect you back so soon, Cass."

Cass stopped pacing and sat across from my parents. "It seems the Protectors no longer welcome us."

"What do you mean?"

"Egan has kicked me and the other lacarnians out. He claims we have aided those on the outskirts of the woods in their attacks on the humans."

My father slammed his fist on the table making me jump. "That is ludicrous. The lacarnian members of the Protectors have done no such thing!"

"It does not matter to Egan. He hates us."

On cue, I heard my mother try and calm the two. "Now I am sure 'hate' is going a bit too far, Cass."

"No, Maddie, it's not. I've seen the way he looks at us and our children of mixed blood. We are disgusting to him. I have no doubt he would rid Velrune of all of us if he could."

"He showed no such signs before we elected him as leader of the Protectors. I can assure you of that, Cass."

"I know, Maddie, you would not have put him in charge if he had. However, he is a sly one and hid his true feelings well."

Father stood and paced as he spoke. "We can speak to him, Cass. Get him to reinstate the lacarnian members."

"No, Julian, do not put yourself in his line of sight. We will withdraw for now. The chiefs of the forests have agreed it is best for the lacarna to return to the deep woods. We have never relished holding a position of enforcement. Perhaps he will let us be if we are out of his way."

Father nodded his head. "We will go along with the chief's wishes, Cass. Those of us in the forest want to do everything we can to remain in harmony with the lacarna."

"I know, Julian. You, and those like you, will always be welcome among us."

Cass scooted her chair back to stand. "Now then, where did that curious little daughter of yours go?"

I popped off the floor and ran to Cass. "Right here, Cassy!"

She grabbed me when I neared, flinging me into the air then catching me. "So you want to know what I did in the big city, huh? Well, let me tell you about all the things I saw."

Max raised his hand. "So there really were lacarnians in the Protectors?"

Alexandra nodded. "At one time, yes. After that day, however, the lacarna stayed clear of the humans, allowing only the Immortals to live with them. Unfortunately, that did not satisfy Egan. He wanted full access to the forests, something the lacarna would not allow. To that end, he tried to find a way to force the lacarna to follow his commands."

"After several failed ideas he, learned of the Lifestone. Using deceit, he was able to locate the holder of the stone and take it from him. Then, without knowing its full potential, he tried to create something that could control the lacarna. The resulting surge of energy ripped a chasm through one of Velrune's largest forests, killing dozens of humans and hundreds of lacarnians.

"Egan attempted to hide, but the lacarna hunted him down. They gave him to the Immortals so they could pass judgment on his actions. All of the Immortals attended the sentencing, even the children. It took place in a flat, grassy area outside of this forest, not far from a small lacarnian community. I remember it well. The five council members of the Immortals stood in half-circle around Egan, who faced them on his knees. The rest of us stood in a large half-circle behind Egan. We, the children, were let up front so we could see the proceedings. It was the eldest of the council who addressed Egan."

"Egan, you stand accused before your fellow Immortals of misusing the Lifestone, causing the death of many, and the destruction of a great forest."

"I swear I intended no harm. I only wanted to find a way for the humans and the lacarnians to live peacefully together."

"By creating living stones that would be forced onto the lacarnians in order to control them?"

"I only meant them for the lacarnians who wished to live in the human villages. It gives the humans peace of mind without any real damage to the lacarnians."

"And what of the destruction you wrought?"

"I knew the stone required material to create, but I had no idea it had such power. I would never have used it if that had been the case."

"If you were unsure of the stone's power, why did you choose the mountains by the lacarna's home forest instead of an uninhabited area? There are those that believe you had another motive in mind."

"Please, I beg of you, I truly had no idea of the destruction the stone would cause."

"Egan, your actions, foolish or planned, cannot go unpunished. Many lacarnians died in the chasm created by the stone. We lost several of our fellow Immortals as well. You will be…"

Alexandra shuttered. "I heard a woman in the crowed scream in horrible pain. Then, someone screamed my mothers name and I knew it had been her.

I left the other children, shoving my way through the crowded circle of adults. At the center lay my mother, her face and hands had withered, all color had drained from her body. She wasn't moving. I heard a thump close behind me and a woman shouted in panic."

"William? William!"

More shouts rose from the crowd as other men and woman fell to the ground. I searched frantically for my father.

"Daddy!"

Not able to find him I rushed to my mother's side, bending down next to her. I carefully touched her hand, but she was so cold I yanked it back.

"Mommy?"

"Alex, there you are!"

I was crying so hard I could barely see father so I reached out for him. "Daddy!"

He scooped me up and held me tight against him. "Come on darling, we need to go."

"What about mommy?"

"We will have to come back for her."

A man came running towards us. "Julian, what's going on?"

"Have you seen Egan?"

The man shook his head frantically. "No, he's gone."

"I am sure this is his doing."

"But what is it, Julian?"

"I don't know, and now is not the time to figure it out. We must take the Lifestone and run."

"Julian, we can't leave our friends."

"Until we know what is going on, I am afraid it is our only option. Maddie had the stone. Please, get it and follow me."

"Daddy, where are we going?"

"Far away from here, darling."

Alexandra gave a heavy sigh. Eve leaned forward, speaking

softly.

"Did you go back for you mother?"

Alexandra shook her head. "Afraid of what Egan had in store for us, we scattered, going into hiding. Unfortunately, most never made it. Over the next few days, several more Immortals died. Others, like my father and I, held on longer, though we grew weaker every day. If we had not run across a pair of humans within that first week, I would not have lived either. The humans let us join them for a meal. In thanks, my father shook one of their hands. In stunned horror, he watched the life flow out of the man and into himself. When my father let go, the man fell to the ground, barely alive. My father, on the other hand, felt as strong as ever.

"Afraid, we fled a short distance before stopping to try and understand what had happened to us. Only one thing came to mind, the Lifestone. William brought the stone out and upon examining it we found that the ends had been filed. Egan had to have done this while he had the stone. His original reason, I do not know. He may not have originally planned to use it against us, but in the end, the fine powder chiseled from the stone, had been mixed in water or food at the meeting.

"After we had ingested the powered, our bodies absorbed it and it began feeding on our spirit energy. Why it acted slower in some of us, we never knew, but it allowed us to live long enough to find another source of energy. That is why we, the Spirit Leeches, feed on people.

"We tried to spread what we had found to others as best we could, but many never received the information in time. A few chose to die rather than harm another, even if that person eventually recovered. A small group; however, committed themselves to protecting the stone at all cost, unsure of Egan's plans.

"Over time, an alternate story of what happened that night spread among the humans. It told of how we had betrayed our own and were cursed for it. Egan wanted us marked as outlaws, giving the Protectors a reason to hunt us down. He wanted the stone. While he waited, he used the living stones he had created, what you know as the Controller Stones, to enslave the Iacarna. He worked hard to turn the Protectors and the people against them."

Lysander shoved himself off his stump. "You're saying a leader of the Protectors murdered most of the Immortals, then led the Protectors to hunt the remaining ones down so he could have this stone. I have a hard time believing that. Our goal as Protectors is to protect the people, all of them."

Melody crossed her arms. "You keep saying that, but I've seen little to back it up. You've certainly shown your distaste for Eve and me."

"I may not like the Children or the Iacarna, but I would never resort to the acts that she says happened."

"I'm curious, Lysander, why don't you like us?"

"The Iacarnians are violent, dangerous beasts and the Children go out of their way to support them."

Alexandra gestured towards Eve. "You really think Evangeline is a violent, dangerous beast?"

Lysander stood silent as he looked at Eve. After a moment he turned away. "She hasn't been in our presence, but I'm sure she is capable of it."

Alexandra snickered. "I could say the same of you. You are well trained in fighting after all. Tell me Lysander, how many violent Iacarnians have you actually had to deal with?"

Lysander began to pace the room. Without an answer, Alexandra turned her attention to Max.

"Do you see what Egan has done? The humans are afraid of or even hate the Iacarnians even though nothing has happened between them for centuries."

"I don't understand. Didn't all this happen centuries ago? If these are lies, why have they persisted long after Egan's death?"

"Because Egan is still alive, and he still leads the Protectors. I believe he calls himself Lord Avram now."

Lysander froze. "Now you go too far, Spirit Leech! Not only do you accuse the original Protectors of hideous crimes, but now you say our Lord Avram is the one that committed them!"

"Stolen identities and staged funerals, Egan has done much to conceal his identity. Only a chosen few ever enter into his presence, but I do not need to see him to know who pursues me. I have become well attuned to his vile presence over these centuries. That is why I am still alive."

"You tell quite a story, Alexandra, but do you have proof?"

Alexandra stood. "Not for all of it, but there is one thing I can show you. Maxwell, your father's box."

Max dug the box out of his backpack and handed it to Alexandra. She opened it and retrieved the pieces of bark. She then, in turn, walked to the four corners of the room. Each had a tree with a small hole carved in the trunk where she would placed one piece of bark. With all four placed, she returned to the center of the room, the roof rustling above her.

Max had not bothered to pay attention to the ceiling until he heard the movement above him. Looking up, he saw that the roof consisted of a thick patchwork of tree branches and leaves which were now separating from each other. A small object fell from the center, dropping into Alexandra's waiting hands. Carefully holding it, she raised the object for them to see. Max stared in wonder at the clear, blue tinted oval stone. It was completely smooth except at the ends where it had been crudely filed.

"My father was the first to swear he would protect the stone. I was the last. I have carried it with me for longer than I can remember. I only hid it after your father warned me of the planned attack on our village."

Melody studied the stone. "If the stone was damaged so easily, why not simply destroy it instead of risking Egan obtaining it?"

Alexandra grabbed her backpack and shoved the stone deep inside it. She pushed between them, heading for the door. "Lysander's gone."

The others spun in surprise. After a moment's hesitation, they followed Alexandra. Outside, they found her fifteen feet from the door facing twenty armed Protectors led by Tyco.

Tyco sneered. "Well, well, you must be Alexandra."

Alexandra jerked her head towards Eve. "Run!"

## CHAPTER TWENTY-SEVEN

Max reeled at the unexpected sight of the armed men in the deserted forest. Melody and Eve stood frozen next to him. Alexandra's command didn't even register until Eve bolted to the side, only to slide to a stop in front of four more guards. Tyco shouted to the guards in front of Eve.

"Don't let her get away."

The four guards readied their weapons, causing Eve to take a step back.

Alexandra yelled pleadingly at Eve. "Evangeline, you must do as I instructed!"

The guards moved towards Eve. She looked at Alexandra then Max. The mixture of fear and sadness in her face made Max's stomach knot. Eve closed her eyes as she faced the guards. In disbelief, Max watched as she changed into a large panther in a matter of seconds. A deep growl emerged from her throat. The guards stepped back.

Tyco took a step in Eve's direction. "What are you waiting for? Grab that beast!"

Eve charged forward. The terrified guards dropped their weapons and dove out of her way. Eve ran between them, disappearing through the vine wall a short distance later.

"Worthless fools!" Tyco turned on Alexandra. "You're lucky she wasn't our main objective."

Tyco moved forward. "You're the one we need to worry

about."

Alexandra raised her arms; the grass around Tyco began to grow. "As well you should be."

Lysander ran out from beside the building. He charged at Alexandra, wrapping his arms around her in a tight bear hug.

"We'll have none of that. You know you're too weak to do much anyway."

Alexandra squirmed in his arms. "Let me go!"

Max took a few steps forward. "Lysander, what are you doing?"

"Turning her in per the law, like I said I would."

Tyco stood directly in front of Alexandra. "She is one of the cursed, Max. She's also a thief."

Tyco bent over, peering into her face. "Where is the stone?"

Alexandra stopped moving. "What stone?"

Tyco straightened and backhanded her across the face. "You know what I want, brat."

Alexandra smiled. "Maybe I do, but I am not telling."

Tyco struck the other side of her face. "Do not play games with me, Spirit Leech."

Alexandra tilted her head towards the ground, lifting her hand as much as she could in Lysander's tight grip. A vine tried to wrap itself around Tyco's ankle. He shook his foot free.

"Oh no you don't."

Reaching back, he balled his fist and struck Alexandra in the stomach. She cried out in pain. The knot in Max's stomach grew tighter.

"Tyco, wait, I know where the stone is, I'll get it."

Alexandra gasped. "Maxwell, no!"

Max ignored her, running inside the building. He emerged a moment later with her backpack. He took it over to Tyco who snatched it away.

"Good job, Maxwell. I was worried she might have confused you with her lies."

Tyco rummaged around in the bag, pulling out the stone a moment later, a cruel smile forming on his lips.

"Good job indeed."

Tyco tossed the backpack to the side. He pointed at two of the guards behind him.

"You two, bind the girl. And you," he now addressed the four guards Eve had ran past, "grab the acolyte."

The two guards took Alexandra from Lysander and bound her arms with rope. Max stood in a daze.

"What's going on, Tyco? How did you find us?"

"I'll explain on our way to Moenia. Lord Avram is anxious to get the Lifestone." He walked back to the group of Protectors. "Let's move out. Keep an eye out for the lacarnian, she may come back."

The guards paired up and headed for the vine wall. Max stayed beside Tyco.

"Why are you worried about Eve, she won't hurt anyone?"

Tyco stopped and faced Max. "I was afraid of that. She has you fooled, boy. Even after you saw her true form."

"Her true form? I've never seen her do that before. What is she, exactly?"

"A killer."

Max gave a nervous laugh. "That's not Eve."

"Really, I believe I heard a report about a large panther killing several bandits in the dead lands about the time we passed through."

Max shook his head. "Eve was either with us or Mr. Penna the whole time."

"Lacarnians are fast in their panther form. She could easily have left and returned while he slept. I suppose I should be grateful though. If those bandits had killed you, they would have ruined Lord Avram's plans."

Tyco looked past Max. "Come, Sgt. Harris, we don't have all day."

Max turned to find Lysander kneeling on the ground by Alexandra's backpack. He finished examining an object on the ground before picking it up and placing it in the pack. Standing, he slung the pack over his shoulder and walked over to them, head down. Tyco patted him on the shoulder.

"You may get a promotion out of this, Sgt. Harris. You should too, Max. You're quickly following in your father's footsteps."

Tyco led them to the vine wall where the other Protectors, with Alexandra and Melody held captive between them, waited next to a cleared opening. Max paused to talk to Melody, but Tyco grabbed him by the shoulder and dragged him along.

"You're with me, Maxwell."

They stepped through the opening with the column of Protectors following behind them.

"You did well, Max, tracking down Alexandra and the Lifestone."

"You knew about her?"

"Yes, in fact it was your father who discovered her existence by gaining the lacarnian's trust."

"How did he know she had the stone?"

"He didn't at first. Lord Avram knew the stone would be in the hands of a Spirit Leech and sent your father out to find one. He just happened to get lucky that the one he found held the stone."

"Why does Lord Avram want the stone?"

"Because, Max, that stone presented a great danger in the hands of the Spirit Leeches. After all, they had already betrayed their own kind, who knew what else they would do with such power. If, instead, Lord Avram possessed the stone, he could use it to improve all of our lives."

"If my father was trying to retrieve the stone, then why did he help Alexandra lock it away?"

"Despite her appearance, Alexandra is quite powerful. He could not simply take the stone. He had to convince her to give it to him. Unfortunately, the bandit attack on the village interrupted his plan."

"But Alexandra said that the bandits were sent by the Protectors."

"After the attack, Alexandra figured out what your father was trying to do and believed the attack was part of his plan."

"If she knew my father was after the stone, why did she let me get so close?"

"Enraged at being tricked, she swore vengeance on your family. That is why Lord Avram sent you and your father across the dead lands. We thought the two of you would be safe. Alexandra proved us wrong; however. She found you and hired the bandits to kill both of you. She believed they had succeeded until recently. When she found out that you still lived, she wanted to finish you off herself. Lord Avram decided to use that against her to draw her out. He sent Lysander with you to keep us informed of all that transpired."

Max shook his head. "Her story is completely different. She says it was Lord Avram that betrayed their kind after accidentally causing a great disaster by misusing the stone."

Tyco chuckled. "Max, I know Lord Avram is old, but he is no Immortal. Don't be fooled by her, Max, she's had many years to perfect her lies. If all else, just remember she's only survived by stealing the spirit energy of others. Would anything good do that?"

"I don't know. None of it makes any sense."

"We will arrive at headquarters soon enough, Max. There you can ask Lord Avram yourself about all of this."

Tyco refused to say anything more, leaving Max to his own thoughts.

*What really happened Dad? Were you trying to get the stone for Lord Avram or did you betray them to help Alexandra? I wish Mr. Penna was here to explain things, but, then again, he never said anything about any of this. I always believed the Protectors were just in their actions, but I haven't seen much of that. Eve seems to believe Alexandra's story and she's never been wrong. I just don't know.*

Max took little note of their passage. Tyco kept them at a forced march until reaching the edge of the forest where the sun had long since set. There, Tyco had them stop, ordering them to bed down for the night. Max sought out a spot away from everyone else, noting Lysander doing the same. Laying down he struggled to find sleep. When at last it came, he dreamt only of his father's death.

At first light, they set out across the plains towards Moenia. To clear his mind, Max focused on the rhythmic sound of their footsteps. It did help to an extent, but the fuzzy idea that he had forgotten about something kept nagging at him. Finally, in the afternoon, it came to him.

*Eve! Where has she gone? It's not like her to run off. Although, Alexandra told her to run. She even mentioned she had instructed her to. I have to go talk to her, but how? Hmm, I know, Melody.*

"Hey Tyco, I would like to check on Melody."

"The acolyte? No, you should stay with me, Max."

"But I promised the head of her church I would watch out for her. What harm is she anyway? She was only delivering a message to the village."

Tyco remained silent as he stared at Max, thinking. Slowly he nodded.

"Fine, she isn't really a threat, but be quick about it."

Max stopped, letting the column pass until Melody and Alexandra reached him. Alexandra looked at him in surprise.

"Maxwell, I did not expect to see you. Does the Lt. know you are back here?"

"Yes, I came to check on Melody."

Melody managed a weak smile. "Thanks Max, I'm fine. I don't think they are concerned much about me."

Melody held her wrists in front of her. The rope was snug but not overly tight. However, a quick glance at Alexandra's revealed a courser rope that had begun to rub her skin raw.

Alexandra smirked. "The Children are an irritant at most, Spirit Leeches on the other hand are considered worse than lacarnians."

As much as Max wanted to untie Alexandra to treat the wounds, he knew he could never do such a thing. The guards behind them already watched him suspiciously.

"Alexandra, did you know they would come for you?

"Yes."

"Is that why you warned Eve? Why her and not the rest of

us?"

"They would have treated her worse than me. You, on the other hand, had nothing to worry about. Melody I did not know enough about to trust her."

"If you lied to me about this, why should I believe anything else you said?"

"I did not lie to you, only failed to inform you. A fine line, I know, but I needed you to hear about your father."

"How do I believe your story now? Especially since Tyco tells a different one. He says my father tricked you into trusting him so he could get the stone for Lord Avram."

"Hmph. Your father tricked someone, but not me. He wanted the same thing I did, to set the lacarna free. I had devised a plan to that end, but it was a plan filled with centuries of my hatred. Your father; however, opened my eyes to a better path, one he offered to help me complete."

"What was he going to do?"

"Overthrow Lord Avram and take leadership of the Protectors himself."

"What? My father would never…Why him?"

"I can set the lacarna free of the stone, but Lord Avram would strike out against them, starting another war. Your father, on the other hand, who had the trust of many of the Protectors and the lacarnians, could mediate between them. I have no doubt he could have re-established the Protectors as they once were, with both races jointly watching over all."

"If what you say is true, that my father wanted to help you, why did he take the box away from you, preventing you from getting the Lifestone?"

"Peter believed Lord Avram had grown suspicious of him. The bandit attack on my village proved that. He decided it best that we cease our meetings for a while. He could tell that I was unhappy with waiting and feared that, if something happened to him, I would revert to my original plan. To ease his concerns, I agreed to lock the keys in the box with him as caretaker."

"Was my father right in fearing what you might do without

him?"

Alexandra averted her eyes, bowing her head. "I don't know."

Melody suddenly tensed. "Max!"

Max first turned to Melody and followed her frightened gaze along the column. Lt. Tyco stormed towards them, his eyes fixed on Max. Reaching them, he grabbed Max by the arm.

"It seems Alexandra's conniving ways are already starting to rub off on you."

Tyco pulled Max along the column until they came across Lysander walking by himself. Tyco shoved Max next to him.

"Watch him, Lysander. Make sure he stays away from that Spirit Leech and the other girl."

Without waiting for an acknowledgment, Tyco moved to the front of the column. Lysander, walking with his head down, said nothing. Max thought he seemed as troubled as himself. For the next three days, both marched in silence.

## CHAPTER TWENTY-EIGHT

They reached Protector Headquarters in the afternoon and made their way to the war room where Max first met Lord Avram. Tyco, Max and Lysander entered first, finding Lord Avram sitting behind the table, studying a large map. When he noticed their presence, he smiled with delight.

"Lt. Biros, you have returned. I hope you were successful."

"Yes, Lord Avram." Tyco stepped forward and handed the Lifestone to Lord Avram.

"Excellent. What of the rest of your mission?"

Tyco signaled the guard by the door who then waved the two guards that restrained Alexandra and Melody into the room. Tyco had not allowed Max to see them after that first day. His stomach churned when he saw Alexandra. The sunlight had wreaked havoc on her body, causing burns and blisters. The toes of her shoes were worn where she had been drug after growing too weak to walk on her own. Even now, the guard had to hold her by the collar of her dress to keep her on her feet.

Lord Avram's smile spread even farther. "Good, Alexandra posed a great threat to my plans." Lord Avram let out an unpleasant laugh, making Max cringe. "She is no threat to us now."

Alexandra whimpered as her legs buckled. The guard tightened his grip, letting her hang loosely in her dress. Max caught his breath.

"Sir, she needs a Healer."

"That's Lord, Maxwell, not sir. Do not let her appearance fool you. Given the chance, she would draw the life energy out of the guard, healing herself and leaving me one guard short. "She wouldn't do that, sir, uh, Lord. She only takes energy if she has permission."

"She deceives you, Maxwell, the same way she tried to deceive your father. He; however, did not believe her lies. Surely you trust your father's judgment, Maxwell."

"Yes, but…"

"Good, Maxwell, if you follow his footsteps you will quickly rise in rank. Guards, take the Spirit Leech to the dungeon. Keep her alive for now. As for the acolyte, you can release her outside of the gates, she is of no consequence."

The guards drug Melody and Alexandra out of the room. "For you, Maxwell, a good rest is in order, report to the sleeping quarters at once. I will need everyone in top condition over the next coming weeks."

"Why, what are you going to do?"

Lord Avram raised the Lifestone to eye level. "Make things as they should be. Guard, help Maxwell to the sleeping quarters."

The guard by the door moved in front of Max. "Let's go."

"But?"

The guard shoved Max's shoulder, spinning him around. He gave Max another shove towards the door. With no idea of what he could do, Max started walking. When they arrived at the sleeping quarters, the guard shoved him inside and shut the door, locking it afterwards.

Max stood alone in the room. *Come to think of it, I didn't see anyone else around when we arrived. Where could everyone have gone?*

Max laid down on a bed, his head swimming with the events of the past several days. *Alexandra tells one story, Lord Avram another, both blaming each other. Lysander was spying on us the whole time, and now he doesn't want to talk to anyone. Worst of all, I have no idea where Eve ran off to. For that matter, she's never run away from anything. Why now?* Max rolled over on his side. *I'll have to find her. Maybe Mr. Penna is back, he can help straighten all this out.* Max closed his eyes, falling into a troubled sleep brought on by the exhausting march to the city

In the morning, Max awoke to the same empty room. Walking over to the door, he tried the handle, to his surprise, it unlocked. He opened it to find an empty hallway. He made his way out into the courtyard where the sun shone brightly overhead. From his right, he heard a loud neigh. He ran to the stables.

"Starlight!"

Max checked Starlight over, finding her well groomed and fed. He patted her on the shoulder.

"It looks like you've had a better time of it than me."

Starlight lowered her head, taking a playful nip at Max's ear. Max laughed, thankful for the release.

"I've missed you too girl."

A young boy stepped out of the neighboring stall. "Is that your horse, sir?"

Max rubbed Starlight's neck. "Yep."

The boy handed Max a carrot. "She's a fine horse, if a bit stubborn. When the other soldiers left, they tried to take her, but she'd have none of it."

Max held the carrot out to Starlight who snatched it from his hands. "Where did they go?"

"Don't know. Most of the other soldiers left several days ago. Lord Avram and his commanders left early this morning"

Max nodded at the boy. "You've kept good care of Starlight; think you can watch her a little longer yet."

"Sure thing!"

Max patted Starlight one last time. "Wait a little bit longer girl."

*What is going on around here? I hope Mr. Penna is home.*

At the gate to the courtyard stood two guards. *At least I'm not the only one still here.* The guards nodded at Max, opening the gate. He entered the square and made his way to Mr. Penna's home. He knocked on the door and waited. He knocked a second time with the same results. He sat down on the step in front of the door, head in his hands.

*Now what? Any time I've been in trouble, Eve's gotten me out. If I had a question, Mr. Penna was there to answer it. Now they're both gone. Even worse, Eve may be the one in trouble. Where would she even go? The only places she knows are Alexandra's camp and Melody's church.*

Max raised his head. *The church! Maybe Eve's there. If she isn't, I can at least talk to Melody. Maybe she has an idea of what's going on.*

Max took off running for the church. Strangely, the streets on the north side of the city were deserted, and all the doors and windows of the buildings closed. South of the market he found the opposite, lacarnians filled the streets. Many turned to face him as he ran by, their expressions resembling that of Eve's when she stalked prey. He ran faster.

Max breathed a sigh of relief when he reached the archway to the church. He ran through the empty garden and into the church itself. Inside, Lady Metis stood at the front of the building addressing those packed into the room. Max tried to spy Melody among the throng. Not finding her, he pushed his back against the wall and began to scoot his way along it to the front. He made it to within a few feet of Lady Metis when someone grabbed him, pulling him into the kitchen. Spinning around he saw Melody.

"Melody, thank goodness. Is Eve here?"

"What?" Melody tugged at Max's sleeve. "Let's go to the store room where we can hear one another."

Melody led Max to a small room next to the kitchen where the noise from the main room dissipated. Before Max could ask about Eve again, Melody spoke.

"Why didn't Lord Avram take you with him?"

Max blushed. "I didn't even know he had left until I spoke to the stable boy a short while ago. I guess I overslept."

"Do you have any idea where he went?"

Max shook his head. "No idea."

"He didn't tell you anything at all?"

Max threw up his hands. "No, not a thing. I tried to find Mr. Penna to see if he knew, but he's still not back. All I want to do now is find Eve. I had hoped she had come here."

Melody took a few deep breaths to calm herself. "I'm sorry, Max. It's just that everyone's frightened. Nearly all of the soldiers left the capital yesterday, then Lord Avram left this morning."

"The only thing he said to me was that he planned to make things as they should be and to get some rest for the weeks to come. That's it."

"He must not trust you, Max."

"Why would he not trust me?"

"Why did you come here, Max?"

"I had hoped to find Eve here, or, at the very least, find out what you believe really happened with my father. Either Lord Avram or Alexandra is lying, but I can't tell which."

"That's why he doesn't trust you, Max, because you don't trust him. If you did, you would not question his story. Add to that your friendship with Eve, a lacarnian, and he will never trust you."

"I just want to know the truth."

Lady Metis appeared behind Melody. "I might be able to help you with that, Maxwell. What would you like to know?"

"Do you know why my father gave you that box?"

"Your father left with few words, and I fear what he did say you will not want to hear."

"Please, Lady Metis, I must know what happened."

"Very well, Maxwell. When he gave me the box, your father said that he had lost faith in the Protectors, and, because of that, he had betrayed them. He then instructed me to never give the box to anyone other than himself or a little girl of whom he described in great detail. With that, he left."

"Did you know anything about my father before then?"

"Oh yes, Maxwell. Almost everyone in Moenia knew of your father, along with many of the villages. Your father treated everyone with kindness and fairness, human and lacarnian. Where other Protectors closely followed Lord Avram's orders, your father often went his own way."

"What do you know about Lord Avram?"

"Very little I'm afraid. He is a mystery to many, or at least he was. Melody told me Alexandra's story."

"And you believed it?"

"I am not sure at this point, but there is one piece of it that I can confirm. We had heard rumors that a forest once existed in the dead lands and decided to send diggers to research the area. It so happens that you met the two I sent."

"You mean Zeth and Bastiaan?"

"Yes."

"Did they make it back? What did they find?"

"Bastiaan returned to us, after having hid in a cave for several days. We still have not found Zeth."

"I'm sorry he has not returned, Lady Metis, but did Bastiaan say what they had found?"

"Yes, evidence that a forest once existed where the dead lands now lie. They also believe that the destruction of that forest and the creation of the dead lands both occurred from the same catastrophic event."

"Then what Alexandra said could be true, at least that part of it."

Melody sighed. "If it is true, it would provide a reason why Tyco tried to stop us from returning. The information could have been used to undermine Lord Avram and the Protectors, especially if it led us to Alexandra. An even greater possibility once we knew you were alive."

"So you believe her, Melody?"

"I'm not sure, Max. Doing so would mean our understanding of the Immortals and the spirits is wrong. That's not easy to deal with."

Lady Metis gently laid a hand on Max's shoulder. "Maxwell, you've asked everyone else what they believe. What is it you believe?"

"Honestly, I'm not sure. I thought dad was devoted to the Protectors, that they treated everyone fairly. Since I left Swiftwater, I've seen nothing but the opposite, and now I'm told my father betrayed them. Believing Alexandra means everyone has lied to me. Except maybe Mr. Penna, he never has liked the idea of me joining the Protectors."

Max paced back and forth, his face furrowed in concentration. "I don't know what to believe, and I'm tired of trying to figure it out. Right now I just want to find Eve. I saw her face before she changed. She was ashamed. If I don't find her, she might not come back, and I won't have that. I don't care what she is."

Melody smiled, "Eve couldn't have a better friend. I'll help you find her, Max."

"Thanks, Melody, but where do we start."

"Alexandra warned Eve ahead of time, maybe she also told her where to go."

Max nodded. "You may be right, Melody? I guess I'll have to ask her."

Max pushed past Melody and Lady Metis, making his way through the kitchen and out past the throng of people. He had made it halfway through the garden before Melody caught up to him.

"Max, they're holding Alexandra in the dungeon. How are you going to get in to see her? Lord Avram's surely warned the guards not to let anyone near her."

Max gave a nervous laugh. "Get in? I don't even know where the dungeon's at."

"It's hidden under the Protector's headquarters."

Max's face hardened. "That's a start. Are you still coming?"

"You really trust me, Max?"

"At the moment, you're one of the few I do."

Melody smiled. "Lady Metis was right."

Max stared at her blankly. "What?"

"She said your father always followed his heart and that you are a lot like him. She also told me that I would be a fool not go with you."

"I would understand if you didn't. Who knows what trouble I'll get in to?"

Melody gave a hearty laugh. "Plenty, I'm sure, but I will not let someone go alone who has put so much trust in the Church, or in me. Besides, I still owe you for saving me in the dead lands."

Max felt his heart lighten a bit. "Then let's go. I want to figure out how we're going to break into the dungeon before it gets too dark."

Melody rolled her eyes. "And I kept thinking Eve was the crazy one."

## CHAPTER TWENTY-NINE

"Are you sure about this Max?"

"No, not really. I'm open to suggestions."

Melody sighed. "Nothing here, it's just that this seems a bit too silly to work."

"Normally I would agree, but, like I said, the only guards I saw this morning are at the gate. You saw for yourself that the ones on this side are asleep. I'm betting it's the same for the two on the other side."

"Okay then, let's give it a shot."

Max and Melody each rolled a barrel next to the wall separating them from the Protectors courtyard. Carefully, they stood them upright side by side. Max walked back behind the nearest house to retrieve a third barrel they had found. Rolling it next to the other two, he and Melody lifted it on to the others forming a pyramid. Max tried to rock the top barrel, but it remained steady.

"Thank goodness the first gate was left unguarded or this wouldn't have worked."

Satisfied, he stepped back next to Melody to survey the pyramid of barrels. She nodded at the stack. "Well, this is your idea, so you first."

"What happened to ladies first?"

"I'll be the first to run when they catch you climbing over the wall, how's that?"

Max rolled his eyes. "Right."

Max climbed the stack of barrels. From the top he grabbed the ledge of the wall and pulled himself up. He looked down the length of the wall.

"I don't see anyone coming."

"And you haven't been shot by an arrow yet either."

Max started to laugh, then realized she wasn't joking. "Hurry, before that changes."

"Okay, okay, I'm coming."

Melody climbed the stack and stood on the top barrel. Max knelt, reaching out his hand to help her onto the wall. She slapped his hand away and grabbed the ledge. She pulled with her arms as she jumped and managed to slide her stomach onto the wall. She paused a moment before swinging her legs up behind her. Max shook his head and dropped down off the wall to the courtyard below. Melody, still lying on her stomach, looked down at him.

"Um, I don't know about this."

"You climbed up fine."

"I didn't have to look down then."

Max shook his head. "Fine." He held out his arms. "Go ahead, I'll catch you."

Melody moved to a sitting position with her legs hanging over the ledge. She took a deep breath and shoved herself off of the wall. Max caught her in his arms and lowered her to the ground. She straightened out her robe.

"Thank you, Maxwell."

"I still don't see how you climbed up, but couldn't..."

"So what's your plan now?"

Max stared at her a moment then shook his head again. "I'm assuming that access to the dungeon is from within the building. So, we go in and find it."

"That simple, huh?"

A frantic neighing cut off Max's reply. Melody grabbed his arm.

"Guards?"

"No, Starlight. We must have startled her."

Max ran to the stable and found the horse stomping nervously. He took hold of her halter to still her while rubbing her forehead.

"Calm down girl. It's only me. Don't be frightened."

Melody reached him and pointed at the ground. "We didn't scare her, Max. There is another animal in the stall."

Following Melody's finger, Max watched a small figure dart out from around Starlight's hooves. It stopped under the light of a lantern several feet away from them. Max shook his head while wiping the sweat off of his brow.

"Almost given away by a mouse."

"Max! That's Spook."

"What? It can't be."

Melody crouched down. "Come here, Spook. You remember me, don't you?"

Max couldn't believe his eyes as the little mouse ran over to Melody.

"See, it is her."

Max squatted next to Melody. "Well, I'll be."

Melody examined a piece of cloth tied to Spook's tail. "Who did this?"

Max recognized the cloth at once. "It's a piece of ribbon from Alexandra's hair. Spook must have hidden in her dress when the Protectors took her."

The mouse suddenly turned, running a few feet away from them before stopping and facing them once more. Spook waited a few seconds before repeating the maneuver. Melody slowly turned her head towards Max.

"I think she wants us to follower her."

"Funny, Melody."

"I'm serious. You would be amazed at how smart animals are. On top of that, the Immortals were known to have a great affinity with nature."

"But it's a mouse."

Melody put her hands on her hips. "A few minutes ago we

broke into the most heavily fortified place in Velrune by climbing a stack of empty wine barrels. Now you're questioning following a mouse when you have no idea where you're going to begin with?"

Max glanced back at the wall they had climbed over. "You really think she wants us to follow her?"

Melody took a couple of steps towards Spook. The little mouse turned, ran a few feet more then stopped, facing them once again. Max groaned.

"Eve's never going to let me hear the end of this. Ok, new plan, we follow Spook."

Max joined Melody and followed Spook as she scurried along a sparse trail of hay that led to an open door in the side of the main building. Sticking his head in, Max saw a mound of hay stacked in the center of a small room. On the far wall he saw another door leading farther into the building.

"Huh, I hadn't noticed this door before."

"You really didn't have a plan on getting us in did you, Max?"

"Well…"

Spook ran through the room.

"There she goes, we'd better keep up."

Max jogged after the mouse. Melody rolled her eyes and followed.

Spook led them through hallways, rooms and even down a flight of stairs. Max and Melody ran as hard as they could to keep Spook in sight, until she shot through a small hole in the wall of a dead-end hallway. They slid to a stop and caught their breath. After a moment, Max studied the wall.

"Now what?"

Melody felt along the wall. "My job with the Church is to validate rumors. Mostly they're false, but every now and again one rings true."

Melody pushed on a brick, sending the wall swinging inward. "Secret passages inside Protector Headquarters, I guess I'll mark that rumor as true."

The false wall revealed a spiral staircase leading down. Following for several flights, they arrived at a heavy wooden door. Taking a deep breath, Max pushed the door open. On the other side was a small room with a small lock box and a pair of guards sitting in chairs next to another door. The sound of the door opening startled the guards from their sleep. The one on the left jumped to attention.

"Who are you?"

Max stood as straight as he could and tried to sound important. "I'm Sgt. Maxwell Laskaris, I need to speak with one of the prisoners."

"Haven't heard of you, now get out of here."

Melody shouted from behind. "Hey!"

Max tried to turn around, but was shoved forward. Steadying himself, he found Lysander standing next to him with a backpack slung over his shoulder.

"I need to speak to one of the prisoners as well."

"Sgt. Harris, we thought you had left with the others."

"I had other duties to attend to. Now, if you will let me pass."

"I...I'm sorry sir. Lord Avram directly ordered us to keep everyone out of the dungeon until his return."

"Is that so?"

Lysander stepped forward and grabbed the guard, lifting him off the ground with ease. The second guard reached for his sword, but Max intercepted him. Unsheathing his own sword, he held it at the guard's neck.

Lysander shook the guard he held. "Keys."

The guard reached a shaking hand down to his belt. He unfastened the ring of keys, dropping them to the floor.

"Good, now I think it's time you took a little nap."

Lysander let go of the guard, striking him on top of the head before he could reach for his weapon. With the first guard unconscious, Lysander turned to the other one. The second guard swallowed hard.

"Wait, I'll be quiet."

Max removed his sword from the guard's neck. The guard

sunk to his knees, his focus on Lysander.

"I won't do anything, I promise."

Lysander nodded. "I know you won't. Max?"

Max swung the blunt edge of his sword, striking the guard on the back of the head. The guard fell flat. Max bent down and verified that he was unconscious. Lysander patted Max on the shoulder.

"It's okay, Max. If this goes badly, they can at least say they put up a fight."

Max stood. "What are you doing here, Lysander?"

"The same as you I would guess, trying to get answers."

Melody stormed up to Lysander. "Answers? Couldn't you have gotten those without having turned us over to the Protectors?"

"No, I couldn't." Lysander bent down and grabbed the keys. "Coming?"

Melody shook her head. "I don't trust you. How do I know you aren't going to lock us in one of those cells?"

"I understand your concern, but I have little time to convince you otherwise."

Max stuck out his hand. "Will you at least give Melody and I your word that you will let us leave?"

Lysander shook Max's hand. "You have my word, if it still means anything to you."

"It does for the moment."

Lysander nodded then turned to the lock on the door, trying one key after another until it unlocked. He swung it open and stared blankly down the dimly lit tunnel.

"I'm not sure which cell she's in."

Max shrugged his shoulders. "That's okay, we'll follow Spook."

"What?"

Max pointed at Spook who sat on her haunches just beyond the arch of the door. Lysander stepped back in surprise.

"What the... is that the mouse Evangeline had?"

Spook turned and hurried down the corridor. The others gave

chase, winding through a dizzying maze of intersecting corridors lined with cells. Finally, Spook stopped in front of a cell and waited. When they reached her she darted between the bars.

Inside the cell, Alexandra lay in a fetal position on a stone slab carved out of the rock wall. The skin on her face and hands had drawn tight to her bones. Her burns remained untreated. Spook climbed onto the slab, tickling Alexandra's face with her whiskers until she woke. Seeing the mouse, she spoke in a raspy voice.

"Hey, Spook. Did you find them?"

Max stepped close to the bars. "If by them you mean us, then, yes."

Alexandra jerked in surprise. She pushed herself into a seated position.

"Actually, no, I did not mean you."

"Then who? Eve?"

Alexandra winced as she nodded. "Yes."

"Where is she supposed to be?"

"Outside the west gate, along with the people from my camp."

Melody stepped beside Max. "Did you plan for this to happen?"

"Lord Avram, the stone and I all needed to come together. This was one of the possibilities, though not the one I had hoped for."

Max heard Lysander grunt behind them. "I thought as much."

Alexandra gave Lysander a curious look. "You I certainly did not expect."

"I need answers from you, honest ones."

"Does it matter what I say? You do not trust me."

"I will this time."

Lysander slid the backpack off of his shoulder. Crouching down, he opened it. Max tensed. "What are you going to do, Lysander?"

Lysander reached inside the bag. "Alexandra, I brought someone else along with me. She misses you terribly."

Lysander pulled out a doll worn by decades of use. It was old, but well taken care of by a loving owner. Not the least bit of stuffing shown from the several meticulously sewn stitches, nor could a single stray thread from the clothing be seen.

Lysander held the doll in front of the cell's entrance. Her eyes wide, Alexandra slid off the bench and fell to her knees at the cell door. She stretched her arm between the bars, trying to grab the doll.

"My doll? Don't hurt my doll!"

Lysander held the doll inches outside of her reach. "I'm not going to hurt her, she's already very sad. You left her behind; she doesn't think you love her anymore."

"No, that's not true! I didn't mean to leave her. I'd never do that."

Max stood speechless at the sudden transformation in Alexandra. *She's centuries old, and knows more than I ever will, but she still is just a scared little kid.*

Lysander turned the doll to face him. "She told me she might trust you again, if you're completely honest with her."

Alexandra slowly pulled her hand back and sat on the floor, nodding as she wrung her hands together.

"O…okay. Anything she wants."

"Well, she wants to know if you told the cat-girl and her friends the truth when you were in the big forest."

Lysander turned the doll back to Alexandra whose eyes locked on it. "Of course I did. You were there, Emma. You know I told them everything, just like we saw it."

"What do you really want to do with the Lifestone?"

"To fix what that stupid Egan did to my friends. They should be free, not trapped in cities wearing collars."

"Isn't someone going to get hurt if you do that?"

Alexandra wrung her hands even harder, causing the wounds from the rope to bleed. Lysander gave her several seconds to respond. When she failed to he pulled the doll away from the cell to put it back in the bag. Alexandra shot forward, hitting her head on the bars as she stretched her hand out for the doll.

"No!"

Max saw a wave of pain cross Lysander's face. He stopped to listen. Alexandra spoke between sniffles as tears freely flowed down her face.

"I...I have to get rid of...Egan. He has to pay for killing mommy and daddy. Peter promised he would help me free the cats if I left everyone else alone, but...he left me."

Lysander held the doll in reach of Alexandra's straining hand. She carefully took hold, pulling it back to her chest where she wrapped her arms around it. Lysander stood and walked a short distance down the corridor, but not before Max glimpsed the tears on his cheeks. He tossed the keys over his shoulder.

"Let her out, Max."

Max grabbed the keys, unlocked the door and swung it open. Alexandra didn't even notice. She sat gently rocking side to side with her faced buried against the doll. Melody slipped past him as he turned to Lysander.

"That doll is what I saw you grab back at the village, isn't it?"

Lysander nodded

"How did you know it meant so much to her?"

"Not long before my wife's death, she gave a doll to my daughter, Agalia. After my wife passed, Agalia wouldn't let go of that doll for anything in the world. Unlike me, Agalia was too young to have many memories of her mother. But that doll, that doll kept her connected. By holding it, she could hold on to her mother."

"That morning in the forest when you saw me standing over Alexandra, I was watching her sleep. There, curled up sucking her thumb, I began to see the disguise she wore. Agalia had worn the same one, tough around the other adults and her friends, then crying herself to sleep at night.

"Alexandra may have been alive for over 600 years, but she stopped living the night her mother died, and that stone did whatever it did to her. With her parents, and most of her kind dead, that doll is all she has left. Losing that doll would mean losing what she had of a childhood before everything went to hell."

Lysander came back to the cell. "I did not enjoy doing that to her, nor what Lt. Biros did in the forest. I did not believe he could be so cruel. Please know that."

Max nodded. "I believe you. I saw the look on your face when Tyco hit her. You wanted to beat him to a pulp, didn't you?"

Lysander bowed his head. "I needed to know the truth, without any doubt, before I could turn against everything I had followed my whole life. Although, now that I have verified Lord Avram's crimes, I'm not sure what to do."

Melody stepped out of the cell. "To start with, we need to get Alexandra's help. She mentioned those from her camp are waiting outside the gates."

Max nodded. "Yes, and Eve is supposed to be there too. I want to see her, and I want to find out what else Alexandra had planned. Lysander?"

"Do you really think she can stop Lord Avram?"

Alexandra lifted her head, rubbing the back of her sleeve across her eyes. "I can stop him, not easily, but if you help me, I can. I...Peter and I figured out a way to fix everything."

Alexandra tried to stand, but her legs had weakened too much. Melody rushed back inside the cell and took hold of her hands. "She needs to draw energy to heal."

Alexandra pulled back from Melody. "Not from you, any of you. You will need your strength. My followers outside will help."

Lysander entered the cell, scooping Alexandra up in his arms. "Then let's get you out of here."

Max looked both ways down the corridor. "Uh, does anyone remember the way back out?"

Alexandra rolled her eyes. "Oh for the love of...Spook?"

Spook jumped off the bench where she had been observing them and scurried out of the cell and down the twisting passageways.

## CHAPTER THIRTY

Max stood by the stable, arms crossed. "I guess I never considered how we would get back out."

Lysander snickered. "You didn't toss a few wine barrels over the wall for the return trip?"

Max turned to Lysander. "You saw that? Wait, how did you get in?"

"The front gate of course. Lord Avram assigned me to keep an eye on you, so the guards didn't question me."

Melody sighed. "They're going to have questions this time. I shouldn't be in here in the first place, and you're carrying a criminal."

Alexandra, half asleep, struggled to talk. "Go check the gate, Spook."

Spook scurried off while the others watched in disbelief. A few minutes later, she returned, climbing Lysander's pant leg and onto Alexandra's chest. Alexandra, her eyes closed, listened to her rapid squeaks. When Spook stopped, Alexandra opened her eyes.

"Head for the gate, the guards are not an issue."

The others looked at each other, shrugged their shoulders and walked to the gate. Once there, they found the guards bound and gagged and a young lacarnian girl, torch in hand, standing in the center.

"It's about time, follow me."

The lacarnian, whom Max recognized from Alexandra's camp, led them to the west city gate. The guards normally stationed there were absent, allowing them to pass through unhindered. After walking another 100 yards, the girl stopped.

"It's safe."

All around them torches blazed to life. A group of Lacarnians stood around them, illuminated by the flickering light. He recognized several from Alexandra's camp including Lycoris who stepped forward and greeted them.

"The others are restless, I'm glad you arrived when you did. How is she Mr. Harris?"

"She's asleep and needs immediate attention."

"Bring her this way."

Lysander followed the woman off to the side. Max turned to the girl that had led them to the camp.

"You were expecting us?"

"We had a plan to retrieve Alexandra ourselves; however, one of the watches reported seeing the two of you sneaking into the compound. When she heard the report, your friend was convinced that you would bring Alexandra to us, and that we should wait. It appears she was right."

"My friend? Do you mean Eve?"

"Over here, Max."

A weary, ragged Eve stepped out of the shadows wearing worn and ill-fitting clothes. Melody inched away from Max, taking hold of the lacarnian girl as she did.

"I think we'll go check on Lysander and Alexandra."

Eve watched the two go then walked over to Max. "I'm sorry, Max."

"It's okay, Eve. I know now that Alexandra told you to run. After seeing what they did to her, I'm glad you did."

"No, no, Max, not that." Taking hold of her tail she stared at the ground. "I mean about not telling you I could change."

Max laughed. "That was a bit of a surprise, even from you."

"Max, you're not getting it. I really am a beast, just like the Protectors said." Eve began to tremble. "In the canyon, I was the panther you saw. I was the one who attacked all those people."

Sobbing, Eve buried her face in her hands. Max took a firm hold of her shoulders.

"Eve, look at me!"

Eve, shocked at Max giving her a command, looked up at him.

"Eve, why did you kill those men?"

"Because they were going to hurt you."

"Did you enjoy it?"

Eve's eyes widened. "N…No, Max. I don't like killing anything."

"Then why are you ashamed?"

"Max, I'm part animal. A wild and dangerous beast that kills people."

"Then what do you think of me, Eve? You may have been born with the capability of hurting people, but I've spent years training to do so. I wasn't born with claws, but instead choose to carry swords forged to hurt others."

"That's not the same. You did that to help people."

"And that's all you have ever done. Eve, I grew up hearing stories of the great things my father did, but those were only stories. You were the one I learned from. I watched how you protected people, how you respected all living things, how you put aside a person's background to see who they really were. Eve, you're the reason why I've strived so hard to protect others. I thought becoming a Protector like my father would be the best way for me to do that. You act as if you're below me because you change into a big cat when all along I've strived to be as strong and good as you." Max shook his head. "I'm still not there."

Eve sobbed into her hands. "Maxy."

Max pulled her in tight against him. "Since the first day we met, you have never questioned my friendship. I'll do nothing less for you."

They stood, eyes closed, arms wrapped around each other, for an untold time. Neither of them wanted to let go. It was the unexpected voice of Mr. Penna that finally interrupted them.

"Years ago I thought I lost my closest friend. Perhaps he did not go as far as I feared."

Max opened his eyes to find Mr. Penna standing a short distance behind Eve. "Mr. Penna, you're back! Wait, how long have you been here?"

"Long enough to know your father would be very proud. I know I certainly am, of both of you."

Max and Eve let go of one another, both their faces a slight shade of red. Eve dried her tears, her usual smile returning. Max crossed his arms.

"Where have you been Mr. Penna?"

"I had a hunch that I needed to satisfy."

"That didn't answer my question."

"I will tell you more later, but first I would like to know all that happened in my absence. You both look like you had a bit of a rough spell."

Max scoffed. "You could say that. Actually, Eve, I don't know what happened to you after you left the forest village. You look exhausted, and what's with the clothes?"

Lysander and Melody walked up behind Max. "We wouldn't mind hearing that ourselves. Everyone else around here is too busy."

Max's face flushed even more. "How long have you two been listening?"

Melody winked at Max. "Don't worry, Max, we kept our distance until you two separated."

"So you were watching?"

Eve grabbed Max's arm. "Come on Max, let's go find a place to sit, and I'll tell you what happened."

Eve dragged Max over to an open, grassy area. The others followed them, sitting in a circle to hear Eve's story.

"When Alexandra and I stayed behind in the cave, she warned me that the Protectors would come after us. She told me when that happened to run back to her camp and tell everyone. I don't think she expected them to arrive so soon."

Max shook his head. "You ran based on that?"

"I remembered making those handprints with Alexandra along with a lot of other stuff. She was my friend, Max. I trusted her with my life. I still do. So, I ran, even though I hated leaving you, Max."

Melody leaned forward. "Did Alexandra want to get caught?"

Eve nodded. "I ran to the camp and told them what had happened. Without asking me any questions, they grabbed supplies they had already packed and headed for Moenia. Along the way, they told me that Alexandra wanted Avram to get the stone. She had hoped she would avoid capture, but had laid out a plan for them to set her free if she didn't."

"Why would she want Avram to have the stone after hiding it from him for so long?"

"Max, she and your father wanted to use the stone to free the lacarna. Unfortunately, before they could figure out how to provide it enough power, Avram ordered the attack on the village. They hid the stone and went their separate ways.

"Later, Alexandra figured out a way to power the stone by somehow involving Avram. She tried to get word to Peter, but the bandits got to him first. Not knowing who else to turn to, she went into hiding."

"Why did she need my father?"

"They said it was because both the lacarnians and the Protectors trusted him, and that he wanted the lacarna freed as much as she did."

Max bowed his head. "So my father really did help her." He raised his head. "Did you know any of this Mr. Penna?"

"Not in detail. I knew your father wanted to free the lacarna, in fact, many humans did, including myself. However, Peter decided to actually do something about it. He did not want to involve me, but I told him I had already managed to make my own trouble. He never told me what he had done; only that he had betrayed Lord Avram."

"Why didn't you tell me this, Mr. Penna? I've spent all this time trying to join the Protectors, like my dad, not knowing he had turned against them."

"Your father did not turn against the Protectors, Maxwell, he turned against Lord Avram. He believed they could be brought back to their purpose, but it would take someone who believed in those ideals, someone who saw no difference between the lacarna and the humans. That is why he made me promise not to tell you the truth about the Protectors, or about himself. He hoped you would take his place by your own decision and not anyone else's influences."

"How am I supposed to do that when I barely know what is really going on?"

"You will have to do as your father intended, Maxwell, and go with what you believe to be right."

"I don't know what that is or what my father had intended to do. Lysander, is Alexandra awake? I want to talk to her."

"No, not for a few more hours."

Mr. Penna stood. "Then I suggest you rest, Maxwell. You have had enough thrown at you for today. In fact, we should all rest. I have a feeling the next couple of days will push everyone to their limits."

Max stood. "As much as I would like to sleep, there's too much to think about. I'm going to wait for Alexandra. Lysander?"

"She's this way."

Lysander led Max to where Alexandra lay asleep under the watch of Lycoris. The others followed curious of what Alexandra planned. They took seats around her and waited for her to wake. When she opened her eyes a few hours later, she seemed unsurprised to find them waiting for her.

"I assume you all are not here to see how I am doing."

Max shook his head. "You had me worried earlier, but now I only want to know what you and my dad had planned."

Alexandra sat up, her skin no longer bone-tight and the color, what little she had in the first place, had returned. Not all of her strength had yet returned; however, as she pointed a shaky hand at Eve.

"I am going to destroy those accursed Controller Stones."

Eve gasped and unconsciously took hold of her collar. "How?"

"The Lifestone created them from a single massive stone, so they share a link. By using the Lifestone to destroy one, I can destroy them all."

Max grew angry. "If that is all it took, why did you involve my father? Why didn't you do it yourself years ago?"

"When it first came to my mind, I wanted to, even though I knew releasing the lacarna with Lord Avram at the head of the Protectors would lead to another war. The lacarnians would win in the end, but the inevitable loss of life on both sides stayed my hand, for a while. I had almost given in when I met your father. He is the one who found a way in which, if done right, only a few will die."

"Only a few? Who?"

"Avram and those foolish enough to protect him."

"All of the Protectors will come to his aide!"

"Not if they are prevented from reaching his side."

"How do you plan to do that?"

"Avram has taken care of that for me. I know what he intends to do with the stone and where he intends to do it. The place is perfect for separating him from any help."

Max paced back and forth. "Even if you can pull this off, what of the chaos that will follow? Won't the lacarna attack the Protectors for the years of mistreatment?"

"I have already spread the word of what I am attempting to do among the lacarna, asking for their patience. Also, those in my camp will spread out in the city to quell any disturbances."

"But how can you be sure? What about the Protectors, who will stop them from attacking the lacarna?"

"Most of the Protectors are away from the city, the rest will not likely take action so outnumbered."

"They will return sometime, and without a leader."

Alexandra sighed. "Unfortunately, that is where your father

was supposed to come in. The Protectors, and many humans, trusted him. He had planned to take over as leader once I had taken care of Avram."

Mr. Penna nodded. "So that is the betrayal Peter spoke of."

Max stopped and stared at Mr. Penna. "My father would really have done this?"

"Yes, Maxwell, I believe he would have. He cared for both races, believing them to be equal. He wanted the lacarnians free."

Alexandra stood and walked over to Max. "The Immortals founded the Protectors as mediators between the races; their members consisting of both lacarnians and humans. Your father wanted to uphold that principle. The only person he would have betrayed is Avram, a murderer of many."

"And now he is dead."

"Yes, but, you are not. Maxwell, you are young, but you are Peter's son. Your name carries more weight than you could know."

Max froze in disbelief. "You think they'll listen to me, let alone follow me? I'm only a kid."

"Really? Maxwell, look around you, people have already begun to follow you."

"What are you talking about? No one is following me."

Eve's hand shot up. "I am."

"Eve, quit fooling around."

Melody raised her hand too. "I told you earlier, anyone that calls me a friend, I'll help. Lady Metis also believes in you, which means you have the Children of the Immortals behind you as well."

"But..."

Mr. Penna stood, giving a slight bow. "Your father honored me with his friendship, I will do no less for his son."

Lysander remained seated as he scanned Max from head to toe. "Kids are idealist fools who run away when things get tough. You, on the other hand, have done whatever you could, despite the rules and the danger, to stay true to your friends. I can only hope to do the same. Lord Avram has led the Protectors astray. I want to try and restore their purpose. I know many others who feel the same way."

"Lysander?"

"Max, that story I told you of the Spirit Leech, that woman survived because a lacarnian healed her. Other lacarnians offered to help my wife and child, despite my distrust of them. I have been unsure for some time, but watching Eve has cleared much in my mind."

A rare smile formed on Alexandra's lips. "I knew you had more to you than big muscles, Lysander. You see, Maxwell, people will listen to you. I saw your father in you that night you entered my camp. With Lysander next to your side, you will give the other Protectors something to consider, at least long enough for us to explain what has happened."

Eve bounced up and down. "Besides, Maxy, we'll be there to help you."

Max looked at everyone again, then nodded to Alexandra. "I really don't know about this, but I want the same thing you do. "He sighed. "Why not, at least I'll have Eve to get me out of trouble, again."

Alexandra's smile broadened. "I will never compare you to your father again, Maxwell Laskaris, for that would only lessen who you are. Now, tell the others to be ready in the morning, I still need to rest."

Everyone began to find a place in the camp to sleep except for Eve who took hold of Max's arm before he could go.

"You know, I never did explain the clothing. You see, the problem with changing into my panther form is that my clothes get torn up. When I change back, I have nothing to wear."

Eve let go and walked away, looking over her shoulder as she did so. "I haven't run around completely naked like that since I was a little kid."

Max watched her walk off, the troubles of the coming events, for the moment, forgotten.

## CHAPTER THIRTY-ONE

At dawn, Alexandra called everyone to the center of the camp where they waited anxiously. Rested and healed, she began giving out orders.

"Those remaining here will spread the word of our actions to the lacarnian in the city. If we succeed, lead them to the forest. If any attempt is made to harm a human, you are to do whatever is necessary to stop them. We cannot give the humans any more reason to fear us if this is to work. Lycoris?"

The old lacarnian came forward. "Miss?"

"Please, do what you can to lead the lacarnians from here out, whether we succeed or not."

"Yes, Miss."

"Dismissed!"

The majority of the lacarnians left the camp and entered into Moenia while three remained standing beside Mr. Penna along with two large panthers. Alexandra turned to Max and the others.

"Avram will reach the outcropping within the next few hours. We need to leave now."

Max shook his head. "I think you skipped something. What outcropping?"

"It extends from the base of the Mountains at the south end of the dead lands."

"The southern mountains? It would take over a day to get

there by horse, three by foot."

"Two by horse and four by foot to be exact."

"Then how are we supposed to get there in time?"

Alexandra smiled mischievously. "We are not. We are getting there before they do."

Max snickered. "I think your head is still a little fuzzy."

"I am fine, Maxwell. You see, Mr. Penna's foresight has brought us another option."

At hearing his name, Mr. Penna walked over to the group, followed by the lacarnians and panthers. Max crossed his arms. "So what have you been doing?"

"If only you had been this inquisitive during my classes."

Eve giggled beside Max. He tried to elbow her, but she easily dodged out of the way. Mr. Penna cleared his throat.

"If you are ready?"

Max straightened, forgetting for the moment that this wasn't one of Mr. Penna's classroom lectures. He waited for Mr. Penna to continue.

"I am sure Evangeline told you that, years ago, I helped many lacarnians escape Moenia, many of whom came from the forest of Urania. I did my best to find them good homes and kept records of their placement. I had hoped that, one day, things would change, and I would have the opportunity to reunite them. The events that transpired during our trip here led me to believe the change I had been waiting for was coming. So, with records in hand, Neysa and I set out to track down any I believed could help in the challenges that might lie ahead. The ladies before you are those we could find in the short time we had." Mr. Penna indicated to each of the lacarnians in turn. "Meet Lalita, Effie, Anemone, and our four legged friends, Callie and Cassia. They are how you will reach the mountains before Lord Avram."

Max shook his head. "I don't understand."

Effie spoke. "Though we seldom care to do so, we can carry a rider when in our panther form."

Eve bounced up and down. "You can change too?"

Lalita, Effie and Anemone all nodded. Max's eyes widened as he pictured a saddle on their backs. "I'm not sure I can do that."

Lalita smiled at Mr. Penna. "We were given a nice home and will do what we can to repay that favor, especially if it means a chance for freedom for our brothers and sisters."

Max shook his head. "Even if we do this, we still won't arrive in time."

Mr. Penna smiled. "Have I never mentioned a lacarnian in panther form is the fastest animal on Velrune? I must be slipping in my old age. Now, Lysander, you will ride on either Callie or Cassia. They are the strongest and the only ones capable of carrying you. Remember, Lysander, they are ladies, treat them that way."

Lysander bowed slightly. "Of course, but, um, how do I…"

A wry smile formed on Alexandra's lips. "Unfortunately, they are not as suited for riding as a horse. Basically you straddle them, lay flat against their backs, wrap your arms around their necks and hang on for dear life."

For the first time, Max saw Lysander nervous. "Uh, huh."

Effie stepped over to Melody. "I'll take the acolyte."

Anemone came over to Max. "Then I will take the boy."

Eve's ears laid back. "Wait." Eve shoved herself between Max and Anemone. "I'm taking Max."

Alexandra took Eve by the hand. "No, Evangeline, he is too heavy, you will take me."

Eve eyed Anemone closely. "But…"

"We have little time, Evangeline, we need to get moving. Come, I already have another set of clothing for you in my backpack."

Alexandra tugged on Eve's hand until Eve sighed and followed her. "Fine."

"Good. Melody, please carry the rest of the clothing I have packed for the other three. Now then, is everyone ready?"

Everyone nodded. Max watched in awe as the three lacarnian girls transformed into panthers. Eve, tail in hand, looked nervously at Max. He gave her a big smile.

"You're going to protect me like always aren't you?"

Eve returned his smile. "You bet, Maxy."

Letting go of her tail, she transformed like the others, stunning Max. *Wow!*

Her tan fur was silky smooth except for a thick, red tuft that covered her head and ran partway down her back. Her tail remained the same bushy red as before her change. Arriving at her face, he became transfixed by her eyes, the one green, the other blue.

*I've always marveled at her grace and agility, but everything fits perfectly in this form. This really is Eve.*

Max felt a light touch on his arm. With great effort he turned his head away from Eve to find Alexandra standing beside him, almost as transfixed as he.

"Now do you see what the lacarna are, Maxwell Laskaris? Now do you know why it was us humans that strove to learn from them?"

"She blends right in with the planet while I feel like such an outsider."

"She is connected in a way we humans can never be, but that does not mean we should not at least try."

Alexandra walked over to Eve and carefully climbed onto her back, making sure to lean forward towards her neck. "Try not to sit straight up, it will put too much weight in one spot."

The others, except Mr. Penna, followed Alexandra's example. Max looked back over his shoulder at Mr. Penna.

"Aren't you coming?"

"I am no fighter. I will stay here to help Neysa and the others. Do not worry, Maxwell. I have no doubt you will succeed."

Max felt a wealth of confidence rise in him. He missed his father, but he felt just as proud to have Mr. Penna there. Alexandra snapped her fingers to get his attention.

"One more thing, do not, at any point, sit up while the lacarna are running."

Lysander shifted on Callie, a look of terror in his eyes. "And why not?"

A tiny laugh escaped from Alexandra, it sounded a lot like Eve's when she was up to no good. "Because the wind will tear you right off of them"

"Exactly how fast do they go?"

Alexandra drifted off into thought for a few seconds, returning with a mischievous smile. "You will see. Just remember to hang on tight."

Max groaned. *Now I know why she and Eve are such good friends. They're both trying to get us killed.*

Alexandra tightened her arms around Eve's neck, took a deep breath then let it out. The others shared a look of uneasiness and tightened their own grips. Excitement carried in Alexandra's voice.

"Okay, here we go. 3…2…1…"

Anemone surged forward. In the first two seconds, her speed matched that of Starlight at a full run. The next second, she traveled at a speed Max could not have imagined. In the fourth second, she hit full stride. The sensation was bizarre. Max had his head turned sideways lying flat against Anemone's back. To his right rode Melody on Effie. It appeared as if they ran in place while the world flew by in a blur of colors.

Above him, the wind blew across his head in a deafening roar. Below him, the rhythmic breathing of Anemone eased the tension of the wild ride. He felt as though he floated in a dream, losing any sense of time.

## CHAPTER THIRTY-TWO

Max felt Anemone begin to slow down. Unlike when she started, it took her close to a minute to come to a complete stop. Lifting his head, Max saw the cliffs of the southern mountains looming a short distance in front of them, with the start of the dead lands to their immediate left.

Taking great care, Max climbed off of Anemone. Behind him, he heard a loud thud. Turning, he saw Lysander pushing himself off the ground.

"I'm walking back. I don't care how long it takes me."

Eve circled back to them. Alexandra still sat on her, wearing a small smile. "Just imagine if they could have hit full speed."

Max's head still whirled from the strange experience. "They can go faster?"

Alexandra slid off of Evangeline. "You guys are heavy, even I slowed Evangeline down a little."

Max tried to imagine going even faster, but failed. "How long has it been since we left Moenia?"

Alexandra headed towards the cliffs. "An hour and a half."

Max and the others followed. "But that's over..."

"One hundred and sixty miles, approximately."

Max stopped in his tracks. "Wow!"

Alexandra paid no attention; instead she pointed to a path leading along the mountain cliff to a plateau in front of them. "At the back of that plateau is the cave where the Controller

Stones were created."

They followed the three foot wide path. Seventy feet along it, Alexandra pointed to another path that split off and led down into the valley below.

"I expect Avram and the Protectors to come from that direction. Lalita, go check it out."

Lalita leapt down the path while the rest walked another sixty feet to reach the plateau. There, Alexandra gave Melody the pack that contained Eve's clothes.

"Take Evangeline in the cave so she can get dressed. You too, Effie."

Melody looked puzzled. "What about the rest of them?"

An unfamiliar voice came from behind Max, startling him. "Anemone and Lalita are staying in their panther form. As for us, we do not wear clothing."

Max spun around, stumbling back a step when he saw the two large beings that now stood in place of Callie and Cassia.

"What…?"

Alexandra curtsied. "You should feel privileged, Maxwell. Callie and Cassia are purebloods. Their form is that of the original lacarnians."

Max studied the two. Standing on two legs in a slightly crouched position they were still a few inches taller than him. Their heads remained that of a panther's while thick, heavy fur covered their bodies. Under the fur, and nearly masked by it, moved well-toned muscles that could put Lysander to shame.

"From the story Mr. Penna told Eve, I thought both her parents were lacarnians?"

"They were, but one of her grandparents must have been a human. Only one, however, or she would not have the ability to change. There are few like Evangeline, Maxwell, but the purebloods are almost non-existent. In fact, I know of no others."

Eve emerged from the cave waving towards Alexandra. "Ready!"

"Good. Ah, and here comes Lalita"

Lalita ran to Cassia, making several growling sounds. When she finished, Cassia relayed her message.

"Lalita says that the wind carries the scent of the Protectors. We have less than an hour before they arrive."

Alexandra nodded. "That gives us enough time to prepare."

Max faced the valley below. "Why did they come through the dead lands instead of on top like we did?"

"Avram likes a show. He and his commanders will come up here while the Protectors watch from below. That is why I wanted to confront him here. When we strike, Melody will use her barrier to block the path from below, cutting any aid from the Protectors."

Melody gave a nervous nod. "I can try, but it will take all my focus to keep it in front of me. I won't be able to do anything else."

"I will have Cassia stay with you. Anyone already on the plateau that tries to get to you will have to go through her."

Alexandra walked over to several large boulders piled next to the cave. "Myself, Lalita, Effie and Anemone will hide behind here. The rest of you will hide in the cave and wait for me to confront Avram."

Lysander surveyed the area. "You've thought about this for a while haven't you?"

"You have no idea. There is one problem though. There are no plants here. There will be little I can do until the rest of you can subdue Avram and his captains."

Max swallowed hard. "Okay, but this isn't going to be easy. I know Tyco's strength, and I bet the captains are even stronger."

"I know, Maxwell, but I am afraid of what Avram has planned if we do not succeed."

"If what you have told us is true, it can't be good. I'll do my best to help."

Alexandra bowed low before them. "Thank you for believing me."

The lacarnians bowed too. "We thank you as well. We know many humans do not like what the Protectors have done, but few have cared to help us."

"I'm a Protector. It's my job to help everyone, or at least it's supposed to be. Besides, my friends have helped me enough. It's time I do the same for them." Max faced Eve and smiled. "Even if they are always getting me in trouble."

Max saw a tear start to form before Alexandra turned away. "Let us get into place." She headed for the boulders. "Oh, my friends, when I had them, called me Alex."

Max watched Alexandra walk behind the boulders followed by Ellie, Lalita and Anemone. "We'll wait for your move, Alex."

Max, Melody, Eve, Lysander, Callie and Cassia, entered the cave and spread themselves out along the wall, staying out of the light from the entrance. They waited in silence for Lord Avram to arrive. Eve heard them first, her ears perking up as she caught the sound of their voices. Not long after, Max heard them moving outside the cave. Eve signaled that two guards had taken positions just outside the entrance to either side. Lord Avram's conversation with the others on the plateau could now be heard by all of them.

"Well, Tyco, we will soon be rid of all of those horrid beasts."

"Yes, Lord Avram, it hasn't come soon enough. I'm tired of seeing what they have done to us humans."

"You have seen little in comparison to all that I have witnessed over these many years."

Lord Avram's voice grew louder. "Protectors, we have suffered enough at the claws of the lacarna. Today I bring you the end of these vile creatures."

Max heard multiple soft footsteps come from the right side of the cave, followed by the unsheathing of swords immediately outside.

"The only vile creature here is you, Egan. The lacarna wanted to live peacefully with us, but your hatred led you to betray your own kind."

"Alexandra, you are quite the surprise. I knew your followers would try to rescue you, but not in time for you to come here."

"Have you forgotten how fast a lacarnian can run," mocked

Alexandra, "or did you think you had gotten rid of those that could change?"

"It does seem an oversight might have occurred."

"I would call it more than just an oversight. You got careless. People began to see past your lies. Peter was not the only one to betray you."

Avram sighed. "Staying in control has become tiring in my old age, but in a moment that will no longer matter. The truth will die with you along with the rest of the lacarna. humans will finally have peace and their children will be pure."

Max's blood boiled. *He really wants to kill the lacarna! Alexandra's telling the truth about him, about my dad.*

Max had heard enough. Signaling to Lysander, he quickly stepped out of the cave. Whirling to the right, he took a quick swing at the back of the guard's head with the flat of his sword. Lysander similarly dropped the other guard. Max quickly surveyed the rest of the plateau.

Lord Avram and Tyco stood with a bound lacarnian girl at the edge of the plateau. His three captains; Leander, Thanos, and Agamemnon, stood at the center with five guards standing along the cliff wall on both sides of the cave. Max's stomach tightened as the reality of fighting trained men sank in.

Lord Avram turned from Alexandra to him. "Don't tell me you are involved in this as well, Maxwell. I had hoped you would see through her lies. Perhaps you still might, given time to think things through. Leave these fools, and I will make you a Lieutenant like your father."

"Like my father? Didn't he betray you?"

"Maxwell, Maxwell, your father fell prey to that evil little brat. I do not fault him for that. The same goes for you."

Max's face flushed red, his grip tightening on his sword. "You do not fault him, yet you had him killed?"

"A misunderstanding, Max."

Tyco, staring coldly at Max, stepped forward. "I warned you this might happen, Lord Avram. That beast has had him wrapped around her finger for years, long before he met

Alexandra. Just another example of what those blasted lacarnians have done to our kind."

Max seethed with anger. "Eve has shown me more of what a Protector should be than I could ever learn from you, Tyco."

Lord Avram sighed. "I see what you mean, Tyco. Enough of this, dispose of Alexandra and that mangy cat, but leave the boy."

Tyco drew his sword and advanced towards Eve. "I've wanted to do this for some time. Let's see what you've got you filthy cat."

Max raised his swords. "I'm not going to sit idly by while you hurt my friends."

Tyco stopped. "You would actually draw against me to protect that thing."

"You and anyone else who would try to harm her."

"Very well, Max. I'll teach you one final lesson."

Tyco charged while Max readied himself for the attack. A blur flew by Max, barreling into Tyco and knocking him onto his back. Eve stood at Tyco's feet, her tail flicking fiercely back and forth.

"It is I who have something to teach you." Eve extended her claws and waited for Tyco to stand.

Max saw a glint of fear in Tyco's eyes as he regained his footing. "You see, Max, they are born predators."

Max paused to take in the creature before him. Her red, cropped hair was a mess, her ears were laid flat and her waving tail made approaching from behind a risky prospect.

*Tyco is right, she is a wild beast, always has been. It's the reason why we had such crazy adventures. But, what's wrong with that?*

The memory of Eve crouched on his chest, purring, in Mrs. Tassi's storeroom flashed in Max's mind.

*Yes, she's wild, but there's so much more.*

A big grin formed on Max's face.

"You know very little about Eve, Tyco. She is a good and loving friend to me and many others. You are right; however, about how she was born a wild beast designed to protect herself

# Outcasts of Velrune

and others. I'm glad I'm the one she's chosen to protect. Good luck, Tyco. You're going to need it."

Eve launched herself at Tyco and the two became entangled. From the right, Alexandra and Callie rushed Lord Avram throwing him into a panic.

"Guards!"

Captain Leander moved to intercept Callie and Alexandra. Lysander and Max tried to resume the charge themselves only to have Captains Thanos and Agamemnon block them. Melody ran to take her position on the path with Cassia hot on her heels and Effie, Lalita and Anemone engaging the remaining guards. At that point, Max lost sight of the surrounding battle as the mighty form of Captain Thanos filled his view.

Thanos advanced with slow, strong swings of his sword. Max met Thanos's forceful blows accurately, but each one left him stunned for the briefest of moments. He recovered only in enough time to block the next one. This continued for several minutes until a final blow knocked Max to the ground. A crooked smile appeared on Thanos's face.

Lysander stepped over Max. "I think this one's a little big for you, Max. Let me play with him while you go help the others."

Thanos and Lysander took a powerful swing at each other, their swords meeting in a deafening clang. Max rolled left to get out of the way and found Captain Agamemnon lying on the ground. He was either unconscious or dead, but, at this moment, Max didn't care which.

Max's training with Tyco had not prepared him for the surrounding chaos of an-all out fight. To his left, Melody struggled to block the path leading down to the plateau with her barrier. Behind Melody, Effie fought to keep a pair of guards from reaching her. To his front right, Callie still engaged Captain Leander while Alexandra searched for a way past them.

He could hear the rest of the battle raging on behind him and hoped Eve still stood among those fighting. Knowing he couldn't take the time to check on her, he dodged around Lysander and Thanos to make his way towards Lord Avram.

He had a brief glimpse of him standing at the edge of the plateau. He gripped the head of the lacarnian girl with one hand and held the Lifestone with the other. Before he could contemplate what Lord Avram was trying to do, two guards stepped in front of him, raising their weapons to attack.

A loud scream from behind the guards froze everyone. Other screams from around the plateau joined the first, Eve's among them. To his right, Callie fell to her knees in agony.

Max shook off the shock, and stabbed at the guard to his left, striking him below his chest plate. The movement brought the second guard back to the fight. He took a swing that Max blocked with one sword while pulling his other out of the first guard. The guard swung again. This time Max dodged around to his side, striking the back of the guard's leg. As the guard fell, Max spun, taking a step towards Lord Avram before a painful impact to his back knocked him to the ground. From where he fell he saw Spook scurry across the ground towards Lord Avram.

A hard kick sent Max rolling onto his back. Above him stood Tyco, breathing heavily and wavering a bit. Claw marks gouged his armor and the left side of his face. Blood flowed from where his ear and eye had once been. With both hands wrapped around the hilt, Tyco raised his sword above his head.

A yell of pain rose from Lord Avram. "You accursed rodent!"

Tyco hesitated. "Lord Avram!"

Tyco's body jerked then stiffened. He hung there, sword high above his head, for what seemed like an eternity. Finally, he went limp, the sword falling from his grip. Max used the last of his strength to deflect it inches from his face. Tyco's body was tugged from behind and fell, leaving Eve standing in clear view. She retracted her bloody, broken claws then stumbled forward, dropping to her knees beside Max. Struggling to talk, she lay her head down gently on his chest.

"Hi, Maxy."

# CHAPTER THIRTY-THREE

Max lifted his head. Eve had several cuts, bruises and a small tuft of hair missing, but otherwise seemed okay. He lowered his head.

"Just once, Eve, would you let me save you?"

"Nope."

Lysander's voice rang out. "Drop your weapons and stay where you are!"

Max tried to move. "What's going on?"

Struggling, Eve pushed herself to a seated position. "Lysander has a knife to Lord Avram's throat"

Melody arrived at Eve's side. "You two are a mess." Melody checked Eve's cuts. "Nothing serious. Eve, help me sit Max up."

Together Eve and Melody pulled Max upright. He cringed in pain.

"My back."

Melody checked his back and gasped. "This needs immediate attention. Alexandra!"

"In my pack there are some salves. Do what you can with those. I cannot use any of my strength to help. Callie, untie the girl and use the rope on Lord Avram."

Melody ran to retrieve Alexandra's pack. Max tapped Eve on the shoulder.

"Can you spin me around so I can see what is happening?"

Once Eve had him turned the right direction, Max could see

Lysander standing behind Lord Avram with a knife next to his throat. In front of them, Callie untied the lacarnian girl and used the rope to bind Lord Avram so tightly that he could barely breathe. Max saw fear in his eyes as he spoke between constricted breaths.

"This is pointless. My Protectors will not let you leave here alive."

Alexandra approached Lord Avram. "They will not be your Protectors for much longer."

Melody returned with a jar of salve. Tearing the back of Max's shirt, she smeared the cool gel over his wound.

"I'll do what I can, Max, but, as I've said before, healing is not my strong point."

Max felt Melody's hand on his back and the pain slowly lessoned.

"There, Max, I've stopped the bleeding. Hopefully, Alexandra will take care of the rest. Otherwise, you will have to wait until we get back to Moenia."

"What about everyone else?"

Tears filled Melody's eyes. "We lost Lalita." She wiped the tears away. "The others have various injuries, but nothing life threatening. They're helping guard the path onto the plateau."

Eve's head swiveled back and forth frantically. "What about Spook? She ran off while I was fighting Tyco."

Max nodded at Lord Avram. "I saw her running his direction after I fell."

Melody gave a strained laugh. "Yeah, she bit Lord Avram, stopping whatever he was doing to the girl. It also let Lysander slip in behind him."

Eve looked at Melody expectantly. "Well, where is she now?"

Melody started to sniffle, but stopped herself. "Lysander flung her back towards the mountainside."

Eve tried to stand. "Where?"

Melody held Eve down. "I'll go look for her. You stay here."

As Melody left, Max focused on the events at the edge of the plateau. Alexandra had calmed the lacarnian girl Lord Avram had brought and now studied the girl's collar.

"What is your name?"

"Han...Hannah."

"Well, Hannah, I think it is time we got rid of these blasted stones."

Lord Avram struggled to free himself. "No, you can't do that! The lacarna will slaughter us if you remove those stones. Guards!"

A few of the close Protectors started to move. Lysander inched his knife closer to Lord Avram's throat. "Stay where you're at."

Alexandra shook her head as she smiled at the girl. "The lacarna will not harm the humans."

Lord Avram carefully turned his head to face Max. "Maxwell, you have just seen what these beasts are capable of, don't make the same mistake as your father. You must not let her do this."

"My father did what he thought was right and so do I." Max smiled at Eve. "I know there is much more to them than their animal side."

Alexandra picked up the Lifestone from where Lord Avram had dropped it. With her other hand, she clasped the stone in Hannah's collar.

Max looked at her curiously. "What are you doing?"

"The Lifestone feeds on life and creates it. Lord Avram used it to create the controller stones as living entities; it can also destroy them. Do not worry Max, she is in no danger."

Alexandra closed her eyes. A slight glow appeared in the center of the Lifestone. When Alexandra let go of Hannah's collar, the stone was gone.

"There, that is better."

Max starred at the collar. "It's gone." Max shook his head. "But how are you going to get all of them?"

Remember, the stones were created from one mass and share a link. Destroying one with the Lifestone, destroyed them all.

"You mean..." Max looked at Eve's collar, the stone had vanished. Eve, seeing his stare, felt for herself. Her eyes widened.

"They're all gone?"

Lord Avram shouted hysterically. "You've doomed us all! The lacarna will not live peacefully with us after what we have done to them. I'm sure they have already started slaughtering humans."

Alexandra faced him. "You are right."

Max and Lysander's jaws dropped. "What?"

"They will live in a place free of humans, but not one brought about from human blood. It will be a new place made solely for them."

Lord Avram looked at her nervously. "What do you mean a new place?"

"I guess it is not really new, I am, after all, only restoring what you took away many years ago."

Lord Avram's brow furrowed. Max shared his confusion, but beside him a wave of excitement washed over Melody. "You mean, you're going to recreate the forest Avram destroyed, don't you?"

"Yes."

Lord Avram shook his head. "Impossible. That would take more power than you or anyone else has. How are you…?" Horror filled Lord Avram's face. "Maxwell, you must stop her, she is going to sacrifice the lives of the Protectors to…to create plants!"

Alexandra's face flashed red. "No, I am not like you. I will not use the lives of others so carelessly." Alexandra fixed her eyes on Max. "I promised your father I would not, nor do I want to."

Lord Avram quieted. "Please, Maxwell, do not trust her. The lives of the Protectors are the only way to supply the stone with so much power."

Alexandra voice softened. "Maxwell, I am of the original line of humans, the ones unaffected by the disease. I have much more for the Lifestone to feed on." Her eyes grew cold and hardness entered her voice. "Thanks to Avram's treachery, I also learned how to channel the energy from others too, namely his."

All color drained from Lord Avram's face, he struggled to speak. "Never! I won't help you."

Alexandra walked over to him. "You have little choice."

"My guards will not let this happen."

The Protectors on the path began to move forward. Cassia and the others readied to fend them off.

*No, I can't let them fight.* Max raised his arm. "Melody, help me."

Melody pulled Max to his feet, keeping an arm around his waist to help steady him.

"Move me to the edge."

Melody helped him walk to where Lord Avram sat bound. Clearing his throat, Max spoke as loud as he could.

"Lord Avram, I, private Maxwell Laskaris, charge you with having failed in your duty to protect all peoples, lacarna and human as per the Protector's code. In addition, you ordered the murder of one of our own, Peter Laskaris, my father."

Lysander relaxed his knife a little. "And I, Sergeant Lysander Harris, charge you with betraying your brethren, the Immortals, the murder of hundreds of lacarnians and the destruction of their home centuries ago.

The Sergeant leading the Protectors up the path commanded them to stop.

"Lord Avram, does this boy speak the truth?"

"Of course not you fool, they're mad. Forget about my life, stop them."

Alexandra rushed towards Lord Avram. "Melody!"

Melody let go of Max, who fell to the ground. Running to Cassia she formed her barrier before the guards could reach her.

Alexandra yelled at Lysander. "Get clear."

Holding the Lifestone in one hand, she grabbed Lord Avram's shoulder with the other. He squirmed beneath her grip.

"Untie me!"

The light in the stone intensified until it engulfed them in a bright, blue light. At Alexandra's feet, grass sprouted, spreading in an outward arc that flowed down into the dead lands like a ripple in a pond.

Lord Avram screamed in pain. Around Alexandra, flowers rose from the grass. As they did so, Lord Avram's skin began to shrivel and tighten around his bones. His hair first grayed then fell from his scalp.

Down in the valley, saplings sprouted from the ground. The Protectors who had gathered there milled about in wonder at the growth. They forgot about Lord Avram, whose body slowly dissolved on the plateau above, one layer at a time. His skin went quickly, then his muscles and finally his bones. Below, the saplings grew into small trees sending the Protectors running in different directions as they tried to avoid them.

Above, Alexandra fell to her knees as the Lifestone now fed on her. She began to shrivel like Lord Avram. A wide variety of plants, the likes that Max had never seen, sprang up from the ground in the valley. Then the growth slowed. Max shivered as a mournful wail arose from Alexandra.

"Nooo. It's not finished."

Lysander rushed towards Alexandra. "That thing is going to kill her."

Anemone bounded from behind Melody, reaching Alexandra before Lysander. Placing her head against the stone her body disintegrated as a new wave of plants burst forth below before stopping once again.

Lysander stood frozen in his tracks, but Callie started towards Alexandra. Melody screamed at her.

"That won't be enough! The stone is far too powerful for us."

Lysander shook himself free. "She won't stop until the forest is complete or that stone kills her."

"Then stay away from the stone. Touch her instead. I think she can act as a valve, keeping it from completely destroying us."

"Are you sure?"

Melody dropped the barrier, no longer concerned about the

guards who stood in fascination at the growing forest. She ran to Alexandra, grabbing her hand. Alexandra's body stopped deteriorating as the color slowly drained from Melody. Below, the plants and trees grew once more.

After half a minute had passed, Melody went limp, letting go of Alexandra. Lysander ran forward, yanking her away. Melody struggled to stay conscious.

"She's so strong. If we can supply her, she can finish it."

Lysander turned to the others. "Help her!"

Without hesitation, Callie, Effie and Eve formed a line, each following Melody's example. As Alexandra drained them, Lysander pulled them free. Below, the forest grew thick and tall. The tops of the trees reached above the cliffs on either side.

Then, to their amazement, a few of the Protector's silently came forward, lending their bodies to Alexandra. However, as fewer volunteers came forward, Lysander tried to wake Alexandra from the trance she had fallen in.

"Alexandra, you've done enough."

She did not respond.

"Alex, I'm the last. You will need me to heal yourself. Let go of the stone."

Alexandra drew a small breath. "I can finish it."

"Not without dying."

Alexandra managed the weakest of shrugs. "I should have died a long time ago."

Lysander's hands clenched. "But you didn't, and you're sure not going to now!"

Lysander grabbed the stone, yanking it from Alexandra's hand. He jerked in pain as he instantly turned pale. With a guttural yell, he slammed the stone into the ground, shattering it into thousands of glistening shards.

Lysander sat hard on the ground, catching Alexandra as she slumped over. "Take what you need."

Alexandra touched the side of his face just long enough for her body to return to normal. Lysander, with what little strength he had left, wrapped Alexandra in his arms. Max, along with the others, dragged themselves to his side where they sat in wonder at the forest in front of them.

Several minutes passed before Eve turned to Melody. "Melody, did you find Spook?"

Melody reached into a pocket inside her robe and pulled out the little mouse. "I found her near a rock. She must have hit it when Lord Avram flung her."

Eve cupped her hands so Melody could lay Spook in them. The mouse no longer breathed. Max took Eve in his arms as she sobbed. Feeling a tear roll down his own cheek, he realized how much he had grown attached to their little friend.

Footsteps came from behind, then Max heard the sergeant speak.

"What you accused Lord Avram of earlier, is it true?"

"Yes, though it is a long story."

"One you must tell, for you have assisted in the death of our leader."

"It was necessary to right a wrong committed long ago. His death has set the lacarna and the Protectors free."

"And that is the only reason your story will wait. We are returning to Moenia immediately. We do not know what havoc the lacarna are causing."

Alexandra's eyes fluttered open. "I have put people in place to keep peace. They are being led into the forest as we speak. One of your own, Mr. Penna, is assisting as well. In fact, your absence will give things a chance to sort out on their own."

Max scooted around to face the sergeant. "My father, Lt. Laskaris, knew the lacarna were not the beasts Lord Avram made them out to be. It was he who set this plan into motion years ago. We merely completed the task that he could not. We believed the same as he, that the Protectors purpose is to watch over everyone, human and lacarna alike."

"I knew your father. He was a friend to all and well respected among us. We knew he also disagreed with Lord Avram's control of the lacarnians. Many of us did. It does not surprise me he had the courage to change things when the rest of us did not. It seems you are of the same mold. Sgt. Harris, I assume you believe this boy as well considering your involvement and accusations?"

"Yes. The lacarna are not as Lord Avram told us. Maxwell, Eve and a few others many years ago have shown me that. In fact, I would trust Eve as I would you. Lord Avram led the Protectors away from their true purpose. With Maxwell's guidance I would like to see us redeem ourselves."

The Sergeant nodded. "We will need to hear the whole story, but the forest the little one has created below will go a long way in your defense. Now, despite your assurances, I am anxious to return to Moenia."

"I agree, but we are too weak to move at this time."

A female voice came from the cave entrance, startling them.

"That, I can help with."

All turned to see who had spoken. In front of the cave opening stood a woman whose beauty, transfixed Max.

"Who are you?"

"I am Rhea, one of the Creators."

# CHAPTER THIRTY-FOUR

Max gave a heavy sigh. He thought he'd figured everything out to this point.

*Now some woman appears and tells us she's a Creator? I don't think I can handle much more.*

Max turned to Alexandra. "Uh, Alex?"

Alexandra gave a light tap on Lysander's arm. "Let me go, please."

Lysander unwrapped Alexandra from his arms and helped her stand. Brushing what dust she could off of her dress, she wobbled a few steps before managing a small curtsy.

"Welcome, Rhea, my name is Alexandra."

Rhea returned the curtsey. "Thank you."

Max scratched his head. "Do you know who she is, Alex?"

"Remember the drawings in the cave?"

Max nodded "Yeah."

"Did you notice I skipped one at the very beginning?"

"Uh…"

Melody nodded. "I did. It looked like a hand above the people. Why did you skip it?"

"Because, I was unsure of its meaning. We had nothing that referenced it. We only speculated that it was the hand of the true Creators placing us here."

Rhea smiled. "Your interpretation is correct. After we created your ancestors, we placed them here between the mountains.

We had intended to leave no knowledge of our existence."

Lysander tried to stand, but his legs quickly gave out. "How do we know you are who you say you are?"

Rhea started walking towards Eve. Max reached for his swords only to realize he had no idea of what happened to them. Eve's ears twitched nervously but she remained still.

"It's okay, Max."

Rhea bent over and gently touched Spook who Eve still cradled in her hands. "Such a brave little creature."

Rhea placed her hands over Spook. A second later Eve jumped with surprise, startling Max.

"Eve!"

Eve giggled. "Maxy, look."

Rhea removed her hands, revealing Spook standing on her hind legs. She sniffed at the air then climbed to her usual perch on Eve's shoulder.

Melody stared in wonder at Spook. "Sa…satisfied, Lysander."

"Yeah, that will do it."

Alexandra wobbled back to the others and eased herself to the ground.

"Why did you not want us to know about you? Why have you come now?"

Rhea lowered her head. "I would like to tell you everything, but my time is limited. I can only tell you of what, I am afraid, will reflect poorly on my brothers and sisters."

Rhea laid her hand on Eve. Max watched the wounds close shut and the bruises fade away.

"We wanted to create our own paradise, a place to relax and enjoy. We picked this planet as our starting point. From its soil we created a variety of vegetation, much like Alexandra has done."

Rhea moved next to Max and laid a hand on his shoulder. A warm sensation flowed through him erasing the pain and soreness, filling him with fresh energy.

"We then created various creatures; some to amuse us, others to keep a balance with the vegetation. We had few rules in regards to our creations, but one exception restricted the creation of a form like ourselves."

Rhea moved on to Lysander and then the few Protectors who had joined them in creating the forest, healing each in turn.

"Then, a small group of my colleagues decided they could evade the rule by making a creature that, while having the ability to communicate with us, was mostly animal in nature. Thus they made the lacarna."

Rhea reached Lalita, who lay motionless in the middle of the plateau. She bent over her for several seconds before shaking her head and returning to where Max and the others sat.

"When the others learned what had been done, they were jealous. They saw the lacarna as monsters and set about to create a form true to themselves, the humans. Arguments rose as to which was the better creation."

Rhea sighed heavily. "The debate lasted for years until a fateful decision was made on how to settle the issue. Both creations were gathered and placed here in this ring of mountains to see which could survive the best. When both seemed to be flourishing, opponents on either side tried to sabotage the other. They interfered with the lives of the lacarna and the humans, trying to get one to destroy the other."

Alexandra's eyes lit up. "The disease on the humans."

"That was one attempt, giving the lacarna the power of the Lifestone was another. Then, an illness struck us. Its cause unknown, but its effects devastating. We began to die off. In concern for ourselves, we all but forgot our creations."

"Recently, a select few of us came to the conclusion that we cannot save ourselves from this disease. Our creations; however, might live on. In secret, we started to watch your proceedings. We soon realized that, despite the animosity between the two creations, there were those trying to bring them together. They showed more effort at a peaceful solution than we ever had."

Max shook his head. "I think we still have a long way to go."

"Perhaps, but you are out of time."

Alexandra cocked her head to the side. "What do you mean?"

"Few of my brothers and sisters are left. If we do not release you from this prison you will not find us before we are gone. Our knowledge of this world and where we came from will disappear."

"How much time do we have?"

"A year, perhaps."

"Max shrugged. "That should be plenty of time."

"Unfortunately, there are complications. Those of us left make our home far from here, and we are too weak to travel. I am only here through great effort. Then there are those few who would see that our mistakes are buried and forgotten. Your trip to find us will not be easy."

Max felt a chill run down his spine. "There are those as strong as you who wish to see us destroyed?"

"Yes."

Max swallowed hard. "But, you don't?"

Rhea smiled. "No, though it was wrong for us to create such beings, you have every right to exist. That, and I want the world we created to be enjoyed. You deserve it after what my brothers and sisters have done to you."

Melody looked questioningly at Rhea. "What else is there beyond the mountains?"

"More than I can describe. Where you live is but a speck on Velrune. The life here, a fraction of the things that exist beyond your home."

Rhea's body began to fade from view. "No, not yet!"

Rhea scrunched her face as if she was thinking very hard, her body solidified.

"I have little time now. Listen to me well. In two weeks, I will open a pathway in this mountain, allowing you access to the rest of Velrune. Survival outside of these mountains will not be easy, but you must do it in order to find us."

Alex stood. "How will we find you?"

"I will try to guide you where we can, but I warn you to beware of others. They have set plans into motion to destroy everything. They will try to lead you astray. Avoid their lies and reach us before it is too late."

Rhea's body began to fade again. "My time is nearly over."

Rhea held out her hand, the shards of the Lifestone rattled on the ground before flying to her and reforming.

"This will buy us some time. If you reach us, you may reclaim it."

Rhea stepped next to Alexandra. "I can do one last thing before I go."

Rhea gently touched Alexandra's forehead. "You carry the history of our creations, invaluable information to us and them. I know it has been a curse to you, so rest for a while my little one."

Rhea removed her hand from Alexandra's forehead who sat frozen with a distant, lost expression on her face.

"Lysander, I have borrowed much of her memory to return to my people. It will lift a heavy burden from her, but it will also leave her confused. Please, take good care of her until you meet me again. Now, I must go. Good luck and do not delay."

Rhea faded from view, leaving them all stunned. Alexandra shook her head.

"Where'd the beautiful lady go?"

Lysander picked Alexandra up, sitting her on his shoulders. "Home I believe, which is where we need to head."

Alexandra sat silently for a few seconds then started to sniffle. "Wh…where's that?"

"Back in the city. You have lots of friends there."

Melody ran over to where she had dropped Alexandra's pack when retrieving the salve. She returned, pulling out Alexandra's doll.

"Here you go, sweetie."

"Emma!"

Effie, Callie, Cassia, Anemone and Hannah gathered around them.

"Do you want a ride back?"

Lysander frowned. "No! I mean, I'm fine with walking, thank you."

Alexandra bent over Lysander's head. "Aww, come on, it's fun."

The sergeant joined them. "First, I have not introduced myself. I am Sgt. Pax. Second, while I do not envy riding a lacarnian, I believe it wise that we return as quickly as possible to the city. We need to show a presence and prepare ourselves for re-establishing our order."

With reluctance, Lysander nodded. "Agreed."

Eve winked at Alexandra. "You can ride on me."

"Ooo, goodie."

Lysander chuckled. "I told you there was still a kid in there, Max."

Max smiled briefly, but then nodded at Lalita's body. "How are we going to bring Lalita back?"

The Protectors that had helped them earlier stepped forward and spoke to Effie. "If you will permit us, we will carry her back."

Effie nodded. "Thank you."

Sgt. Pax turned to a nearby Protector. "Lt. Tabbar, see to gathering those below and make all haste towards Moenia, but stay on the ridge. We are going ahead."

Alexandra bounced up and down on Lysander's shoulders. "Let's go already."

Everyone else was just as impatient as Alexandra, but not for the joy of the ride. All were anxious to know what had transpired in Moenia in their absence. Lysander and Sgt. Pax mounted Callie and Cassie, Eve carried Alexandra, Effie carried Melody and Max once again rode Anemone. Hannah, unable to transform, remained with Lalita and those carrying her body.

## CHAPTER THIRTY-FIVE

They arrived at Moenia's gate two hours later. Outside stood two lacarnians from Alexandra's camp. Seeing Alexandra, they ran towards her with great excitement.

"You did it! The stones are gone and the forest has re-grown. We're free!"

Alexandra slipped off Eve and ran behind Lysander. "Who are they?"

The two women looked at each other in confusion. Lysander rubbed the top of Alexandra's head.

"She's lost a lot of her memory. We'll explain later. Right now, we need to know what is going on inside the city."

Max and Sgt. Pax joined Lysander to hear the lacarna's response.

"Most of the lacarnians have left for the forest. A few with human partners have remained."

Sgt. Pax shifted uneasily. "Have there been any incidents?"

"Six or seven lacarnians bound their masters wanting retribution for their mistreatment. We convinced them to hand their masters over to Neysa and Mr. Penna at the Protectors headquarters until a proper jury could be established. Other than that, both races have been staying out of each other's way."

Sgt. Pax relaxed a little. "Thank you for your report. Things are going better than I expected, but we need to re-establish order as quickly as possible. For starters, the Protectors need new leadership. Lysander, we are both next in rank and well known in Moenia. We will have an official vote later, for now I propose we jointly take lead."

"I...I don't know if I'm much of a leader."

"You are as qualified as anyone else. I also want Maxwell holding an advisory position. His father's name carries great weight with both races, and he is the most familiar with the lacarna. If we are to move forward successfully, we will need their support. Without the stones, we are no match for them. Maxwell?"

"Of course, Sgt. Pax."

"Good. Now as for the lacarna, does anyone lead them?

The two lacarnians looked at each other again. "That would have been Alexandra."

Max shook his head. "Yeah, that's not going to work. What about Lycoris? Didn't Alex tell her to take over if something went wrong?"

The two nodded in unison. "Yes, and others will listen to her."

Lysander turned to Sgt. Pax. "I think we should have her meet us at headquarters. It sounds as if we have some things to take care of there anyway."

Max nodded. "Yes, but I don't think we should stay there. It is too secluded from the lacarna. Is there a place in the market we can use?"

Sgt. Pax thought a moment. "There is small warehouse near the center that will work. The rest of the Protectors, when they arrive, should still use the headquarters. I don't want us to show any type of force."

Melody partially raised her hand. "Don't you think the biggest thing we need to do is spread word as to what has happened. Confusion only scares people."

Lysander nodded. "Not to mention there is the whole thing with Rhea."

Lysander turned to the two lacarnian women. "Notify everyone of our plans to set up in the market, and tomorrow we will hold a meeting to try and explain everything."

The two took off running for the city. Lysander then turned to Melody. "Can you watch Alexandra for the next few days? I have a feeling I'm not going to have any free time."

Melody smiled. "Sure, but I'll bring her by often. I think you and Eve are the only two she really remembers much."

Max nearly fainted when he saw Lysander smile. "Thanks, Melody."

Eve bounced up and down. "What am I supposed to do?"

Max laughed. "Follow me around to keep me from doing anything stupid like usual."

Eve giggled. "That's not easy, but I'll try."

They set about their plans, first meeting with Mr. Penna, Neysa, and Lycoris. Afterwards, they established a new headquarters in the market warehouse and began laying out plans for moving forward.

The following day, Max, Melody and Lysander told their stories, including meeting Rhea, to a large crowd in the market. They also told of their plan to reform the Protectors as it was originally intended, with both human and lacarna members.

Many were uncertain what to make of their tale, although the newly grown forest was a little hard to ignore. While a lot of the humans feared the lacarna being completely free, few mourned Lord Avram's death. After the meeting, both races once again separated with the lacarna heading into the forest.

Two days later, the rest of the Protectors returned to the city. Lysander directed them to their old headquarters and together, with Sgt. Pax, set to work reorganizing and establishing new rules for the fair treatment of all. Max, Eve, Neysa and Mr. Penna worked night and day speaking with both races about moving forward as equals.

Several days later, the first of the lacarnians to volunteer to join the Protectors came forward. While a few human Protectors left in protest, most welcomed their new sisters-in-arms.

Melody, besides keeping an eye on Alexandra, worked with Lady Metis in rebuilding the Children's relationship with the

Protectors. They were also the first humans to be allowed by the lacarna into the new forest, soon followed by select members of the Protectors.

Near the end of the second week, Max felt as if he had traveled farther during that time than he had since leaving Swiftwater. Every day he made a trip from headquarters into the city or out into the forest. At least Eve and Spook spent most of their time with him. The two provided endless entertainment.

He occasionally ran into Melody and Alexandra too. He had to laugh as he remembered how Alexandra had acted when they first met. She had changed completely. Free of centuries of painful memories, she once again behaved like a nine year old child. She also drew close to Lysander and even began insisting on staying with him whenever he was not out and about. For his part, Lysander treated her as his own daughter. He seemed happiest when she was with him. In fact, Max had left the two of them together a few hours ago, both laughing as Lysander took a break from his duties to play with her. Now, late in the evening, he wandered down the dimly lit hallways of headquarters alone.

*I miss the days in Swiftwater; sleeping in late, running around the plains with Eve. Hmm, we need to get back to her swim training. I think I miss those nights the most. She's was so much calmer then, and that scent...*

Max stopped walking, his thoughts interrupted by a strange feeling. He stood still for a brief second then twisted his body hard to the right. A dark mass flew by him, grazing his shirt. A joyful laughter ensued from behind him.

"You're finally getting better, Maxy."

Max relaxed and turned around. "I had to get better, I got tired of..."

Eve barreled in to him, once more knocking him flat on the floor with her face inches from his own.

"...hitting the floor."

Eve purred softly.

*Okay, that's a little different.*

Groaning, he propped himself to his elbows. "You're never going to stop doing that are you?"

Eve smiled. Suddenly, the hallway started shaking violently. Eve slipped forward, and, for a brief second, their lips touched. As the quake ended, Eve jumped to her feet, her face flushed.

"Are you okay?"

Max stood, his own face bright red. "I wonder what that was about."

Eve bounced and grabbed her tail in excitement. "Do you think Rhea opened the mountain path?"

"I hope so, or we have a completely different problem on our hands. We need to find Lysander. I assume you're ready for another adventure?"

"Yep, I've been getting bored lately. It's no fun when you're not in trouble."

Max rolled his eyes. "Yeah, yeah." He held out his hand. "Let's just go already."

Eve smiled and took his hand. Together, they walked down the hallway.

"By the way, Eve, do you wear perfume? I've never seen a bottle, but you always have this nice spring-like smell about you."

"That's just me." Eve's devilish grin appeared. "I guess next to you, anything smells nice. I mean, I did track you for miles in the dead lands."

Max shook his head, sorry that he had asked, but as she leaned her head onto his shoulder he noticed her purring had grown much louder.